Barbara A. Luker

the
right
one

Black Rose Writing | Texas

The author grants the final approval for this literary material.

First printing

This is a work of fiction. Names, characters, businesses, places, events, and incidents are either the products of the author's imagination or used in a fictitious manner. Any resemblance to actual persons, living or dead, or actual events is purely coincidental.

ISBN: 978-1-68513-276-7
PUBLISHED BY BLACK ROSE WRITING
www.blackrosewriting.com

Printed in the United States of America
Suggested Retail Price (SRP) $21.95

The Right One is printed in EB Garamond

*As a planet-friendly publisher, Black Rose Writing does its best to eliminate unnecessary waste to reduce paper usage and energy costs, while never compromising the reading experience. As a result, the final word count vs. page count may not meet common expectations.

For Susan, my sister and my friend.

AUTHOR ACKNOWLEDGEMENTS

This book wouldn't have been possible without the help of some special people in my life....

Many thanks to Gustavus Adolphus College graduate, Tyra Ericson, who provided valuable editing services for the book. I hope the experience was valuable for you as you find your path in life.

Continued thanks to my beta readers Nancy, Susan, Barb, Maureen, and Francine. Each of you have been a great bellwether for me and I appreciate all of your comments, criticisms, and support on this writing journey.

Finally, for all those who have enjoyed my first two books and shared reviews and kind comments, thank you. Your support and appreciation for my writing has pushed me to continue on this creative journey.

Dreams don't happen overnight and they don't happen without the help and support of an army of friends, family and colleagues. To all those who made this book possible, thank you.

the right
one

CHAPTER ONE

"Hey lady."

Lost in her thoughts as she stared at the seemingly endless cloud cover outside the plane window, Andi didn't hear the child's soft voice at first.

"Lady, do you want to play Go Fish with me?"

Only the slight tug on the sleeve of her jacket brought her attention back to the inside of the plane, where a young girl stared back with large brown doe eyes.

"Honey, leave the poor lady alone," her mother said gently as Andi smiled down at the child sitting on the woman's lap. "I'm so sorry she bothered you. It's a long flight and I've run out of ways to entertain her."

"It's all right," Andi said kindly. The woman and her husband were traveling with three young children and had done their best the entire flight to keep the kids from annoying other passengers. Now well into the trip to Texas, the children were getting restless. "I should warn you, I'm a pretty mean Go Fish player," Andi told the child.

Backing away in fear, the little girl's eyes opened wide. Obviously, Andi should have chosen her words more carefully. She'd forgotten how literal children can be. The child looked nervously at her mother for backup.

"Honey, she's not mean at all. She meant she's a great Go Fish player, that's all. I'm sure she's very nice, but let's leave her alone, okay?"

The girl hesitated for only a moment before crawling off her mother's lap onto the empty seat between them to stare expectantly at Andi.

"I promise I'm a nice person and if you still want to, I'd love to play with you. Why don't you tell me the rules?"

"Hey, you said you knew how to play," the little girl said with surprising astuteness for a child of maybe five or six.

"I did, but when I was younger, we played Go Shamu instead of Go Fish."

"You mean like at the water park? I saw Shamu when I was real little. He splashed water on me," the child said with more interest.

"Exactly. In my family, instead of saying 'go fish,' we say 'go Shamu.' Would you like to play Go Shamu with me?"

"Mommy, can I?" she asked excitedly.

"If you're sure..." her mother directed to Andi. There was no mistaking the look of hope on her tired face.

"It will be fun," Andi told her with a warm smile. "My name is Andi. What's yours?" she asked, turning her attention back to the little girl.

"Madison," the child told her as she tried to shuffle the deck of cards in her tiny hands before Andi gently took them from her and did it herself. "Isn't Andi a boy's name?" the girl asked sweetly.

Dealing the cards, Andi clarified. "My real name is Andrea. Andi's my nickname. Do they call you Maddie?"

"Nope. Daddy said they named me Madison after my Grandma. She's dead."

"Sorry to hear that."

As they had been talking other children seated nearby, including Madison's two brothers seated across the aisle with their father, had peered over seat backs and around corners and it wasn't long before Andi was entertaining a whole group of children with her version of the classic card game. The girl's mother joined her husband in a now empty seat across the aisle as the couple offered grateful looks for the break. Nodding back, Andi suspected they really wanted a stiff drink and a nap; something she wouldn't have minded herself.

It had been a hectic month preparing for her transition from Minnesota to Texas. Between the insane hours she was putting in at work and trying to pack up a house full of belongings, she was emotionally and physically exhausted, yet stretching out on a nice comfortable bed and sleeping for a solid twenty-four hours was not in the cards. Once the plane landed, she only had the weekend before reporting for work as the newest trauma surgeon at Austin's Presbyterian Medical Center.

Sleep deprivation came with the medical degree and Andi was used to it. Years of studying and working around the clock for days at a stretch had taught her to sleep when and where she could. Even a quick nap was, more often than not, a luxury. When her residency was over and she started as a trauma surgeon at the Mayo Clinic, she had hoped for a more regular sleep pattern, but being on call at all hours of the day and night made that impossible. At the beginning of her career, racing to the hospital in the middle of the night had been exhilarating, but as with most things in life, the luster soon wore off and Andi had learned to function with as little sleep as humanly possible.

Her new position in Texas, while still requiring her to be on call, might finally provide for a stable routine and allow her to sleep in her own bed most nights. At least that's what she was hoping when she accepted the position and turned her life upside down to move to Texas.

Minnesota born and raised, living in Texas wasn't something she considered in the beginning. A nature lover and an athlete who loved all sports and activities winter related, how could she possibly give up the land of ten thousand lakes and four distinct seasons to live in a dry, hot, and dusty state? Still, in the end and after weeks of weighing the pros and cons, the offer was too good to pass up. She turned in her resignation at Mayo and left behind family and friends for a world of cowboys and ten-gallon hats.

The decision finally made and contract executed, she hadn't looked back; that was until now. Once the plane left the runway in Minnesota, doubt had eaten away at the corners of her mind once more. She was growing more nervous as the miles passed until the little girl interrupted her thoughts. Playing cards with the children seemed to be the tonic she needed to take her mind off her worries, and the rest of the flight was stress free until the plane taxied to the gate in Austin.

Following the rest of the passengers to baggage claim, Andi scanned the throngs of people waiting to welcome loved ones, searching for the single friendly face she knew in all of Texas. She and Carol had been roommates and friends since their freshman year at the University of Minnesota, but had lost touch as Andi worked around the clock after medical school. Losing the friendship that had meant so much to her had broken her heart, yet her attempts to find Carol and her husband had been stymied by their apparent frequent moves around the country. It was pure luck when, just weeks before her departure, a mutual friend mentioned that Carol and her family were now living in Austin. One quick phone call was all it took to renew their friendship, and Andi was very much looking forward to their reunion.

It didn't take long to spot Carol in the crowd; the "WELCOME DR. TAYLOR" sign held high above her head was a dead giveaway. Texas wasn't home, but seeing Carol instantly made Andi feel less lonely and she waved back excitedly before collecting her luggage and making her way to Carol for a long-overdue and heartfelt hug. The familiar scent of Carol's favorite perfume took her right back to the last time they had seen each other when neither of them knew where life would take them. While Andi had already become a doctor, her plans back then had also included a husband and a house full of children. Carol wanted nothing more than to be a dedicated career woman until meeting David and realizing she wanted nothing more than the family she now had. They were both happy with their choices and the sacrifices they had made, and now they were back together again.

"Welcome to Texas," Carol said with an accent she didn't have the last time the friends had seen each other. How long would it take before y'all punctuated Andi's own Minnesota accent she wondered?

"Thank you so much and it is so wonderful to see you again! My God Carol, you look like you haven't aged a day since graduation."

It was true. She still looked like the fresh-faced young coed Andi had first met so many years ago.

"Oh stop," Carol said in embarrassment.

Andi realized from the faint blush of excitement on Carol's cheeks, the compliment had pleased her.

"I wish I could say the same about you, but..."

"But what?" Was Carol about to tell her she looked as old as she felt at the moment?

"But you, my dear... wow. Andi, you were always a pretty girl, but you have definitely grown into your looks. You're beautiful! You must have to fight the men off with a stick."

As with any close friendship, it was as if no time had passed since their last meeting and locking arms, they each grabbed a suitcase and headed to the curbside passenger area where Carol walked up to a large black SUV chauffeured by her husband David who had waited patiently while listening to a football game on the radio. After another reunion with David, they were finally on their way.

"I really wish you'd consider staying with us tonight, Andi. You don't want to be all alone on your first night in town," Carol implored as the miles from the airport to the city flew by outside their windows. "We've got the room if the kids double up and it will give us a chance to catch up after all these years."

"It's a wonderful thought and I appreciate the offer more than you know, but I only have the weekend to get my new house in order before starting work on Monday."

"Why don't I help you?" Carol suggested. She had always been the first one to help anyone she thought was in need. It was the quality that had initially drawn so many of their friends to Carol and it seemed nothing had changed in the years since they were apart.

"That's so nice of you, but honestly, I need the weekend to decompress. It's been a madhouse for me the last few weeks and I just need some peace. All I was planning on doing was putting away some clothes, making up my bed, and booting up my computer. These next few weeks are going to be crazy busy and if the hours are anything like they were at Mayo, I probably won't be home much. I'm going to just concentrate on the basics for this weekend, but I wouldn't mind an invitation for dinner now and then."

"Still can't cook, huh, Andi?" David asked with a deep-throated laugh from the driver's seat. The running joke among her friends had been she could take a body apart and put it back together blindfolded, but couldn't make scrambled eggs. While her cooking skills weren't quite that dismal, she had learned to take the teasing with grace.

"I'll have you know I make a stellar peanut butter and jelly sandwich," Andi quipped as they all laughed. "Besides, what's the use of learning to cook if I'm never home to do it?"

"What man is going to marry you if you don't know how to cook?" David said before Carol punched him in the arm and looked nervously back at Andi.

"He didn't mean that Andi. I'm sorry. David, tell her you're sorry."

"Sorry Andi," he said sheepishly before turning his attention back to the road as Carol continued to glare at him.

"It's okay. I understand I'm not what most men expect in a wife and that's okay. I chose a different path and I know that means I have to sacrifice some things to do what makes me happy. Not every woman's destiny ends in marriage, but then again, not every woman can be a surgeon either."

Andi's college friends, all of whom had been happily married for years, had doggedly tried to set her up with suitable men for years. She had willingly gone along with their attempts; after all, she had no time to meet men herself, but those setups had never worked out and it was all on her. It just wasn't fair to the guys who didn't understand what being a trauma surgeon entailed, and the constant relationship failures had long ago taken a toll on her mental health.

It seemed nearly impossible to find a man willing to put up with her crazy work hours and, after years of disappointment, she and her friends had all just stopped trying. Her dream of a husband and family appeared to be just a pipe dream. However, now that the issue had come up again, leaving Carol and David uncomfortable and Andi embarrassed, it seemed easier on all of their parts to change the subject. They transitioned seamlessly into making plans for activities they could do once she settled in.

"Your house is just ahead," David said as he turned the car into an upscale housing development.

Her original plan had been to stay in a hotel for a couple of weeks while she worked with a realtor to find a home of her own, but those plans changed when the realtor found a relatively new home in a subdivision close to the hospital that was about to come on the market. With only pictures and video of the home to go by, Andi had made a snap decision to buy the property sight unseen. It was unlike her to make a hasty decision, and she hoped she wouldn't come to regret it. David slowed the car before turning in the driveway of her new home and Andi let a whispered "wow" escape her lips. The curb appeal of the massive brick house had sold Andi even before seeing the interior photos, but the pictures hadn't done it justice. The home was beautiful. Lovingly attended to both inside and out by the previous owners, every inch of the home was sheer perfection, though thousands of square feet more than she needed. Was that a sign that Andi hadn't yet given up on that pipe dream?

"This place is a mansion," David said as he got out of the car to help her with the bags. "What are you going to do with all this space?"

"Oh my goodness, I'd hate to clean this house," Carol said. Carol had been the first person to offer the couple's services in readying the home and she and David had already been in and out of the house several times as they prepared for Andi's arrival, but compared to their more modest home, Andi's house was enormous. "I'll admit it is beautiful and I wouldn't mind having it myself," Carol said with a wink at her husband, "But what were you thinking, Andi?"

Although said with a smile, the comments stung a bit. The house was gorgeous and even if she never had a family to fill it, Andi was proud of her purchase.

"I guess I'll hire someone to clean for me and if I ever get time off, it's going to be fun to fill it with furniture." There was nothing she liked better than spending a day wandering around a furniture showroom. "Until then, I'll try not to get lost!"

Leading the parade to the front door, Andi used the code provided by her realtor to let them in. The massive foyer was just as she remembered from the photographs. Dominated by a gracefully curving stairway to the upper floor and flanked by twin sets of French doors, the foyer opened to the sunroom on one side of the house and a formal dining room on the other. The dining room was a luxury she might never use, but something her own mother had always wished for. It was an impressive welcome to the home.

As they made their way to the back of the house, David was quick to point out another room that might be equally useless to her - the kitchen.

"Maybe I better explain this next room, Andi," he teased as they walked into the large chef's kitchen.

"Again, not funny David," Carol said as she glared at her husband while trying hard not to laugh herself.

"What do you mean? She's probably never been in a kitchen," he teased before pointing to an area next to the stove. "At least it has a microwave!"

Giving Andi a quick tour of the house, the trio made their way back to the front door to say their goodbyes.

"I almost forgot," Carol said. "We stocked the fridge and pantry for you and David picked up your new car. It's already in the garage and the keys are next to the phone in the kitchen. I don't think there's much else you need right away except help to unpack. You said the moving truck arrives tomorrow, right?" Before Andi could answer, she continued. "Please take me up on my offer. It will go so much quicker with us both working to unpack."

"Thanks guys. I really appreciate your help with everything and I'm going to pay you back somehow, but for now, the unpacking will have to wait until I get more free time."

"Well, if you're sure, but if you change your mind, you know how to reach me," Carol said before offering a warm hug. "We wanted to give you a welcome to Texas gift and I just couldn't think of what to give you, but David came up with the perfect present. Honey, do you have the envelope?" she asked her husband.

"What's this?" Andi asked as she accepted the envelope David pulled out of his back pocket.

"It's a bit of home and a welcome to Texas gift," he said. "Open it later."

"Ok and thank you again."

"If you change your mind about help this weekend, call me," Carol offered once again. "And you'll come over to ours for a barbeque next weekend, right? We want to introduce you to all of our friends so you won't feel so lonely."

"That's so sweet, but you know you don't have to do that," Andi told her as they walked arm in arm out to the car.

"Nonsense. We want to," Carol assured her. "It's going to be so nice having you in the same zip code for a change. I've missed you more than you know."

"Come on Carol. Let's leave her to it and try to beat the traffic home. Don't be a stranger Andi."

"I won't and thanks you guys for the ride and everything else. I'm looking forward to your party."

"Oh honey," Carol said before giving Andi's hand a quick squeeze through the open car window, "you're in Texas now. It's not a party–it's a barbeque!"

"I'll try to remember that," Andi told her with a laugh. "Drive carefully and I'll see you guys soon. Thanks again!"

Watching the car disappear around the corner, an unexpected wave of loneliness washed over Andi before she turned to go back inside. Stopping to look up and down the street at the empty neighborhood, she realized that on a beautiful Friday night, not a single neighbor was outside. Had everyone started their weekend early or maybe it was just too blasted hot to leave their nice air-conditioned homes? Either way, she had asked for peace and quiet and that's what she was getting.

· · ·

By late the next afternoon the moving truck with the rest of her belongings, having arrived only a few hours later than promised, had pulled away and the house, which had echoed with every sound in its emptiness the day before, now seemed crowded and chaotic with the maze of boxes just waiting to be unpacked. It seemed every available space, including the oversized double garage, was full of boxes. Thank goodness she was in Texas and not Minnesota, where the brutal weather made parking in the garage a necessity. Intent on getting the house set up before starting her new job, Andi began opening boxes, looking for the few things she needed most for her bedroom, bathroom and office space. It wasn't much, but at least it was a start.

Finishing by making up her bed, she collapsed onto it and stared at the tray ceiling above. The large ceiling fan circled gently overhead, stirring the air just enough to make it feel cooler than it really was and the gentle hum of the fan motor was the only sound in the house until her cell phone rang. Seeing her parent's number on the caller ID, she broke into a smile.

"Hi Mom."

"Hi, honey. You sound tired. Are you all settled in?"

"Not exactly," she admitted. "The truck arrived a few hours ago and I've been trying to make a dent in the mountain of boxes with little luck."

"I knew we should have come with you."

Like Carol, her mother had spent weeks trying to convince Andi to let them accompany her to Texas to help get the house set up. It wasn't until she promised a visit that her mother had backed off on her efforts.

"It's fine Mom. Nothing a bit of time and energy can't solve. But I have my bedroom unpacked, the bathroom is mostly ready to go, and I set my computer up in my office. What else do I need?"

"Have you been to the grocery store yet? You need to eat, even if it's just those horrid frozen dinners you seem to live on."

"Mom, I just got here last night. I haven't had time to go to the store even if I knew where the store was. Besides, Carol and David were nice enough to stock the fridge with the basics. I have enough peanut butter to get me through a month."

"Maybe you'll learn how to cook before Dad and I come down?" her mom asked hopefully. Unlike David's playful teasing, it mortified her mother that her only child was so helpless in the kitchen.

"Don't count on it."

"Dad wants to say hello too." Andi could hear them talking in the background as they passed the phone.

"Hi, honey. So is Texas as big as you expected?" her dad asked.

"Well, I don't know about that, but it's sure hotter than I expected. Minnesota heat is nothing like this and it's going to take some getting used to."

"Well, at least you have air conditioning. Have you met any of the neighbors yet?" he asked.

"Not yet, but then again, I've been pretty busy since I got here, so maybe later."

Having heard tales of Texas hospitality, she was disappointed none of the neighbors had knocked on the door to extend a welcome to the neighborhood.

"I'm sure you'll make friends with everyone in no time."

She hoped he was right. Although she wouldn't be home much, it would still be nice to say hi to a neighbor or two when she was coming and going each day.

"Well, honey, we'll let you go for now, but if you need anything, call us. You know how much your mother wants to be involved. If it's okay with you, we're thinking of coming down in a couple of months. That should give you enough time to get settled before we barge in on you."

"You don't need to ask my permission, Dad. I'm happy to welcome you whenever you want to visit. I'll call you at the end of next week and let you know how things are going, okay? Love you both."

"Love you too Andi. Make us proud."

As they ended the call to the same encouraging words her father had offered throughout her life, Andi felt yet another stab of loneliness. Her entire family had lived within an hour's drive in Minnesota, and now she was all alone and a thousand miles away.

Suddenly she remembered the gift David had handed her the day before and she hurried downstairs to dig through the mess on the hall table, looking for the envelope. Kicking off her sneakers and collapsing into the nearest chair, she peeled open the envelope and pulled out a single sheet of paper. As she unfolded it, a smaller piece of paper fell into her lap.

"Welcome to Austin! We know you'll be missing Minnesota already and wanted you to feel a little more at home in your new city. We've signed you

up as the newest member of the *Austin Hockey Association. Yes, they have hockey in Texas! We know you always have your hockey gear handy and when you're ready, we encourage you to join one of the adult leagues, but until then, we reserved a spot for you at one of the Association's Sunday morning pickup games. They play every Sunday before the Cowboys game. We hope you'll make new friends who share the same love of hockey you have. The ticket is for this Sunday morning and it will get you in the door, but it's up to you to make new friends! Love, Carol and David."*

What a wonderful surprise! They were right, of course. After years of playing the sport, her hockey bag was never far away. To some it had seemed silly, but one thing that had influenced her decision to accept the job was learning hockey is a growing and increasingly well-loved sport in Texas. Back in Minnesota, she had skated regularly, although it wasn't as competitive as in her formative years.

The paper that had fallen out of the envelope was a ticket to play the next morning and she saw Carol had signed her up for the advanced skater's group. Maybe Texas wouldn't be so bad after all.

· · ·

Even though she was tired, the lure of getting her skates back on helped propel Andi to get up early the next morning and head to the rink. Being a stranger in the nearly empty women's locker room prompted a few curious looks in her direction from those already dressing, but mostly the women were welcoming. After the initial flurry of greetings, they went back to their conversations and Andi concentrated on getting dressed for the game. Pulling her University of Minnesota sweater over her head, it startled her when a newcomer appeared at her side and introduced herself.

"Hi, you must be new. I'm Susan," the woman said as they shook hands and Andi realized the Texas accent that had bombarded her since the plane touched down was nowhere to be found.

"Nice to meet you. I'm Andi. You don't sound like you're from Texas."

"Nope. Wisconsin for me. And I would guess you're from Minnesota, right?" she asked, giving a nod to Andi's jersey.

"Yup, but you won't hold that against me, right?" Andi said with a chuckle. The Gophers and Badgers had had an ongoing rivalry for decades.

"Heck no. Most of us are transplants from someplace or another at these games and we try to hold our own against the true Texans. So did you play?"

"A bit in college. You?"

Until she knew more about other players, Andi didn't want to brag too much about her hockey career. Everyone in her extended family, her parents included, had grown up with a pair of skates on their feet, but Andi had been the one with the most skill. She had been a captain on her college team that won the national championship three years in a row, which ultimately had led to an invitation to join the women's Olympic team.

"I wish. Mostly just backyard pond stuff, but I've continued to play. Had a few lessons when I got down here—they have an excellent program to teach adults the game—but I'm really not that good."

"Is it all women this morning?" Her question elicited a full belly laugh from Susan.

"Hate to break it to you, but until you arrived, I was the only woman in our group. The rest of these ladies are in the beginner's league. I suspect I was put in the advanced group just so they could say they had a woman on the team. Hockey might be a fast-growing sport in Texas, but it's still pretty male-dominated. How did you end up in Austin?" Susan asked.

"I just got a job at Presbyterian Medical Center," Andi told her without elaboration.

"That's terrific. Good for you," she said. "Now, if you're ready, I guess it's time to join the guys."

Susan led the way as they exited the locker room to an arena so massive it sported four separate sheets of ice that were all in use on this busy Sunday morning. Putting her heavy gloves on, Andi started her warmup skate as the men that were already warming up cast curious glances her way. Her helmet on and hair tucked in, she wasn't sure how many other players even realized she was a woman. It would be fun to see their reactions.

Two men appeared to be designated captains and, with only the cursory question of what position each of the other players preferred, they assigned Andi to the third of the three lines that rotated in and out of the game. She took a spot on the bench as the game began.

Carol and David's note had said she was in the advanced group, but most of the players were not exactly what Andi would call advanced with one exception. Strong and lean, the man had the perfect physique for the game of hockey. After just moments of watching, she recognized he also had the skills to match. The first time he touched the puck, he buried it in the net before the goalie even realized the shot was coming. It was quite obvious that somewhere down the line the man had played competitively, and Andi expected him to dominate the game. However, she was more than surprised to note that after that first easy goal, he continually passed the puck to the other players, even though he could have easily scored most times the puck hit his stick. His display of good sportsmanship and his obvious talent made it fun to watch the guy play.

By the time it was Andi's turn to hit the ice, she was eager to show what she could do, but an ill-advised pass changed all that. The first pass her way flew by her; picked off by a player from the other team, who easily scored. Several of her own teammates glared at her as they skated past. Their disdain served only to ratchet up her competitive nature. She held nothing back the next time the puck came her way.

Trapped in the corner with a couple of players from the opposing team, she cleared the puck and showed off her stick handling abilities all the way down the ice before burying it in the back of the net. Expecting high fives for her goal, she instead found the players had stopped to stare at her as they leaned on their sticks in apparent disdain. It wasn't exactly the impression she had been hoping for. She skated back to the bench with her head down until hearing their comments, just as the horn sounded for the end of the first period.

"*Pretty impressive!*"

"*Wow, great job!*"

"*Where'd you learn how to skate?*"

"*Want to be on my team next week?*"

Keeping her head down, she couldn't help but smile to herself as she skated to keep loose until the second period began. She also removed her helmet for the first time, shaking her long hair loose as she did so. It was hard to miss the looks of surprise when the other players realized she was a woman. Trying to hide her laughter at their reactions, she kept her head down. Minnesota had a well-established hockey development program starting with the youngest of players, but even there the male dominated side of the sport was still king. It wasn't often, but even with her skill level, she had been the subject of gender bias in the sport and it appeared things were no different in Texas. The irony of it all was that the negative comments she heard on the ice when these men realized she was a woman almost always came from men who would never have her level of skill.

While she might never be as strong as a male player, her skating speed often exceeded that of the men she played with. She knew she could have played and succeeded as a pro. With medical school on the horizon, the only option available to her after college had been the Olympic team, but when the invitation came to join the team, she had made the tough decision to choose school over the Olympics. The disappointment at having to turn down the invitation had faded, but she would always remember the sting of having to say no to the offer.

Being a woman wasn't the only strike against her in the world of sports, however. Blessed with good looks, she had always turned a man's head, but in the world of sports, that wasn't always such a good thing. Not only was she forced to work against the stereotype of women playing hockey, but she also had to deal with the ongoing perception that a pretty woman couldn't possibly have skills. Luckily, a little demonstration was usually all it took to convince them she was for real.

By the time the second period started, Andi's team was catching up and, to at least score a goal or two to even things up, she didn't hesitate to take shot after shot and by the end of the second period it was a tie game.

Now that the men were talking and joking with her, she felt more comfortable, at least when she wasn't on the ice at the same time as the best player from the other team. Whether or not by the design of their captain, she frequently battled for the puck with the man. After one particularly inspired effort between the two of them, Andi freed the puck and buried it in the net with a wicked slap shot. As her teammates celebrated the goal with fist bumps all around, her opponent slammed his stick to the ice in frustration and went to his bench amid jeers from his teammates for being beaten by a woman. Watching him from the corner of her eye, Andi hoped it wouldn't become a problem.

The third period was just underway when a skirmish erupted in the corner furthest from the bench. In a no-check game, it was unusual for tempers to flare, but two men had been taking cheap shots at each other all morning and now that their tempers had finally gotten the best of them, a fight was underway.

Watching safely from the bench with no intention of getting involved, Andi expected the fight to end when the combatants tired of trying to stay up on their skates. The bigger man had a good hold of the hockey sweater of his smaller opponent before both men crashed to the ice in a tangle of skates and discarded gloves and sticks. Andi had seen it all before. Players normally popped back to their feet after a fight, but not this time. The smaller of the men lay sprawled on his back and he wasn't moving. A hush fell over the rink. That alone was an ominous sign in the otherwise loud environment.

Even if she had missed what started the scuffle, there was no missing the pool of blood staining the ice around the downed player. Grabbing a towel and leaping over the boards, Andi called for someone to dial 911 and skated quickly to where the man lay, stopping just short of the rapidly congealing blood stain. Kneeling at the injured man's side, she calmly assessed the situation as blood poured between the man's fingers as he clutched at his neck.

The man's eyes were as big as saucers as he looked from one face to another before Andi peeled his hands away from his throat and immediately applied direct pressure on the wound to stem the steady pumping of blood. The towel Andi was holding quickly became soaked. A player's skate had sliced his throat - a rare but potentially deadly hockey injury.

"I know you're scared, but I promise you I'll do my best to make sure you'll be okay," she said confidently, using the voice all trauma surgeons adopt when they need a victim to remain calm. "I know this probably hurts like hell, but I have to press hard to get that bleeding under control. Try not to move your head if you can, okay?"

Offering only the slightest nod of his head to show he understood what she was saying, he stopped moving. Every patient she worked on had looked back at her with that same pleading look. Knowing they could die, they all wanted to believe that she would save them.

"Get me more towels," she said.

No one moved.

"More towels now!" she shouted to break them out of the stupor they all seemed to be in before several players skated to the bench and returned with more towels. She could tell the pressure she was applying was stemming the flow of blood, but she didn't dare release her hold for a better look. If the cut had penetrated all the way to the internal jugular vein, the man had only a minute or two before he would bleed to death right there on the ice.

The rink had gone deathly silent except for the faint sounds of crying coming from those in the stands while the players emptied the benches to stand guard around the injured player.

The boards became lined with the faces of spectators from the other rinks who watched the drama unfold. Counting the seconds ticking by, she prayed the ambulance would arrive in time. Finally, the familiar wail of a siren cut through the air.

"He's been down three minutes by my estimation, and I'm pretty sure it's only the external jugular. Hang a bag of saline and get an IV started so we can replace some fluids he's lost."

As the paramedics worked to follow her directions, one of them finally asked, "Are you a doctor?"

"Yes. Presbyterian Medical Center. As soon as you have that IV going, let's load and roll."

With the IV in and fluids being forced into the man's body, Andi could feel a weak but steady pulse begin beneath her fingers once more. His condition was still critical, but at least he was stable enough for transport. With her hands still firmly applying pressure, the paramedics loaded him onto the stretcher and wheeled him to the ambulance as the other players watched helplessly and called out best wishes to their friend.

Minutes later, they were on their way to the hospital with the siren warning other drivers to get out of the way. With Andi still in her hockey gear, the paramedic looked like he wasn't sure what to make of her.

"Do you want me to take over pressure for you, doc?"

"Thanks, but I don't want to take any chances by making a switch. You could do one thing for me though," she told him.

"What's that?"

"Could you help me get my skates off?"

She wanted to be ready to move as soon as they arrived at the hospital.

"Which hospital are we going to?" she asked as the skates finally came off, leaving her in stocking feet.

"Presbyterian is closest, so we're heading over there. I don't think I've seen you there before."

"Actually, my first day is tomorrow," she said with a wry grin.

"Talk about baptism by fire," the paramedic said as he continued to monitor the patient's vitals. The patient's eyes moved frantically from one face to the other before landing on Andi's once more.

"How are you doing? You hanging in there, Mark? That's your name, right?" The other players had called him by name as they left the ice. "You're doing great and we're almost at the hospital," she told him before her eyes once more moved to the equipment monitoring the man's vital signs. The numbers weren't good, but they were holding steady.

Not expecting an answer, she received none in return and smiled down at him once again, hoping to give him a bit of encouragement as they arrived at the hospital.

Sunlight flooded the interior compartment of the ambulance as medical personnel pulled the doors open at the emergency department entrance. All business as they listened to the paramedic relay the patient's medical condition, her attire still surprised the medical staff, and one doctor demanded to know who she was.

Not releasing the pressure on Mark's neck, she identified herself. "Dr. Andrea Taylor."

"The Dr. Taylor who's starting here tomorrow?" he asked with raised eyebrows.

"Yes. This is Mark. Sorry, I don't know his last name. It appears to be the external jugular. I brought the bleeding under control just under a minute from the time of injury. Mark is lucid and alert and he has a steady and strong pulse, but he needs to get to surgery immediately."

To his credit, the doctor didn't flinch at her direction and instead barked out his own orders before they hurried inside with the patient.

"Dr. Taylor, would you like to assist?" he asked.

"I don't technically have privileges until tomorrow."

"I think we're safe to say that won't be a problem," the doctor said with a smile. "Your reputation precedes you."

"If you're sure?" She didn't want to cause any legal entanglements with hospital protocol before she had even started.

"I assure you it won't be a problem and knowing your skill level, I think you're just what we need to save this man's life."

Occasionally it was good to have a reputation, and it turned out this was one of those instances. The Medical Center Chief had recruited her to their facility because of her advanced skills that had already garnered nationwide attention. Being recognized by her peers was certainly satisfying, but more than anything, her satisfaction came from the look in the eyes of family members when they learned she had saved the life of someone they loved who should have died.

After verifying the patient was stable, hospital staff whisked him up to the surgical floor, where preparations had already begun for Mark's surgery. Turning her hold on his neck over to a resident, with strict instructions not to lessen pressure for even a moment, she exchanged her hockey sweater for the scrub top handed to her and scrubbed up next to the ER doctor.

"Hell of a welcome to Texas, Dr. Taylor," he commented. "I'd shake your hand, but well, you know. I'm Brian Miller, Assistant Chief of Emergency Surgery. When did you get to town?"

"Hi Brian. Please call me Andi. I've been here since Friday night. Thanks for letting me scrub in on this one. I was playing hockey with the patient when he went down, and I appreciate being able to see his care through."

"Aha. That explains your outfit when you got to the ER. Damn good thing you were there or he probably would have bled to death. I know you have vascular certification, so I am going to let you take the lead. Maybe I can learn a trick or two from you."

Entering the operating theater, Dr. Miller took a moment to introduce her to his team before they got down to the task at hand and the room quieted with only the steady hum of the equipment breaking the silence.

"All right everyone, let's save a life today," Andi said before accepting the scalpel and taking her first good look at the wound. Soon she let herself relax in the comforting familiarity of what she did best.

. . .

Hours later, it was over. Mark had made it through the delicate surgery with flying colors and as the nurses bundled him up for transport to the recovery room, Andi stripped off her gloves and gown. She rolled her neck, trying to release some of the tension that had built up from the hours of tedious work repairing the wound to Mark's neck.

"Really exceptional work, Dr. Taylor," Dr. Miller exclaimed as they walked together from the OR.

"Thank you. It wasn't exactly the way I had planned to spend the day, but it turned out well."

In a borrowed pair of scrubs, her hockey clothes tucked safely in a bag at the nurse's station, she looked down at the booties on her feet.

"That's right," Dr. Miller said as he followed her gaze. "You didn't have any shoes on when you arrived. What was that all about?"

Explaining that she had been wearing hockey skates in the ambulance elicited a chuckle from the man.

"I'd sure like to get my skates back before I leave," she told him. Good, comfortable skates were hard to come by.

"I'll have the ER desk track them down for you, so don't worry about it. And we'll get you a ride home. I'm sure you'd like to salvage whatever's left of your weekend."

"That would be great, but I'll hang around until Mark is out of recovery and then I can add him to my rounds tomorrow if that's okay with you. But for now, if you can direct me to the waiting room, I'll see if any of Mark's family have shown up and let them know he's doing okay."

A nurse appeared at her side and guided her to the nearby family waiting room, which was packed with familiar faces from the hockey game. Unlike Andi, they had changed into their street clothes, but there was no mistaking the worry on their faces as members from both of the teams stood up when she entered the room.

Dressed in her scrubs, she wasn't sure if they recognized her or not until Susan addressed her.

"Wow! You didn't tell me you were a doctor," she exclaimed.

"I am. Now, are any of you Mark's family by chance?"

A young woman holding a small child in her arms walked forward with tear-stained cheeks.

"I'm Jennie, Mark's wife. Is he okay?" she asked with fear in her eyes.

"Hi Jennie. I'm Dr. Taylor and I operated on your husband. He's going to be fine."

The room seemed to breathe a collective sigh of relief at her words.

"He's in recovery and everything went really well with the repair to his neck. He's got a pretty angry looking incision right now, but in time the inflammation will fade and the scar will be barely noticeable. I expect he'll make a full recovery."

"Can I see him?" she asked with just the beginning of a smile.

"The nurse will come and get you when he's ready for visitors. He'll be in the hospital for a few days just to make sure there are no complications, but then you should be able to take him home. I'll check in on him tomorrow morning to make sure he's doing okay. Do you have questions for me before then?"

"I don't think so, but Doctor thank you so much for saving my husband!" she exclaimed as she pulled Andi in for an awkward hug, juggling her child between them.

Before Andi could make her escape from the room, several of the players stepped up to offer their thanks for saving their friend. Last in line was the man who had so impressed her with his skills on the ice. She had noticed him watching from the corner of the room as she talked to Mark's wife, and the look he gave her was unsettling for its intensity.

On skates he was an impressive figure, but here in the hospital, even without his protective equipment and dressed in casual clothes, he was still stunning. Just a touch over six feet in height, with a trim and hard-muscled body that showed he most likely worked out as much as Andi did, she couldn't take her eyes off him. He wore his dark hair longer than most men and kept a light beard that had become so popular in the last few years. Whether that was by design or just because it was the weekend and he hadn't shaved, she didn't know, but it wasn't heavy enough to hide the slight scar on his chin, either. Large chocolate eyes and full lips that any woman would want to kiss completed the look. She imagined he had a tough time fighting off women.

"Thanks for your quick thinking with Mark," he said as he shook her hand.

"You're welcome," she told him. He was still holding her hand.

"I'm Ryan Jacobs."

"Andi Taylor," she replied before gently pulling her hand back from his grasp after what seemed an uncomfortably long period.

"Guess we were lucky you were there this morning. Am I wrong, or was that the type of injury that could have killed him?"

"You're not wrong. Sometimes it helps to be in the right place at the right time."

"From the way you were skating, I don't think it was just luck you were with us this morning. You've got some serious hockey chops."

"Actually, I was thinking the same thing about you," she admitted. "Did you play professionally?"

"Only in juniors. Blew out my knee and that was the end of my career. How about you? I mean, where did you play?"

"Not professionally, but I played a bit in college." Still not ready to admit the extent of her abilities, especially now she knew Ryan had played professionally, she said nothing further as those who remained in the waiting room started talking amongst themselves again.

"You're from Minnesota, right?" he asked.

At first she suspected her accent had given her away, but then remembered her University of Minnesota hockey sweater.

"Guilty," she admitted. Ryan had only the slightest of Texas accents. "But I'm thinking you're not originally from Texas either, right?"

"I'm Canadian. Settled here about six or seven years back when I started my company."

"Oh. What kind of company?"

"Dr. Taylor, can I pull you away for just a moment?" Turning around, she saw one of the scrub nurses standing at the door.

"I'll be right there," Andi told her before turning back to the handsome man in front of her.

"It was nice meeting you, but I have to go," she said with more than a touch of regret. Ryan was certainly attractive, and she wouldn't mind getting to know him better if her life was different, but ultimately history would be sure to repeat itself and it was best to just not go there.

As she began to walk away, Ryan reached out and touched her arm.

"Will we see you at the game next Sunday morning?"

"I'm not sure. Having just started, I don't know what my schedule will be," Andi told him even though she would love to play again.

"I hope to see you soon and thanks again for what you did for Mark."

Leaving the waiting room, she took one last glance back into the room to find him watching her as she walked out. If they hadn't just met, she would have described the look in his eyes as desire.

Several hours later, she left the hospital. Her patient was stable and awake and speaking with his family, and she knew he would be in excellent hands overnight. The cab driver raised a questioning eyebrow when she entered the cab with skates in hand and booties on her feet before depositing her at the rink to collect her gear - none the worse for wear but having lost a whole day of unpacking.

Once again, her new neighborhood was quiet, with not a soul in sight by the time she turned on to her street. Maybe the realtor hadn't known what she was talking about when she said the area was full of young families. It wasn't the sole reason Andi had bought the house, but it had been a nice selling point and she was strangely disappointed. Her neighborhood back in Minnesota had been alive with activity throughout the day and her house had been in the middle of a group of neighbors that regularly scheduled block parties so everyone could socialize together. They weren't events she had made often, but those she had attended had been enjoyable. It didn't appear that would happen in Austin, though.

The phone was ringing as she entered the house, and she rushed to answer it.

"Dr. Taylor," she said rather breathlessly.

"Hey Andi," came Carol's welcome voice. "I was just about to hang up, figuring you had gone out. David wanted me to call and find out if you took advantage of our little welcome gift."

If only they knew.

"I did, and I can't thank you enough. After spending all day Saturday unpacking, it was just what I needed."

"Did you win the game?" she asked.

"Not exactly."

"What does that mean?"

"We never got to finish. There was a medical emergency."

"Oh no. Is everyone okay?" she asked.

Sparing her the more gruesome details, Andi gave her the cliff notes version of how she had spent the day.

"See, fate meant for you to come to Texas," Carol said confidently. "If you hadn't been there, that man might have died."

Laughing at her positivity, Andi wasn't so sure fate had anything to do with it.

"Whatever the reason, it looks like he'll be okay. I'll check in on him tomorrow when I start work."

"But with all that drama aside, did you make any new friends? I'm willing to bet there were a couple of good-looking guys there, right?"

"Carol! Is that the reason you signed me up? To set me up with a guy? I thought we agreed that wouldn't happen anymore."

"I know I agreed to that, but that was a few years back and things have changed now. You're older and more settled and, for heaven's sake, you're in Texas where the men are gorgeous. You can't fault me for trying. David knows a couple of men who play and even he agrees there's one or two that would be a good match for you."

"So now you're dragging your husband into it too?" Andi teased. As frustrated as she sounded, Andi knew they weren't being malicious. Carol just wanted Andi to be as happy as she and David were.

"Come on. I know you had a good time. Weren't there at least a couple of men who caught your eye?"

"That's never been the problem." For Andi, the difficulties had always been after a man was around long enough to realize her work always came first.

"So there was nobody you found attractive?" she asked with dogged determination.

"I didn't say that," Andi said slowly as she imagined the excitement that statement would generate in her friend.

"Ha! I knew it. Who was he?" she asked.

"Nope. Not going there. If I tell you his name, the next thing I know, you'll have us on a blind date and I'm not going down that road. Besides, I doubt if I'll see him again, so it's a moot point."

"Andi, you take all the fun out of matchmaking, but I'm not giving up yet. We've invited all kinds of single men to the barbeque next weekend, and we'll just see if we can find you a good old Texas boy to spend your lonely nights with."

"You are incorrigible," Andi told her with a smile. "But I'm still looking forward to your party... oops... I mean, your barbeque! And speaking of food, I have had nothing to eat today, so I am going to beg off for now and make myself a sandwich. Thanks for checking in on me and I'll talk to you in a few days and let you know how work is going."

"You're going to do great, Andi. Talk to you soon."

CHAPTER TWO

Walking in the door at her new job the next morning was not as dramatic as Andi's arrival the day before had been, but it was nice when a few people actually recognized her. Dr. Miller was the first to greet her, and she was grateful for a friendly face as he escorted her to the office of her new boss, Chief of Emergency Surgery Dr. Everett Thompson.

"Dr. Taylor," he said as he rose from his desk and extended his hand. "Welcome to Austin. We're excited to have you join us."

Dr. Thompson was everything she would expect from a Chief of Surgery. Late sixties, tall with a strong jawline and sharp angles to his face, he carried himself like a man with a military background, leaving no doubt he was in charge. The cut of his salt and pepper hair was also military regulation, and his firm handshake fully engulfed her own small hand. He reminded her of her dad.

"Thank you very much. I'm excited to be here."

Motioning her to be seated, he sat back down and studied her from across the expanse of his messy desk before pressing his hands together in a praying motion. He said nothing. For the briefest of moments, she wondered if he was having second thoughts about hiring her.

"I was going to ask if you're ready to go to work, but from what I've seen, we already benefitted from your services over the weekend," he said when he finally spoke again. The look on his face was rather nondescript.

Was he angry she had operated on a patient before her clinical privileges had actually begun?

"That's true, and I apologize if I overstepped my bounds by doing so," she admitted. "It certainly wasn't my intention when I came in with the patient. Wait a minute. What did you mean? What did you see?"

"Didn't you show her Brian?" he asked Dr. Miller before turning his computer screen her direction.

There for the entire world to see was a video of the incident the day before at the rink. How could she not have expected it? Of course, someone with a smartphone had captured the whole thing and put it online. The video started with Mark on the ice and her skating to his side and didn't end until the ambulance pulled away.

"The only thing that would have made it better was if someone knew who you were. Look at these comments... all wanting to know your name," Dr. Thompson said excitedly.

"I'm sorry, sir. Obviously, I didn't intend to have my actions show up on social media."

"I don't think you understand what I'm saying, Dr. Taylor. This is a good thing. It's just too bad we couldn't benefit from this kind of publicity. It's great for our fundraising efforts. Now, as for you doing surgery before your official start date, I guess we'll just let that go. While technically you didn't yet have privileges, I can't argue with the outcome, so I'm not worried about it. Our philosophy of care is that we do what's best for the patient and I think you both made the right decision. In fact, Dr. Miller tells me your skills are even more impressive than we thought."

A quick glance at Dr. Miller's nodding head showed he concurred.

"Thank you. I appreciate that," she said, trying to be humble in acceptance of the praise but knowing that her abilities with a scalpel were the reason they had offered her the position.

"Our plan for the day is to have you shadow Dr. Miller to learn how we operate - no pun intended - and then we'll set you free tomorrow. We already have a couple of surgeries lined up for you, and you'll have time today to meet those patients and review their charts before tomorrow.

Pretty simple stuff just to get a scalpel in your hand. I wish I could give you more time to get acclimated but we're short-staffed as you know."

"I'd like to check in on my patient from yesterday if that's okay with you both," she asked.

"It's first on our list for today," Dr. Miller said. "I knew you'd want to follow up with him."

"Thank you for that."

Dr. Thompson answered her next question without even having to ask.

"You're certainly free to choose your own team for the operating room, but we want to get you in there right away, so for now I've assigned a handpicked team for you until you get to know the people here and decide who you'll work best with. We have top-notch staff, but I know it's important for you to feel you can trust and depend on the men and women in the trenches with you."

Aha... so he was military at heart! He stood to show the meeting was over and shook her hand once more before he walked them to the door.

"Thank you for your time, sir."

"We're expecting big things from you, Dr. Taylor. Let me know if you need anything."

"I will."

If she thought the cordial meeting with Dr. Thompson showed how her day would go, she was way off base. The calm of the meeting dissolved into the chaos of a Level One trauma hospital, leaving Dr. Miller's detailed hospital tour in tatters as they were called from one trauma to another. Eventually, the sheer volume of patients meant she was on her own.

Many of the staff seemed to know who she was even though she had not yet officially been introduced to most, and it was easy to see Dr. Thompson was spot on in his assessment of the trauma staff. Everyone she interacted with was professional and efficient, and they accepted her direction without comment. The staff worked together as a well-oiled machine and things went smoothly from the first moment, at least as smoothly as a trauma department can work. To the layperson, the activity might have looked like chaos, but the well-trained staff remained calm in the face of an overwhelming patient load.

It wasn't long before Andi found herself in her first officially sanctioned surgery of the day... a drive-by shooting that had shredded the aorta of a young man who looked to be barely out of his teens. Being certified in both cardiac and vascular, there was no question she would do the surgery and Dr. Miller happily handed it off to her. This was one of those cases that could go either way and she prayed that her first official surgery wouldn't end in a death.

The surgical team prepared the patient as she watched from the scrub room and briefed the brand-new interns assigned to her.

"This is an extremely complicated surgery. None of you will be directly involved, and I don't want you to get in my way. Find a spot where you can watch and if I ask you to do something, I expect you'll do it without question. Does everyone understand?"

Four heads bobbed up and down in response, even though two looked like they were about to pass out. Andi directed a steely look their way from behind her mask. Normally easygoing with her staff, she knew the surgery would be delicate and risky and she wouldn't have time to hold the hand of an intern who couldn't stomach the sight of blood.

"Are you two going to be okay? I don't want anyone passing out in my OR. Don't even go in if you can't stay on your feet. Do you understand what I'm telling you?"

The heads of the two she was concerned about bobbed up and down, albeit it much slower than they had before. It didn't give her much confidence they would keep their word, but there was no more time to waste.

"Okay, let's go in and remember, don't get in my way."

Barely into the surgery, with only the smallest amount of blood visible, the first of the two questionable interns had already slumped to the floor as the other ran for the door.

Directing her attention back to the patient on the table in front of her, Andi took a deep breath before continuing as two nurses helped the intern from the floor and out of the operating room.

"More suction please."

Accompanied by the sounds of the ventilator and the soft voices of the team, she worked efficiently and quietly. Some surgeons blasted music in the OR, but she had long preferred a tranquil operating room. Few could argue with the results then or now and in the end, she was happy with the outcome. The boy would live.

"Thank you everyone," she told the staff after placing the last suture. "I'll check on him in recovery soon. Does anyone know if his family is here?"

"His mother is in the waiting room," the lead scrub nurse, a woman named Ashley, told her. "Her name is Sofia Morales. Sarah can show you the way if you'd like."

"Actually," Andi told her with a smile behind her mask, "That's the one room I know how to find on my own." Taking off her gown, she threw her gloves in the medical waste bag.

"That's right, you operated yesterday, right? Is it true you came in the ambulance in stocking feet?" Sarah asked with a smile. Obviously, news of Andi's dramatic introduction to the hospital had already found its way around the surgical unit.

"True, although I did originally have hockey skates on. We were in the middle of a game when a player went down with a lacerated jugular."

"Wow! Did he make it?" she asked.

"He made it through surgery yesterday, but I've been so busy I haven't been able to check in on him today. Would you be able to find out for me while I'm talking to this boy's family? His name is Mark, although I never got his last name."

"I'd be happy to do that for you, Doctor. Just stop by the nurse's station when you're done with the family. I should have something for you by then."

"Thank you and thanks everyone," she said, addressing everyone in the room. "You did a really great job and I look forward to working with you all in the future."

Wow! That was almost a 'y'all' and she had only been in Texas a few days.

Heading to the waiting room, it was a surprise to see one solitary person sitting in the corner in stark juxtaposition to the packed room she had walked into the day before. Head down, hands clasped together in prayer, the small, frail looking woman could only be her patient's mother.

Unsure whether to wait until the woman finished her prayer or not, Andi asked quietly, "Ms. Morales?"

Lifting her head as Andi walked towards her and took a seat, the fear in the woman's eyes was substantial. Andi didn't waste any time putting her out of her misery.

"My boy?" she asked.

"He's going to be okay," Andi reported before explaining the boy's injuries and the surgery she had performed.

The woman listened intently before she burst into great, heaving sobs and Andi put her arms around her.

"Thank you, Doctor," she said when she could talk again. Grabbing Andi's hands in her own, she pumped them up and down.

"You're welcome ma'am."

"I don't know what I would have done if I had lost him. He's such a good boy. I raised him right. My son doesn't run with gangs and he doesn't live on the streets. He is a good boy, gets good grades, and he's going to college."

"He's lucky to have such a loving mother."

"But that didn't stop him from getting shot. They told me he was in the wrong place at the wrong time, but he was just coming out of the library. How could they shoot my beautiful baby boy?"

Andi had learned a long time ago there was never any good reason for violence, especially for innocent victims, and she had no answer for her.

"Miguel is going to be okay, and that's what you need to concentrate on," she told her quietly. "He's going to be in recovery for another hour, and then we'll move him to a regular room. Do you have anyone else who can come and sit with you?"

"My sister is on her way from Houston. Can I see my boy?"

"Soon. The nurse will come and get you. It shouldn't be too long. I'll check in on Miguel in a bit, but until then, is there anything you'd like to ask me?"

"No, and thank you, doctor. Dr. Taylor, is it?" she said, looking at Andi's new nametag. They had yet to embroider her name on her lab coat. "Thank you for saving my boy. I'm going to say a special prayer for you when I'm on my knees tonight."

"You're very welcome, and I'll say a prayer for you and your family."

. . .

"Sarah, did you find out about my hockey patient yet?"

"Just finished. His name is Mark Anderson. He's in Room 6422 West."

"Can you point me in that direction?"

The nurse jotted down directions to Mark's room and Andi carefully folded the note and put it in her pocket just as her pager lit up with another urgent call to the ER.

"Thanks Sarah. Tell everyone not to go too far. It looks like I'll be right back up with another surgical patient in a few minutes.

Hoping she still remembered the way, she raced down the hallway to the nearest staircase. It was six floors down to the ER, but she was used to taking the stairs which were most often always faster than waiting for the elevator.

"I'm Dr. Taylor," she said as she exited the stairwell and raced to the nurse's station, not the least bit out of breath. Hockey was a great stamina builder. "You paged me?"

"I did," Dr. Miller said as he walked to her side. "We've got an attempted suicide. Slit her wrist and throat. Luckily, the throat wound doesn't appear to be deep, but this one needs your vascular skills. Patient's name is Stephanie Michaels."

Andi hurried to the trauma bay, where a cursory examination showed Dr. Miller's assessment was correct.

"Stephanie, my name is Dr. Taylor, and I'm going to operate on you in just a few minutes."

As with most of her patients, the girl looked back in great fear. She should have been able to speak, but still she said nothing.

"You're going to have a pleasant sleep and when you wake up, I promise everything will be better. Is there anyone we should call for you?"

She nodded her head ever so slightly before whispering, "Please call my mom."

"The mother's already on her way," a nurse interjected.

"Did you hear that? Your mother should be here soon, so I don't want you to worry about that. Let's get you up to surgery now, okay?"

With more strength than Andi would have expected from someone with those kinds of injuries, Stephanie grabbed her arm as she turned to leave.

"Don't let me die. I don't want to die," she pleaded.

Placing a gentle hand on the girl, Andi did her best to reassure her without making promises she couldn't keep. "I promise you I am very good at what I do and you're in excellent hands. I will take good care of you."

A look of hope slowly replaced the fear in her eyes. It wasn't necessarily a belief that Andi would save her, but at least it was something.

While Stephanie was being prepped for surgery, Andi scrubbed nearby. She couldn't help but think about the power of hope and belief. The will to live and all the power that implied was a real thing and for patients like Stephanie, who were here ostensibly because they no longer wanted to live, she wondered if her words of encouragement would be enough.

"Dr. Taylor? We're ready for you."

Mask firmly in place, gown tied and gloves on her hands, Andi worked to save Stephanie's life - the life she had so willingly tried to throw away just hours before.

The same surgical team was with her again and by now they knew enough about how she liked to work and the surgery went smoothly. Only two of the interns from the morning's surgery were along for the ride, and she wondered if she would ever see the other two again.

When the delicate work of reconstructing the vascular system at both the wrist and throat was complete, she stood back from the table with a satisfied sigh, rolling her shoulders and neck yet again.

"Great job everyone. Is it just me, or do we work well together?" Even covered with masks, she could see the smiles directed back.

"You're very easy to work with Dr. Taylor," Ashley said as she helped Andi remove her gown. "I've been lead scrub nurse for several years and think I can speak for everyone here when I say that you're a lot nicer than most surgeons. And I want you to know that we all saw the video of you at the hockey game. It makes us proud to say we work with you."

As top of the medical food chain, surgeons could be difficult. Many of them developed a sense of importance that went far beyond reality. Sure, they saved lives, but the contributions of everyone involved in the process were equally important. During her residency, Andi had worked with some real jerks who never had a kind word to say to their coworkers. That's not how Andi treated people. Maybe it was ingrained Minnesota Nice, but she had long felt it was important to be kind to those around her.

"Thanks for saying that. You've all had a long day, and I want you to have a wonderful evening. See you tomorrow, okay? Thanks again."

Dr. Thompson had selected the team, but as far as she was concerned, they were hers now and she would have to remember to thank him.

Stephanie's mother had arrived just as surgery was wrapping up and Andi made her way to the waiting room with the good news. It didn't surprise Andi when Stephanie's mother reported it wasn't the first time her daughter had tried to kill herself and said she expected her to try again. A mandatory seventy-two-hour psych hold would give the family some time to find help for the girl before she attempted it again.

After updating Stephanie's mother and checking on her progress in recovery, it was the end of a very long day - at least until Andi remembered she had not yet checked in on Mark. Digging in the pocket of her lab coat to find the room number, she took the stairs to Mark's floor, stopping just long enough to glance at his chart. With visiting hours nearly over, the floor was as quiet as a hospital ever gets and she made her way to his room, giving a soft knock on the door before going in.

Even late in the evening, the room was full of visitors who moved out of the way to allow her to stand at Mark's bedside.

"Hi Mark. Don't know if you remember me or not, but I'm Dr. Taylor. I did your surgery yesterday," she said before offering her hand. His grip was firm.

"Of course, I remember you. Not only are you all over the internet, but you've got a wicked slap shot," he told her as the room erupted in laughter.

Looking around the room, she recognized several faces from Sunday's hockey game and she smiled at them all.

"From what I've been told, you did more than just my surgery. You saved my life. Jennie and I can't thank you enough!"

At the mention of her name, his wife stepped forward. "Thank you again Dr. Taylor."

"You're both very welcome. I was just glad I was in the right place at the right time and could help. Sorry I didn't get here earlier, but it's been a busy day around here and I just got out of another surgery. I took a quick look at your chart before coming in. It looks like you're recovering nicely."

"When can I go home?" he asked with an anxious look at his wife.

"Maybe in a couple of days. You lost a lot of blood, and I want to make sure everything is normal again before sending you home."

"And when can I play hockey again?" As a hockey player herself, she knew how important that was and chuckled at the question.

"That will take a little longer. Maybe in a few weeks, but you have to promise me no more fights!"

"I'll promise for him," his wife said as she looked lovingly down at her husband. "We're not going through this again!"

With a promise to check in on him the next morning, Andi took her leave. Her head down as she reviewed Mark's chart one more time, she looked up just in time to see a familiar and very handsome face turn the corner and begin walking towards her. Ryan sported a potted plant in one hand and a six-pack of beer in the other.

"Dr. Taylor," he said when he realized it was her. The smile on his face grew with each step as he quickened his pace to get to her. "I didn't expect to see you here."

"That's funny since I work here," she said with a touch of sarcasm, although she wasn't sure why she was suddenly so defensive. The man had been nothing but charming each time they had met.

"Well, of course you do and I knew that, but what I meant was its late and I would figure with doctor's hours and all you'd be long gone by now."

"Contrary to popular belief, doctors don't work eight to five and actually I'm just on my way home," she told him before nodding at the six-pack of beer in his hand. "I hope you're not expecting my patient to have any of that."

"What? Ah, no. Of course not," he stammered. His guilty reaction said otherwise. "So, how's Mark doing?"

"He's doing well and entertaining a whole crowd. If you're going to see him, I better let you go because visiting hours are almost over. Nice seeing you again," she told him as she moved past him.

"Dr. Taylor? Andi?" he said. "Would you like to have dinner with me tomorrow night?"

His words stopped her mid-step. Being asked out was the last thing she was expecting in that instant and for a fleeting moment, she considered accepting.

"Thanks, but I don't think so," she said after a lengthy pause. As attractive as Ryan was, something told her getting involved with him would not be a good idea. She had already seen how intensely he looked at her and instinctively knew this was a man who loved deeply. With her very dismal dating history, getting involved with someone like that just when she was starting a new job would be too much to handle.

Her obvious hesitation to the question was all he needed to prod her to reconsider.

"It doesn't have to be tomorrow," he said. "What about Friday, or next week, if that would work better for you?"

"Thanks, but no."

"Are you married? Do you have a boyfriend?"

"Not that it's any of your business, but no. I am not married and I don't have a boyfriend."

"Then why not have dinner with me?"

Did she really owe him a reason? No. But it didn't appear he was going to let it go either. She was flattered by his interest, but it had been a long first day. She was just too tired to deal with it.

"If you must know, I'm not interested in a relationship. I just moved here, have a massive house filled with boxes that need unpacking and rooms that will sit empty until I find time to shop for furniture. Not to mention that I just started this job today and have already put in a fourteen-hour day. I simply don't have time for relationships."

"So, you're saying that if all that were different that you'd go out with me," he said with a grin.

"What?" she said in confusion. "No, that's not what I said. I said I'm not interested in going on a date."

"Well then, we won't call it a date. You must eat. I must eat. Why can't it just be two friends having a meal together?"

"In case you haven't noticed, we're not friends. We just met." Good lord, the man was pushy. Attractive, but pushy.

"But we could be friends. Come on. Isn't it easier to just say yes to me?"

He was right. Saying yes would at least end the conversation and she could go home to her nice comfy bed, but looking into those dark eyes, she knew it wouldn't take much to develop feelings for the man. Even in the short time she had known him, she could tell he was not only extremely intelligent, but funny and comfortable to be around. Combined with his good looks, it was a dangerous combination.

"I'm sorry, but the answer is no," she insisted. The look of surprise on his face left no doubt he wasn't used to being turned down by women.

"Okay, well you have a good night then anyway," he said before turning to continue down the hall and into his friend's room.

Watching him walk away, Andi had another moment of hesitation. She had made the logical decision. She had no time for dating and her history with men had been dismal failures caused by her professional commitments, but something about the man was drawing her to him. Shaking her head to clear such thoughts, she took one last look down the now empty hallway before turning and heading for home.

CHAPTER THREE

A night made shorter by her insane need to stay up working on the seemingly endless unpacking and getting her house in order had left Andi extra tired the next morning. The lack of sleep, combined with information overload of everything she had to learn about her new hospital, made it difficult to get through her second day at work with a cheerful smile on her face, but she soldiered through.

Unlike the previous day, she was only in the operating room one time, but it was a surgery that took nearly all day. The patient had suffered a fall at a construction site and rebar had pierced his body in several parts of his torso and extremities. It took not only her skills, but those of two other surgeons working in tandem to save his life. Even with all that medical expertise, it was still touch and go.

Mid-way through the surgery, while trying to lessen the stiff neck that was developing from being hunched over the patient for hours, she glanced at the gallery above to see Dr. Thompson watching. He joined her in the doctor's lounge after it was all over.

"Great job, Dr. Taylor," he said before offering a cup of coffee. "That's exactly the type of case we brought you here for, and it couldn't have gone better."

"Thank you, sir," she told him as she took a sip of the strong coffee and wondered if he often took the time to watch his staff in surgery.

"Brian told me about the work you did yesterday, and I thought he was exaggerating about your skills. Decided I needed to see for myself," he said to her unasked question. "As it turns out, I don't think he was being generous enough. You are an exceptional surgeon."

"Thank you sir, but of course not all surgeries go that well. The staff here is superb. They deserve a lot of the credit."

"Then you're happy with the team I put together for you? You don't want to make any changes?"

"I am thrilled with them. So, no... no changes are necessary from my point of view. They might have a different opinion, but I think we work very well together."

"That's the same thing they told me about you," he said. "I met with them early this morning and they couldn't say enough nice things about you."

Now that was interesting. All the research she had done on Dr. Thompson before accepting the job was right. He was a good leader.

"That's nice to hear," she told him with a slight smile, "but something tells me that's not the only reason you're here."

"Not only are you an excellent surgeon, but it appears you're quite astute. I have a favor to ask and I wanted to give you as much advance notice as possible. I'd like you to join some of us at a fundraiser for the hospital. It's the Saturday after next and it's being held on a ranch outside of town. The owner is one of the hospital's biggest benefactors and he asked personally for you to attend. It's an annual event to raise money for the hospital. In fact, donations from the event paid for the new wing. I know you are just getting settled and have a lot on your plate, but as a personal favor to me, I hope you'll consider attending."

How could she say no? Not only was he the boss, but he was asking for a personal favor.

"Of course, I'll be there. If you want to send the details over to my office, I'll make sure it gets included on my calendar." She had yet to do more than glance at her office door and hadn't yet met her assistant, but figured that was the best way to make sure she remembered.

"Wonderful, I'll RSVP for you. Again, good job today. Keep it up."

And with that, he was gone, leaving her to wonder who the benefactor was. There was no doubt there was a lot of money in Texas, especially in the capital city of Austin, but why would the man ask for her to attend? She might have an excellent reputation in the medical community, but as far as she knew, that didn't extend outside the boundaries of the hospital and she didn't know anyone wealthy enough to fund a hospital wing who might be involved.

With no further pages to the ER and her construction worker patient stable, she headed to her new office. The first day tour of the hospital had gotten her and Dr. Miller to the hallway door before being paged and this morning's emergency had delayed her visit until now. Opening the hall door, she entered an outer office to find a desk plate identifying her assistant as Lillian Moore. The woman wasn't there, although what appeared to be a fresh cup of coffee sitting on the desk showed she wasn't too far away.

Andi walked by Lillian's desk to the door that already sported a sign with her own name to discover a beautifully appointed and completely unexpected office. Although not her style, the decidedly masculine space featured a large window directly behind the heavy desk with a breathtaking view of downtown Austin. Smaller than Dr. Thompson's office by a good amount, the room was still large enough to provide space for a small sitting area and even included a small private restroom complete with a shower that would come in handy on those late nights when she couldn't make it home. Deep pile carpeting cushioned her every step as she completed the brief tour and hung her lab coat on the coat rack near the bathroom. Taking a seat in the high-backed leather desk chair, she turned to survey her new surroundings.

"I think I could get used to this," she said to the empty room before a woman walked in with a surprised look on her face.

"Excuse me, what are you doing in here?" she asked sternly.

"Are you Lillian?" Andi asked as she rose to her feet.

"I am, but who are you and again, what are you doing in here?"

"Dr. Andrea Taylor," Andi said as she extended her hand in greeting.

The look of horror on Lillian's face would have been comical if she hadn't felt so sorry for her.

"Oh Dr. Taylor, I'm so sorry. I thought you were still in surgery and I wasn't expecting to see you today. I'm Lillian, your assistant."

"Nice to meet you Lillian. I'm sorry I surprised you."

"No, I'm the one who should be sorry," she said. Her face was a brilliant shade of red. "I never should have spoken to you that way, and I apologize."

"Please don't worry about it. I'm sorry I didn't have time to meet you yesterday, but I got called into a couple of surgeries and never came to the office. Let's say we just start over, okay? It's nice to meet you."

"And it's so nice to meet you," she responded as her face gradually returned to its normal complexion. "I guess what they were saying about you is true. You are very nice."

"I don't know who you were talking to, but I like to think so. Why don't we take some time to sit down and get to know each other? Have a seat."

She had shared an assistant with other doctors at Mayo, so having Lillian at her beck and call was a luxury Andi wasn't used to. By the time they were done with their visit, she learned Lillian had been at the hospital for many years and hadn't really cared for the doctor Andi had replaced; a fact the woman didn't freely admit, but one that wasn't hard to understand.

"Dr. Daniels was quite a rigid man, and he made it clear he had no time for the little people like me. I mean people who aren't doctors."

"I'm sorry. This profession is full of men like that, but I am not one of them. I consider the people I work with as part of my team and even though it sounds cliché, everyone on that team plays a vital part in what we do each day. You'll be my right hand trying to keep my life in order every day and I want you to feel you can tell me anything. If I'm behaving badly, tell me."

"Oh, I couldn't do that," she said. "You're a surgeon."

"I'm giving you permission to do it," Andi assured her. "In fact, my mother would insist on it!" she said with a laugh. "Look Lillian... if we're going to be successful, we need each other. This job isn't just about saving patients, it's about being good people and sometimes there is a lot of stress, which may make me less pleasant to be around than I should be. That's when I need you to tell me to snap out of it and put me back in my place."

"If you're sure," she said hesitantly. Obviously, she still didn't think it would be good for her career if she corrected the boss.

"I am. But I also want you to know that those instances will be few and hopefully far between. Until then I hope we can not only be co-workers, but friends as well. What do you say?"

"I say where have you been all my life!" The look of relief on her face was instantaneous.

That out of the way, the pair got down to business and in short order, Lillian had taught Andi most of what there was to know regarding the hospital operations.

"Isn't it about time for you to be going home for the day?" Andi asked her with a glance at the clock on the wall. It was already dusk outside and well past what she would expect the woman's hours to be. "What are your normal work hours, anyway?"

"I didn't really have normal work hours. Dr. Daniels insisted I didn't go home until he did," she admitted.

"That seems pretty ridiculous to me," Andi told her. "You're salaried right?" She nodded. "Which means you were here for fourteen hours or more every day and didn't get overtime for it?"

"Overtime? What's that?"

"Okay, that stops right here. I don't know what you get paid, but I bet it's not even close enough to justify those kinds of hours. From now on you will have set hours... eight to five or seven to four or whatever you want them to be, even when I am on nights."

The look on her face was priceless. "Are you serious?"

"I am, but you should know there may be rare occasions when I ask you to stay longer, but your job should be an eight-hour day and not the hours I put in. I can't even imagine what you did to fill those hours."

"Honestly? I spent a lot of time reading a book," she admitted.

"Well, now you can read at home. Starting tomorrow it's a regular schedule for you. Now get out of here and have a good evening. I'll see you tomorrow morning."

"Thank you, Dr. Taylor," she said, with tears welling in her eyes. "My husband will never believe this. I'll see you tomorrow at eight o'clock sharp."

. . .

By the end of her first week at the hospital, Andi realized a lot of the staff were talking about her. At first she was concerned about the whispered comments, until Lillian assured her that was unnecessary. Coming from the world-renowned Mayo Clinic and being a double certified trauma surgeon to boot, apparently many of the staff expected Andi to be difficult. As word of her interaction with Lillian and her surgical team spread throughout the hospital, she realized she had become an anomaly and even a curiosity, leaving her to wonder about the relationships other surgeons in her department had with their own staff.

Friday was the first relatively calm day for Andi and she pulled into her driveway before sundown, excited to see neighbors out and about. Hoping for an introduction to at least a few of her neighbors, they disappointed her when the family two doors down got into their car and drove away with just a quick glance her way. What in the world was she doing wrong? Lost in her musings about the situation, she barely heard the phone ringing in the house; racing inside to grab it just before her answering machine would have picked up.

"Hi Andi. Are you ready for the barbeque tomorrow?" Carol had impeccable timing.

"Hey Carol. You know, I was just thinking about that same topic on my drive home. What time do you want me to stop over and what should I bring?"

"Even if I thought it was safe to ask you to cook something," Carol said with a laugh, "you're the guest of honor. Just bring yourself. Most folks will arrive around three, so why don't you arrive before then, which will give me a chance to find out how your first week was? Now you're sure you can find the place, right?"

Carol's tendency towards being directionally challenged had resulted in some hilarious misadventures when they were in college. Luckily Andi was much better at directions and if she got lost, she had modern GPS technology as back up.

"Don't you worry about me! I'll be there with bells on."

"Wonderful, but now I must run. There's so much to do before the barbeque, and David is waiting on me for directions. See you tomorrow."

Andi chuckled at the mental picture of what things would be like in the Madsen's house at the moment. Carol would bark out orders to David as she readied for the battle that would be tomorrow's barbeque. Carol had always loved throwing parties and attacked the preparation like a general. Andi knew tomorrow's event would be flawless.

With a whole evening in front of her, she changed into shorts and a t-shirt, intent on tackling the unpacking. She was opening the first box just as the doorbell rang. The sound was unfamiliar, and it took a moment for her to realize someone was at the front door. Hoping to receive a neighbor's welcome, she hurried downstairs.

Opening the door to find not a neighbor, but a small group of people dressed in cleaning company uniforms, Andi was confused.

"Can I help you?" she asked.

"Dr. Taylor?" the woman at the front of the line asked.

"Yes?"

"We're here to help with the unpacking."

"What? What do you mean, help with unpacking? What are you talking about?" Was this some kind of scam?

"Mr. Jacobs sent us. He said we were to help you with unpacking boxes and getting your house set up."

"Mr. Jacobs? Who's Mr....?" Then the lightbulb went off. Ryan Jacobs. The woman was telling her Ryan hired them to help her finish unpacking. But why?

"I'm sorry. But there's been some mistake. I know nothing about this, and you all need to leave. I'm sorry to cost you the job, but this is all a mistake."

"Are you sure, ma'am? You don't have to pay us. Mr. Jacobs has already taken care of that and we can do whatever you need. If you need us to come back tomorrow, we can do that. Whatever works for you is what he told us to do."

"I understand, but apparently Mr. Jacobs got things mixed up. I don't need help. If he's already paid you, I suggest you all go out and have a nice dinner on Mr. Jacobs, but I honestly have no need for your services."

The workers eyed the stacks of boxes in the foyer behind her and looked at her like she was crazy to turn down the free help before shrugging their shoulders and turning away.

Andi closed the door on them and moved to the window to watch as they got into their vans and left.

The nerve of the man! He seemed to have trouble accepting that she wouldn't go out with him. To send these strangers to her home and expect her to let them help was out of bounds. Subconsciously wanting to prove that she didn't need Ryan's unsolicited help, she attacked the unpacking with renewed vigor for the next several hours before falling into bed in the early morning hours, totally exhausted.

CHAPTER FOUR

Saturday morning, the first chance she had to sleep in, the ringing of her cell phone jolted her awake before the sun was even up.

"Dr. Taylor," Andi mumbled into the phone. The sound of breathing on the other end was all she heard. "Hello? Is someone there?"

Suddenly the call disconnected, and she pulled the phone back to look at the caller ID - "Unavailable". It was quite early for a wrong number and now she was wide awake. Pulling the covers up tighter to her chin, her thoughts drifted back to Ryan Jacobs and the gall of him sending the workers to her house. If they had a relationship his gesture would have been nice, but she had spent all of ten minutes talking to him. She didn't appreciate him trying to force her into something she had already said she wasn't interested in. And now that he apparently knew where she lived, she had the unsettling thought that maybe she needed to take a few more precautions with her safety. What if he was a stalker?

Having already dealt with a stalker in Minnesota, it wasn't an experience she wished to repeat. One of her patients, a man named Richard Kelly, had developed an unnatural affection for her. While he did nothing to physically harm her, he had shown up wherever she was and it became unsettling. Whether she stopped for a cup of coffee at the local coffee shop or was at the movies with friends, the man always showed up and more often than not attempted to engage her in conversation, even though she clearly wasn't interested. It eventually became so intrusive and admittedly frightening, she had reached out to the local police, who paid the man a quiet visit before he disappeared from her life. That was a year ago.

Was that situation now being repeated with Ryan? He seemed completely normal, and she didn't think he was crazy, but then again, that's the same thing she thought about the man in Minnesota.

Too little sleep and not enough fresh air all week had left her feeling lethargic and possibly overacting to the situation with Ryan. She needed to run. With no time for hockey, running was her next favorite form of exercise and in the pre-dawn hours, she explored her new Texas neighborhood. With each slap of her foot onto the already hot pavement, her spirits lifted and by the time she turned for home, the music coming through her earbuds and the sweat dripping from her face had finally made her feel alive again.

A neighborhood buzzing with activity greeted her as she made the last turn onto her street. It seemed someone had flipped an imaginary switch and the neighborhood was now a textbook example of suburbia as children played in yards, men washed cars in driveways and dogs were being walked up and down the street. Passing each home, she offered a smile and a quick wave, hoping for even one person to say hello, but her reception was the opposite of what she had hoped for. One woman actually held her children back as if Andi were someone to be feared. Dawdling in the front yard doing post-run stretches to give them one more opportunity to come and talk to her was worthless. Not a single soul tried to say hello and finally she gave up and went inside.

Loneliness threatened to overwhelm her until her phone chirped to announce an incoming email from her father. He had seen the now viral video of the hockey game.

"I'm tempted to comment that the angel of mercy who saved this guy was my brilliant daughter!" he wrote, *"but I know you prefer to stay out of the limelight. Hope you know how very proud your Mom and I are of you. Love you and miss you, Dad."*

Having even that bit of contact with her family made her feel less lonely, yet without friendly neighbors and too busy at work to make friends, Texas was becoming a lonely place. She missed the day-to-day interaction with family and friends and, while grateful to have Carol and David nearby, it just wasn't the same. Still, today was the barbeque, and maybe she would make some new friends. It would be her first social event in Texas and a few hours later, with one last look in the mirror, she headed out the door.

.   .   .

"Hey Andi, welcome," David said as he opened the front door. "Did you have much trouble finding the place?"

"Unlike your wife, I drove straight here," she said with a chuckle. "The house looks great."

"It better look great. Carol has had me working on the landscaping for days. She didn't like the yellow flowers, so I had to plant the red and she wanted all the mulch changed around the bushes and then I had to mow the lawn in a pattern. You've known her longer than I have, so you know what she's like when planning a party. She's in the kitchen and said to send you straight in. See if you can get her to calm down, okay? I'm going to go check on the grill."

"You mean you're going to hide, right?" They had both been through Carol's frantic party preparations before, and she didn't fault him for wanting to hide.

"Can you blame me?" he chuckled before he disappeared.

"Andi? Is that you?" came Carol's voice from somewhere in the back of the house.

"Coming!"

"Hey sweetie," she said as she came around the kitchen island offering air kisses. "Don't get too close. I'm such a mess. You're right on time. Are you ready for a fun evening?"

"Of course, but I should have asked you what to wear. Is this okay?" Andi asked before smoothing down the front of her dress.

"Okay? Oh my goodness, Andi, you are going to have every man in the place panting after you. That dress looks fantastic on you!"

She had thought so too, which is why she choose it. It fit her in all the right places and after being in a boxy lab coat and scrubs all week, it was nice to look like a woman.

"Thanks, but what can I do to help?"

"Nothing. You're the guest of honor and I want you doing nothing more tonight than eating, drinking, and enjoying yourself. And with that being said, how about a glass of wine or maybe a beer? You're not on call, are you?"

"Nope," Andi told her before reaching for a nearby wine glass. "They took pity on me and said I could have the next couple of weekends off while I get used to the place."

"Good for you," Carol said as she poured some wine into the glass. "Maybe next weekend you and I can go shopping, have lunch... you know, make a day of it."

"You know I'd like that very much, but I told my boss I would go to this fundraiser for the hospital. It's on a ranch somewhere. Apparently, the guy who's hosting the event asked specifically for me to be there."

"Who is it?" Carol asked as she busied herself putting appetizers on a tray.

"No idea, but I've been told the host is someone the hospital counts on for donations. Why don't you and David come with me?"

"Seriously Andi? I don't think your boss would take too kindly to you dragging us along with you, especially if it's a hospital function. Besides, David isn't all that fond of hanging out with rich folks."

"Do you think that's all it's going to be? Wealthy donors?" She had been looking forward to the event but didn't relish spending an evening with a bunch of people with whom she would have nothing in common.

"Probably. Aren't they the only people who can afford to attend that kind of event? There are frequent stories in the lifestyle section of the paper about those fundraisers and if I remember correctly, they aren't the type of events David and I attend. Hey, maybe you'll meet someone famous!"

"I'd settle for just knowing who this person is that invited me. Dr. Thompson said it was a man, but we never got around to how this guy knows me and why he wants me there. Still, with the hospital just being certified as a Level One trauma center, it's likely they invited all the trauma staff."

Further discussion on the topic had to be shelved as the doorbell rang and other guests arrived. The sheer number of people was surprising and soon the backyard was full of people laughing, drinking, and enjoying themselves. While David manned the grill, Carol took time out of her preparations to introduce Andi. Pretty soon the names and faces began to blur and Andi concentrated on keeping a smile on her face as Carol introduced her to one person after another... many of them men whom Carol couldn't help but point out were single. Working hard to keep the cringe off her face as Carol did so, Andi realized that many of them seemed thrilled to know she was also single. Obviously, that had been Carol's intention all along.

Even with Carol's matchmaking attempts, the party was enjoyable and it wasn't long before Andi felt comfortable among Carol and David's friends. David's cooking, which had tempted all of their taste buds with a heavenly aroma, finally made it onto guests' plates and she had her first taste of a real Texas barbeque.

When it seemed they had fed everyone, David took a break from the grill to join Andi at the side of the pool, laughing at the delicate balance she was attempting on her lap to keep her drink and dinner plate from spilling onto her dress.

"Are you having an enjoyable time, Andi?" he asked. The heat from the grill had left him sweaty and red faced and she felt for him. The heat of the day had left her feeling sticky as well.

"I am, thank you," she said before wiping barbeque sauce from the corner of her mouth.

"Any marriage proposals yet?" he teased. He had known his wife far too long to be fooled by her more benign reasons for throwing the party.

"No marriage proposals but a couple of indecent proposals," she answered with a laugh. "Texas is certainly full of good-looking men— present company included."

"Thanks. But seriously, did anyone strike your fancy?"

They let their gazes wander over the still packed backyard.

"No, but it's not for lack of interest," she assured him. "It's just bad timing. I just moved here, started a new high-pressure job, and haven't even finished unpacking yet. The thought of starting a relationship with someone is just stress I don't need right now, especially with my track record with guys."

"I think you're being too hard on yourself," he told her.

"What do you mean?"

"The reason you have such a dismal track record..."

"Hey..." she said in mock surprise.

"... no, let me finish. The reason you haven't been successful with guys is they weren't the right ones at the right time. It's not that you can't have a successful relationship, it's that you weren't ready for one. I'm not saying you are now, but it will happen and when you find the right one, he'll fit so seamlessly into your life that you will just know the two of you belong together. Trust me on this."

He had a point. Every man she had developed a relationship with had never felt quite right to her. For whatever reason, she always ended up torpedoing the whole thing when she saw their frustration with her inability to make dates and spend time together. It was always her and never the guy who ended things.

"How did you get so smart?" she asked. "Maybe you could impart a bit of that wisdom to your wife and she would back off on the matchmaking?"

"Never going to happen," he said with a laugh. "Getting you married with a houseful of kids seems to be her number one goal in life these days. I'll try to rein her in, but for now I better get back to work or Carol will have my hide."

As he stood to leave, he waved at someone. Following his gaze, she couldn't believe what she was seeing. Ryan Jacobs had just come out of the house with a very attractive blonde at his side and he was looking right at Andi.

"Ryan, you made it," David said as he walked hurriedly over to greet the late arrivals. As they exchanged greetings, Ryan's eyes never wavered from Andi's and as he walked towards her, she hurried to put her plate down and stand up.

"Andi, I have someone I want you to meet. This is my friend Ryan Jacobs, and this is... sorry, what was your name again?" David asked the woman.

"Trish," she told him. The woman was stunning. Bright blue eyes and what appeared to be naturally blond hair drew Andi's attention to start, but it was impossible to miss her model thin figure with unnaturally large breasts that were pressed as close as possible to Ryan's side.

"Dr. Taylor," Ryan said as he extended his hand to her with an enigmatic smile. "We meet again." She couldn't tell what he was thinking and against her will, butterflies beat a furious rhythm in her belly.

"You already know each other?" David asked in surprise.

"Mr. Jacobs was on the opposing team when I played hockey that first weekend in town." Andi explained. Turning her attention to the woman, she offered a simple "hello."

"Aren't you the woman from the video... the one where the hockey player died?" the woman asked.

"Yes, but he didn't die."

"Oh," she said, obviously disappointed.

Her reaction was enough to dismiss her from Andi's thoughts. Anyone who could think it more exciting to watch a man die on the ice than to be saved wasn't worth further consideration.

"Trish, why don't you go get us a couple of drinks?" Ryan suggested.

"I'll show you where the bar is," David said as he guided her away from them.

Ryan's appearance and friendship with David had stunned her, and she let him know it with clipped words.

"What are you doing here?"

"I could ask you the same thing," he said.

"Carol is my friend."

"And Dave is mine."

They appeared to have reached a stalemate, and Andi realized just how rude she sounded. There was just something about the man that brought it out in her against her will.

"I'm sorry. Can we start over again? It's nice to see you, Ryan."

"You also, although I have to admit, I'm surprised you had the time for a social event. Have you finished your unpacking?" he asked with a wry smile.

She had given little thought to how he would take her sending the work crew away, but was pleased he was being so gracious about it.

"You got me. But seriously, what were you thinking of sending complete strangers to my house? And how did you find out where I live?"

"I thought that since you turned down my invitation for dinner claiming that you had too much work to do getting your house in order, that I would make that excuse go away. Isn't that what you told me?"

"I'll admit I said that, but that doesn't mean I wanted you to send a crew to my house to do it for me," she told him. "And that doesn't explain how you knew where I live."

"Don't you know everything is available on the internet?" he said with a smile as he motioned for her to sit in the chair she had just vacated while he sat in the one next to it. "Property records are public information in Texas. You were pretty easy to find."

"Oh." All her anger about someone at the hospital having leaked her private information evaporated at his words.

"So, how's the party been so far?"

"It's been lovely. I've met many people and everyone's been very kind."

"As beautiful as you look today, I imagine all the single guys haven't left you alone for a moment."

His unexpected compliment caused a bit of color to appear on her cheeks before she turned her head away, trying to hide it from him.

"Your girlfriend seems nice," she offered to change the subject. The woman stood across the pool surrounded by the same group of men who had previously found Andi so interesting, but she could hardly blame them. Most men would have found the woman irresistible, and Ryan probably had several equally attractive women at his disposal.

"She's not my girlfriend and to tell you the truth, she's a bit of an airhead."

"Oh, I thought..."

"Nope, we're not together. She's way too superficial for me."

"Then why did you bring her?" Andi asked, hoping beyond hope he wasn't the type of man who would date a girl just for her looks.

"I keep asking myself that very thing," he said without really answering her question. "So, how have you been?"

"Fine, although I've been really busy at work."

"Why did you decide to move from Minnesota?" he asked. Without her realizing it, they had settled into a pleasant conversation and he didn't seem at all concerned that his date had never come back with the requested drink.

"It was a fluke. I was happy at Mayo and never considered leaving until Dr. Thompson contacted me. Apparently, I operated on a friend of someone who is on the hospital's Board of Directors and that's how they found out about me. After that, the Chief of Surgery offered me a job and when I turned him down, he pursued me for a few months before I finally gave in and here I am."

"Lucky for us, I guess, and certainly lucky for Mark. I think we were all pretty much in awe when you jumped over the boards and took charge while the rest of us just stood around and watched."

"I think that's a pretty natural reaction," she told him. "If you really don't know what's happening, it's hard to respond. It's part of being a doctor. We have to get to where we automatically react."

"Still, it was a good thing you're a surgeon."

"Actually, I'm a trauma surgeon," she said with the same touch of pride she'd had for years about her profession.

"What's the difference?" he asked.

Unless someone was in the medical field, it was a valid question; one most patients and their families aren't concerned about when they are in crisis. Undergraduate, medical degree, residency and all the additional surgical training necessary for certification in many surgical specialties. It had taken her years of training and education to get to where she was, and she laid it all out for him.

"Of course, the best part was landing a job at the Mayo Clinic in Minnesota," she finished with pride.

"Is that all?" he said. The respect in his comment was clear.

"Not quite. At the end of all that training, we also have to be licensed by the American Board of Surgery and pass the general surgery qualifying and certifying exams and then the Surgical Critical Care certifying exam. Then we are finally ready to save lives."

She realized it was important to her he understood what her life had been like to this point.

"So you're the gold standard for a doctor then?" he asked with a smile.

"We like to think so, although I know a few other specialties that think they hold that title," she said with a matching smile.

"So before you arrived Austin didn't have any trauma surgeons?"

"No, I'm sure they did, but now, with a level one trauma designation, the hospital must have trauma surgeons on call twenty-four hours a day in all trauma specialties. I'm double certified in both cardiac and vascular and that's kind of rare even for trauma surgeons."

As they had been speaking, the sun had gone down, and the night had turned substantially cooler. Without their noticing, the crowd had also thinned out as folks made their way home and she and Ryan were the only ones still out by the pool.

"Looks like folks are leaving," she said, even though they could still see people inside. "I better find Carol and David and say my goodbyes." She felt a sense of disappointment at ending their conversation.

"Can I offer you a ride home?" Ryan said, as he offered his hand to help her up.

A shiver went through her at his touch and she had to remember her resolve to not get involved with him. Moving a few steps away, she could still smell the intoxicating fragrance of his aftershave, and the shiver became stronger.

"Thanks, but I drove myself. Besides, I think your date probably wouldn't appreciate having me along as a third wheel."

"Maybe I'm wasting my time here, but won't you reconsider and have dinner with me one night? I'd like to get to know you better," he said.

"While I've enjoyed talking to you, I'm sorry. I'm just not interested in getting involved with someone right now."

"It's just dinner. We can go as friends."

"I don't think so," she told him as she turned to go inside.

"How about this?" he said as he stepped in front of her, blocking her exit. "I'm having a few people over to my house next Saturday for a little get together. Why don't you come? It's an annual thing and we'll have great food and drinks, some music, maybe a little dancing. It wouldn't be a date - just more of a get together - and I promise you'll have a good time. You can bring Dave and his wife if that would make you more comfortable."

Even if she had wanted to accept his invitation, and she realized she actually wanted to, she couldn't. "I'm sorry, but I already have work plans on Saturday that I can't get out of."

"You're not just saying that to get out of my invitation, are you?" he asked with a smile.

"No, it's the truth. But thanks for the invitation."

"Maybe another time, perhaps?" he asked.

"Maybe." It was the closest she had come to agreeing to go out with him and she surprised even herself with her answer.

"Andi, there you are!" Carol said from the patio doorway. "You must be freezing! Come inside, you two."

Carol was right. It was getting chilly out, but inside Andi the slow burn of a fire that had been missing for far too long reminded her the possibility of a relationship could still excite her. She moved to hurry past Ryan before he reached for her arm, stopping her mid-step and pulling her close.

"Can I tell you something?" he whispered in her ear. "But you've got to promise to keep it just between you and me for now."

"What's that?" she whispered back to him. They were so close she could hardly keep her mind on what he was saying.

"I'm going to marry you someday."

Too stunned to reply, Andi stood slack jawed while he walked past her into the house without a backwards glance.

"Who's that handsome man?" Carol whispered as she came closer, causing Andi to stop and look at her in surprise.

"What do you mean, who is he? Didn't you invite him?" Andi whispered back.

"I didn't invite him, so he must be a friend of David's. My god, but he's handsome. What did he say that caused you to have that reaction?"

"It was nothing. I think he's had too much to drink." There wasn't a shred of truth in that statement. She hadn't seen Ryan take a drink the entire time she was with him, but what else could have possessed him to make such a declaration?

"I know you probably want to get home, but hang on for a while and we'll find out more about him."

Even though it was late, Andi waited patiently until the last of the guests had gone and Carol and David could join her in the living room.

"Saw you and Ryan getting kind of cozy by the pool," David said with a smile.

"It's not what you thought. We were just talking."

"Can someone clue me in?" Carol asked. "Who is he?"

"We do business with his company from time to time and he's a really nice guy. I thought Andi might enjoy meeting him," David told her.

"And I know him from hockey. He was on the opposing team when I played that morning."

"He's the perfect guy for you," David said triumphantly.

"Oh my god, not you too David!" Andi said in mock despair.

"How could you have done that without letting me know?" Carol asked her husband. "If it works and we find someone for Andi, I'm all for it, but let's work together, okay?"

"Hey guys? Remember me? Don't I get a say in this?"

"No," they said in tandem before they all erupted into laughter.

"So, was I right? He's a good guy, right?" It was obvious David wanted to best Carol in this competition that Andi seemed to have no say in.

"He's nice, but again, I don't want a relationship right now. You guys have to back off."

"But did he ask you out?" Carol questioned. "He did, didn't he?"

"He did, and not for the first time," she told them.

Carol put down her drink and leaned forward, demanding to know more. It was easier to tell them the truth than to have them keep badgering her, so Andi explained about running into Ryan in the hospital, being asked out to dinner, and the cleaning crew at her house.

"And then tonight, after an enjoyable conversation, he asked me to dinner again."

"Andi, what would it hurt to go out to dinner with the man? It's just one dinner." David seemed to have made it his personal mission to get the two of them on a date.

"Dinner is a date, and I am not interested in dating. He still wouldn't take no for an answer though and he invited me to a small get together at his house next weekend."

"Well, that's something. Good for you!" Carol said.

"Not really. Even if I wanted to accept the invitation, I can't. Remember the fundraiser? I can't back out now, especially after the host issued a personal invitation."

"Who's the host?" David asked.

"No idea. I know it's on a ranch and it's a black-tie event. Who goes to a ranch in formal attire?"

To her surprise, they both laughed.

"Andi, Andi, Andi. You have so much to learn about Texas!" Carol exclaimed. "We don't mean to make fun of you, but in Texas formal attire at a ranch party is pretty normal. You can't really expect these rich folks to walk around in jeans and dusty boots now can you?"

"I guess not, but it's too late for this discussion and I'm too tired," Andi said before forcing herself up from the couch. "Thank you both for a wonderful party. Even though I ate too much, I had a terrific time."

"The next time you get a day off, let's go shopping," Carol suggested as they both walked to the front door. "David, why don't you walk Andi to her car?"

"No need. I'll be fine on my own. Thanks again both of you and I'll talk to you soon. Good night."

CHAPTER FIVE

A terrific weekend topped off by Carol and David's party paved the way for an even better week at work. Everyone had been so nice to Andi that she already felt like part of the team and the next week flew by.

"Do you have any exciting plans this weekend, Andi?" Dr. Miller asked as they walked back to their respective offices. "I know it's your last weekend of freedom before going on call."

"I don't know how exciting it is, but Dr. Thompson asked me to attend a fundraising event. You're going too, right?"

"I didn't know they had invited you to that," Brian said in surprise. "It's an annual event, but unfortunately, I've never received an invitation. Usually it's just the Department Chief's and members of the board. How did you swing that?"

"It was a surprise to me," she told him, mortified now that she had brought it up. "Dr. Thompson said the host invited me, so I guess I assumed they included the entire department. Sorry."

"Don't be. I'm not. My kids have been begging me for a weekend of baseball and the water park. That should be a lot more fun than hanging around with a bunch of people with more money than I'll ever see."

"You might be right and I wish I could get out of it, but..."

"When the Chief asks, you can't say no," Brian finished for her.

"That's right... especially when I just started. I hope it won't be too incredibly dull. At least I'll get to see a real Texas ranch. I guess that's something to look forward to. I'll tell you all about it next week."

Brian continued on to his own office and she walked into hers just in time to see Lillian shutting down her computer.

"Dr. Taylor, I wondered if I would see you before I left," she said as she handed over a stack of messages. Her previous employer had insisted on paper messages and Andi was trying, rather unsuccessfully, to convert her to electronic messaging. Apparently, they still had a way to go.

"Anything in here that can't wait until Monday?" she asked, giving only a cursory look at the pile.

"I don't think so, although there is one message from your mother. She told me she's worried that she hasn't heard from you all week." The smile on Lillian's face showed she had already figured Andi's mother out. "As a mom, you can trust me on this, Dr. Taylor. A two-minute phone call does wonders for soothing any worries about a child. On another matter, I've called the IT folks to come and check your line for all the hang-up calls."

"What do you mean?" she asked absentmindedly as she leafed through the paper messages.

"You've had several dozen calls come in on your direct line and when I answer, I can hear the person breathing, but no one ever says anything. At first I thought it was a wrong number... that happens from time to time, but even though I ask if they were calling for you, no one ever says anything."

"I had a similar call at home early one day last week," Andi told her as she walked into the inner office and took off her lab coat and stethoscope. "Let me know if IT figures it out. And I know you're right about calling my mom. I'll call her in a minute. So, do you have any big plans this weekend?"

"For the first time since I started working here, I am happy to say yes. Bill and I are going on a little getaway. Now that I have regular hours, we finally have the time and we have you to thank for that."

"A thank you is unnecessary. It was the right thing to do, and I know how hard you work all week."

"What about you? You're going to the fundraiser, right?"

Lillian had already confirmed Andi's attendance at the event.

"That's right, but I really don't know what to expect. What do you know about the event?"

"Just what I read in the papers and, of course, the occasional bit of gossip you hear around the hospital. What are you going to wear?"

"I'm not sure. I have a couple of semi-formal dresses, but Dr. Thompson told me it's a black-tie event and if that's true, I need to do some shopping tonight. What do you think?"

"I think you should go shopping. From everything I've read, this is a pretty glitzy event and most of the women wear designer dresses. Do you have anything like that?"

Although she was pretty well off financially thanks to her exorbitant salary and brilliant investment advice from her dad, designer gowns didn't hang in her closet.

"Not even close!" she said with a laugh. "I can't embarrass Dr. Thompson by showing up in a dress that looks like it's from Goodwill. Any ideas?"

. . .

Lillian's suggestion to visit Kate's, the shop of an up-and-coming designer, had been a good one. Her new dress started with a simple fitted black sheath underneath, and dazzled with a collar close to the neck made entirely of crystals attached to a see-through black organza cut in a kerchief style that floated as she moved. The dress left her shoulders bare and came to just above the knee, showing off the toned legs she was more than happy to flaunt.

Fifteen minutes before the car was due to pick her up, Andi nervously paced around the foyer as her new dress floated gracefully around her. After several late nights of unpacking, there finally was room to move, and she took full advantage of it as her favorite pair of high heels clicked a staccato rhythm on the tile in time to her pacing. A bundle of nerves at what the evening would bring, she was so lost in nervous thoughts she nearly jumped out of her skin at the sound of the doorbell.

With one last look in the hallway mirror, she opened the door to see a chauffeur in a black suit and a crisp white shirt.

"Dr. Taylor?" he asked. "I'm Tom and I'm here to drive you to the party."

"Hi Tom. Please call me Andi," she told him. Gazing past his shoulder, she could see a very long and very black limousine. "Holy cow! Is the hospital sending limos for everyone?"

"The hospital?" he said with a raised eyebrow. "Sorry Doctor, but the hospital didn't send me. Your host did. He said you were the guest of honor at the party and I was supposed to take special care to make sure you arrived safely. Are you ready to go?"

"I guess," she said hesitantly as he guided her down the steps and helped her inside the limo. The car was enormous, and she felt foolish sitting there all alone wondering what the neighbors would think if they glanced out their windows. More than anything, she wanted to know who the host of the party was, but Tom had long since gotten in the driver's seat as they started on their way. She could see his profile but didn't know if he could hear her or not with the partition that separated them, so she sat silently watching the scenery, becoming more nervous with each passing mile.

It was almost an hour later when the car finally drove under an enormous set of gates with the name "PrivaTech Ranch" emblazoned in the wrought iron; the ranch was so big it took another ten minutes before they actually pulled up to the party. Gathering her small bag and tucking a few stray hairs behind her ears, she accepted Tom's hand and emerged from the car to the most amazing sight.

The owners had transformed the property into a magical wonderland, complete with twinkle lights and strategically placed spotlights. Lit up like a Hollywood gala, complete with a roped-off section for photographers, the flash of cameras threatened to blind anyone who ventured a look in their direction. Music played in the background while valets were busy helping fashionably dressed men and women from their luxury vehicles and smartly appointed wait staff mingled among the crowd offering refreshments. Standing still for a moment, she tried to take it all in before noticing Tom was still at her side as the valet drove off in the limo.

"If you'd like to come this way, Dr. Taylor, I'll introduce you to your host," he said before gesturing for her to follow him.

"That's okay," she told him, concerned he would neglect his chauffeuring duties for her. "I don't want you to get in any trouble."

"It's no trouble at all and, in fact, my employer has instructed me to stay by your side until you are introduced."

Could this evening get any more bizarre? Who was this person who felt the need to send a limo for her and assign her a personal guide through the crowd? They made their way through the throngs of people before Andi spotted Dr. Thompson. Relief at finally knowing someone washed over her and she gave him a small wave before veering away from Tom to make her way to the doctor's side.

"Dr. Taylor, glad you could make it. My, don't you look lovely," he said as he looked her up and down. "I'd like to introduce you to my wife, Gloria. Honey, this is Dr. Taylor, formerly of the Mayo Clinic."

"Pleased to meet you, Dr. Taylor. Everett has told me so much about you and he's very excited you're here with us in Texas. He's expecting great things from you and I love that there's finally a woman surgeon in the department."

"Thank you ma'am and please, call me Andi."

"Honey, if you'll excuse me for a minute, I need to speak with our host. I'll be right back," Dr. Thompson said as his wife nodded her approval and he gave her a quick peck on the cheek before wandering off.

"Andi? That's a lovely name. Is it short for something?" she asked, getting back to their conversation while Andi watched her husband, hoping to glimpse their elusive host. How he expected to find someone in this massive crowd was beyond her.

"It's Andrea, actually. Named after my grandmother."

"Your parents must be very proud of you. Double certified in trauma surgery. Few women your age can say that."

Obviously, as a surgeon's wife, Mrs. Thompson knew exactly what she was talking about.

"They are quite proud."

"And that's a beautiful dress you're wearing," she said. "Can I hazard a guess that it's one of Kate's?"

"It is, and she's a wonderful designer," Andi told her. "She told me several other guests would wear her designs tonight. Is yours...?"

"Oh, my no. I love her work, but it's all a bit too young for me."

"Do you mind if I ask you a question?"

"Certainly not. How can I help?" she asked.

"I've been trying to figure out what I'm doing here," Andi told her before grabbing a glass of champagne from a passing server. "I don't even know whose house this is."

"Didn't Everett tell you?" she asked with just a touch of exasperation. "Honey, you're the star attraction for this event."

"But why?" It wasn't just false modesty. Her skills were exceptional, and she understood she was an asset to the hospital, but why bring her to this exclusive party?

"The entire process of becoming a Level One trauma center started because of you. We would have tried for the certification eventually, but hiring you moved it ahead exponentially."

"Okay, I get that, but why am I at the party?"

"You've made quite an impression on our host from what I've been told."

"But I don't even know who it is."

"That's strange. I thought you've met several times since you arrived," she said as she looked at Andi in confusion. "Oh, look, here they come now."

Turning to look in the general direction of the older woman's gaze, she saw Dr. Thompson walking their way. It wasn't until he moved closer to his wife that she could see who was with him.

Ryan.

Was he the owner of this massive property? How come he didn't tell her? And not only that, but he was apparently on the hospital's Board of Directors which made him her boss.

"Look who I found," Dr. Thompson said as he joined his wife with Ryan at his side.

"Ryan, it's so nice to see you again," Mrs. Thompson said as she beamed at him. It was obvious from the adoring look on her face that she was a fan of the man.

"Gloria, you look younger than ever," he told her before kissing her lightly on the cheek. "And Dr. Taylor, it's a pleasure seeing you again. Thank you for coming," he said as he held out his hand to her.

She was too stunned by it all to say anything as he held her hand in his own.

"You look lovely. Has Tom taken good care of you?"

The aforementioned Tom had been patiently waiting nearby as she had been talking with Mrs. Thompson. Having completely forgotten about him, she directed an apologetic look his way.

"Yes. Thanks."

Desperately wanting some answers, she listened politely and watched Ryan intently as the three of them chatted away.

Several minutes passed before Dr. Thompson and his wife spotted some friends and wandered off.

"You do look lovely," Ryan whispered into her ear before she moved away from him. "Is that a new dress?"

"You already said that," she told him with a bit of anger. "But what you haven't said is what I'm doing here and why you didn't tell me who you are."

"But I told you who I am," he said with a rather cheeky smile on his face.

"You told me your name, but apparently you forgot to mention you are chairperson of the board of the hospital I work for and technically, that makes you my boss. You didn't think you needed to mention that minor fact? Or even mention that you seem to be incredibly wealthy?"

"Would it have made a difference if I had?" he asked. "If I had told you I had money, or that I was on the Board, would you have gone out with me then?"

"That's not what I meant," she snapped.

"I didn't think you were that kind of woman, but maybe I was wrong," he teased.

"What difference would it have made if you knew those two details of my life? I'm still just Ryan."

"But you lied to me," she said again.

"A lie of omission? Maybe. But didn't you do the same with me?"

"What do you mean? You apparently know everything about me."

"You didn't mention to me you were a good enough hockey player to be invited to join the Olympic team. That's a pretty big deal, but you let me believe you just played a bit in college."

"That's not the same..." she sputtered, knowing full well that he had a point and wondering how he knew.

"True, it's not, but I think I made my point. Why don't we start over again? If I remember, I was telling you how beautiful you look tonight. This is the part where you say thank you and tell me how handsome I am."

"Thank you," she said begrudgingly. "And you look very handsome." Dressed in a stunning midnight blue designer suit, she hadn't been able to take her eyes off the man.

"See! Now that wasn't so hard, was it?" he said with a smile. "Tom, I think Dr. Taylor and I are going on a tour of the ranch. I'll call you if I need you."

"Don't you have guests to attend to?" she asked.

"Actually, in this crowd, they won't even notice I'm gone. Let me show you around."

Tom disappeared quietly into the crowd as Ryan gently touched her elbow and guided her away from the party to the area of the ranch with outbuildings. They walked through several stables before entering a quiet and sparkling clean horse barn with many stalls. The occasional neighing from a stall was the only sound other than the click of her high heels on the floor; an unfamiliar noise that caused a few horses to raise their heads out of their stall doors.

Walking to one stall, she gently patted the velvety soft nose thrust towards her, struggling for something to say to break the uncomfortable silence that had developed between them. Ryan beat her to it.

"Do you like horses?" he asked as he stood nearby, leaning against a stall door, watching her pet the horse.

"They're beautiful animals and when I was a little girl, I wanted one desperately, but it wasn't really practical in town. There was a riding stable my friends and I would go to on weekends, but then I discovered hockey and that was the last time I was on a horse," she told him.

Seeing the intensity of the gaze he sent her direction, she was glad for the distance between them. There was something magnetic about those eyes that seemed to bore into her soul each time he looked at her.

"So do you ride?"

"Technically, I guess so, but realistically, I wouldn't call myself a rider. It's been years since I was on a horse."

"It's a lot like riding a bike... you'll pick it up again once you're back in the saddle. You might just need a refresher," he said as he moved to her side.

Once again, she caught a hint of the aftershave she had already come to associate with him and a tingle went through her body.

"Are you asking me to go riding with you?" she asked before walking across the barn to another stall to put more distance between them. The nearness of him was scrambling her brain.

"That would mean we'd have to spend time together. If I remember correctly, that wasn't something you were too interested in."

"That's not fair!" she said in surprise.

"Aha! So, you are interested in me?" he asked with a smile, jumping at the opening she had apparently just provided.

"What? No! I didn't say that," she said, stumbling over her words as a slow flush crept across her face, causing her to turn away from him yet again so he wouldn't notice.

"Then what are you saying?" he asked softly. She heard his footsteps as he walked over and knew instinctively he was now right behind her, close enough to touch, but keeping his hands to himself.

"I guess I'm saying that I wouldn't mind going riding with you, but since technically you're my boss, it could only be as friends."

Spending time with the man could be dangerous, and she knew it. Still, she couldn't help herself.

"Being friends is a good place to start," he told her before walking away. "Why don't we go riding tomorrow?"

"Tomorrow?" she asked in surprise.

"Sure, why not? I'll have Tom pick you up in the morning."

"Uh, tomorrow will work, I guess, but I can drive myself. I sure don't need a chauffeur."

He laughed.

"Tom's not my chauffeur. He's my head of security and bodyguard."

Ryan's pronouncement helped Andi understand him and his life as a wealthy person more fully, but she couldn't hide her surprise. It was a reaction he was familiar with.

"I hate it, but when you're a public figure, sometimes a little extra protection is called for. But don't worry, you'll get used to having him around."

"While you might be a public figure, I'm not. I'll drive myself. What time?"

"If you insist on driving yourself, how about ten? We can grab a bite to eat first and then get started. It won't be too hot earlier in the day."

"That would be fine."

"It seems we have that settled. How about we rejoin the party?" Offering his arm, they strolled back to join the others, chatting about frivolous things as they walked.

The rest of the evening passed in a blur of faces and laughter, and Ryan never left her side. The odd person out in the group of wealthy donors, Andi was nonetheless welcomed graciously. Of course, everyone had a medical story and many brought the video up. Dr. Thompson's wish to get publicity for the hospital had come full circle. It appeared her actions at the rink had resulted in huge donations for the trauma center.

After an enjoyable evening, the party ended in the wee hours of the morning. Ryan said goodbye to the last of his guests while Andi looked for Tom for a ride home. He was nowhere to be found.

"Ryan, do you know where Tom is? I'm ready to go home."

Truth be told, she was more than ready. The party had been more than enjoyable, but her feet ached and her head pounded from the noise and too much champagne.

"He's around somewhere, but since you're going to be back in just a few hours, why don't you stay the night?"

Had that been his plan all along? Having only recently agreed that they could be friends, her temper flared.

"I am not staying the night at your house," she said heatedly. "Just friends, remember?"

"Don't get angry," he said with a chuckle that made her think he wasn't taking her seriously. "I'm not suggesting we share the same bed. It was an innocent suggestion. You could sleep in one wing of the house and I'll sleep in another. And if you feel you can't control yourself around me, I could station Tom outside my bedroom door for protection."

The gall of the man to think she was worried about her own self-control! Her hands clenched into fists at her side and her jaw tightened in anger. Just as she was about to issue him a stern rebuttal, he broke into a full belly laugh.

"Andi, if you could see the look on your face! Please forgive me. I'm kidding you. Look, it's an hour back to your place, then an hour back out to the ranch. That barely gives Tom any time to sleep, and lack of sleep is dangerous behind the wheel. Would you really want to jeopardize his safety?"

As if they had conjured him out of thin air, Tom appeared at her side.

"Ready to go home, Dr. Taylor?" he asked.

His timing couldn't have been better orchestrated. She looked from one face to the other, wondering if she was being played while wishing she had taken Dr. Thompson and his wife up on their earlier offer of a ride.

"Even if I wanted to stay, I don't have any other clothes. You can't expect me to wear this outfit on the back of a horse," she finally said.

"That would make for an interesting ride, but it's not a problem," Ryan chuckled. "Mary will have something that will fit you."

Mary? The idea of wearing the clothing of one of his many women friends sickened her. Almost as if he was reading her thoughts, he hurried to clarify.

"It's not what you're thinking. Mary is my little sister. She goes to Texas A&M and stays here during the summer. I'm sure she wouldn't mind if you borrowed something to wear."

Feeling sheepish about having jumped to conclusions, she found herself out of reasons to reject his offer.

"If you're sure?" she asked hesitantly, as he nodded his agreement. "Then I guess I'll stay as long as you stick to our deal."

Tom gave his employer a knowing look before he quietly withdrew as Ryan took her arm.

"Wait a minute please," she told him as she veered over to a nearby chair. "My feet are killing me. I need to get these heels off before I take one more step."

Before she could reach down to undo the strap, Ryan knelt in front of her, lifting her leg onto his knee while sliding his hands slowly around her bare ankle. Her breath caught in her throat at his action. Without another word, he gently removed her shoe before repeating the action with the other leg. She froze at the touch of his hands as, for just a moment, his hand slid slowly up her calf before pulling away. As innocent as the action was, it was one of the most sensuous moments of her life. She could feel her desire for the man build within her.

"Better?" Ryan asked as he held out his hand to help her from the chair.

"Yes, thanks," was all she could manage in response. Her body was on fire and she could barely move as they walked side by side into the house so close she could feel the heat from his body.

From the corner of her eye, she saw Ryan watching as she took in the beauty of the room they had just entered. Leaning against the doorframe, arms crossed in front of him, he smiled as she viewed it all. The house was spectacular, but nothing like she expected from such a wealthy man. His house was actually a home. Photos that she assumed were family and friends dotted the room, and while the room was decidedly masculine, it was also inviting.

"Your home is lovely."

"You know, you're the first person who has been here who has called it a home instead of a house. I appreciate that. This might sound weird, but since I became successful, people judge me like a thing and not a real person. But you're different."

"Maybe the only reason you think I'm different is that when we met, I didn't know you had money," she reminded him.

"Maybe, but something tells me it's more the kind of person you are. You see things in people others don't. I think I quite like that about you."

Once again, the intensity of his look was unsettling, and she turned away from him to look at the pictures on the piano, hoping that agreeing to stay the night hadn't been a mistake. Maybe it was all the champagne she had drunk or the late hour, but she could feel her attraction to the man growing.

"Is this your family?" she asked, trying to get past what she was feeling by picking up a photo of a man, woman, and four small children.

"What's left of us, yes."

"What do you mean?"

"That was my dad," he said before coming to her side and pointing to the man in the picture. "He died just a few months after the photo."

"I'm so sorry. He looks so young. Was he ill?"

"He died in a work accident. He fell four floors from a scaffolding at a construction site."

"Oh my God, how horrible!" she exclaimed, remembering the construction worker she had just recently operated on.

"Funny thing though, he initially survived the fall and was even talking to the rescue crew. But there was no trauma center for hundreds of miles and the local hospital couldn't save him. If there had been a doctor like you, he might be alive today."

The pain in his voice was palpable.

"Is that why you are so involved with the hospital? Why you put on the party tonight?" She wanted to ask if that's why she was here in Austin, but didn't dare.

"Partly. But mostly because it's the right thing to do. I've been given so much and want to give back. Since I will never be a doctor, I help in other ways."

"Is your mom still alive?" she asked. The woman was beautiful, and it was easy to see where Ryan got his good looks.

"She is. She and my two brothers and their families still live in Canada. Mary is the only family I have nearby, but we all have regular contact. I'll go up there in the winter when I need a dose of snow and they come here when the snow gets to be too much for them."

"How did you end up in Austin, of all places?"

"Pure chance," he said. "A couple of buddies and myself were investigating a business venture at the time and by the end of the week, I had fallen in love with the place. Then this property came on the market right when my company took off and I never left."

"You said your sister is in college?"

"She's a sophomore at A&M and she's brilliant. Working on her engineering degree and already she puts me to shame."

"You're an engineer?"

"Nope. Not even close. I'm in information technology. Started out as a software programmer in my brother's basement... not like Steve Jobs did with Apple in a garage, but close to it. In reality, I didn't plan for this to be my life, but I stumbled upon some innovative ideas and suddenly my life turned upside down."

"PrivaTech? That's your company, right? I saw the ranch name on the sign when we arrived."

She hadn't connected the ranch with the company at first, but most everyone had heard of PrivaTech. The company had launched a program that stopped ninety-nine percent of all the spam and phishing emails and phone calls that had clogged up the internet and it was a global phenomenon.

"So, you've heard of us?" he asked. "We've had a lot of publicity lately, so I guess that's not surprising."

"I actually have your program on my phone and I love it. All the spam calls have completely stopped. Most of the time now I actually feel safe answering my phone again."

"I'm glad you like it, but even though that's the part of the company that is generating all the publicity, it's not really what we do. Our primary focus is designing security systems."

"You mean like for the military?"

"No. Personal security... home, vehicle, other property, and for employers to keep their employees safe."

"I don't understand," she admitted.

"We've developed a device that workers attach to their clothing and if they are getting too close to an obstacle, or too close to the edge of something, it emits a warning device."

"You mean like your father?"

"Yeah, like my dad. If he would have had something like this, he wouldn't have been so close to the edge of that building. And there are other variations that are designed specifically for a variety of different jobs... factory workers, highway workers, jobs that have a high number of on-the-job deaths or injuries. Each one developed to alarm under certain conditions that could cause injury to the individual. We even have a prototype undergoing testing now that senses changes in body chemistry when danger is present and it can notify authorities of the need for emergency response."

"You mean like one of those 'I've fallen and can't get up' buttons?"

"Not exactly. Ours works to sense increased blood pressure and heart rate along with other stress indicators and automatically distributes a signal. For instance, take a woman who is walking home alone on a dark and stormy night. Suddenly, she senses someone following her. Her heart rate goes up. Her step quickens. She's not in danger yet, but she senses something out of the ordinary and she's on alert. That's the first signal sent. The company would find her location using satellites and monitor the signal for escalating signs of danger. If the situation warranted and her fear levels became extreme, that would trigger sending help to her location."

The excitement in his voice was intoxicating.

"That's interesting. How would your system distinguish between the body's reaction from fear and danger to something else that might trigger increases in each of the indicators you are keying in on... like, for instance, something enjoyable?"

"You mean like sex?" he asked with a smile. "That's one reason this sensor is still only a prototype. We haven't perfected the metrics enough to eliminate that situation. Can you imagine the publicity that would get? Couple engaged in intimacy and police burst into their bedroom?" His deep-throated laugh filled the room.

"I've heard it said that any kind of publicity is good publicity, but something tells me that's not always the case," she told him with her own laugh, which was followed almost immediately by an embarrassed yawn.

"I'm sorry Andi, I've kept you up far later than I intended. Let's get you to bed."

The conversation had been so pleasant she hadn't even realized that another hour had already gone by.

"Your room is upstairs and to the right," he told her. Stopping only to grab some clothing from his sister's room, they were soon in front of the doorway to her designated bedroom.

Accepting the pile of clothing he handed over, the moment suddenly felt awkward between them, like ending a date and not knowing if you should kiss the guy or not.

"Pleasant dreams, Andi," he finally said, before giving her a gentle kiss on the cheek. As surprising as it was in light of their friendship agreement, it was perfectly innocent.

"Good night Ryan, and thank you for a wonderful night."

Closing the door carefully, she leaned against it before emitting a long sigh. There was something about the man that made him hard to resist. Still knowing her track record with men and sensing that Ryan was someone she would never want to disappoint, she understood she would have to stick to her guns and they would remain just friends. And if that wouldn't work, then she would end things before one or both of them got hurt.

Andi woke early the next morning after dreaming of Ryan all night. Lounging in bed, the birds outside her window already singing their early morning songs, she thought about him and wondered if he had also dreamed of her. He had been the perfect gentleman all evening long, but the thought of being friends with the man was troubling knowing that her attraction to him seemed to increase each time they saw each other.

Having watched him interact seamlessly with the rich and famous of Texas, she had to admit she didn't fit into his world and never would. Not that people with money intimidated her; in fact, it was the opposite, but she couldn't help but think they had only tolerated her because of Ryan. Would getting involved with Ryan mean that would be the world she would become part of, and if so, was it something she could handle?

It was still quite early, but as she was now wide awake, there wasn't much else to do but get up and face the morning with Ryan. After a nice long shower, she ran her fingers through her still-wet hair before tying it up in a heavy ponytail and stepping into the jeans and t-shirt Ryan had borrowed from his sister. The clothes of a sophomore in college fit her perfectly. All that hockey and running stairs at the hospital were definitely keeping her fit and trim. With just a light touch of lipstick, the only makeup she had in her small handbag, she made her way quietly downstairs, trying not to wake the household.

Expecting to see remnants of the party everywhere after such a late night, it was a surprise to find nothing. Carol would have been so jealous. All evidence of the massive party—tent, lights, flowers, dirty dishes, and food and drink—was gone, as if the event had never taken place. If that's what money could buy, she was all for it.

The house was deathly quiet, and she realized maybe she should have stayed in her room, but then she got the first whiff of freshly brewed coffee. Following her nose into the kitchen, she discovered Ryan already seated at the table, coffee cup in his hand as he read the newspaper. Unshaven, his hair still tussled from sleep, he had never looked more attractive.

"Good morning," she said softly, so as not to startle him.

"Good morning Andi. I didn't expect to see you up so early," he said as he stood and motioned for her to join him at the table. "Can I get you a cup of coffee?"

"That would be heaven," she admitted with a sigh. "But please stay where you are. I can get it myself if you just tell me where..."

"Cups are in the cabinet to your right," he said before sitting back down and folding the paper. "You must be a morning person to be up so early after such a late night."

"Actually, it's the opposite," she told him before joining him at the table with her coffee. "I was always more of a night owl, but life as a doctor has a way of changing all that."

"Are you hungry? I could make you anything you want as long as it's toast or cereal."

She couldn't help but laugh. It sounded exactly like something she would say.

"Are you laughing at me?" he asked with a smile.

"Kind of. I'm fine with just coffee, but I take it you can't cook?"

"I can grill, but I've been told that's not the same as cooking."

"Boy, are we a pair," she admitted. "I don't cook either, and my family and friends never hesitate to tease me about it. I survive by eating a lot of microwave dinners. How about you?"

"Well... I have a cook. Yeah..." he said at the look of surprise on her face, "I have staff in the house... although most everyone has Sundays off. That's why it's so quiet around here this morning. Normally, there are people everywhere."

"How many staff do you have?"

"Well, you've already met Tom, then there's my cook Jackie, and a couple of housekeepers and about a dozen more on the ranch."

"That's quite a large staff to take care of one man," she said, realizing too late how condescending it had sounded. "I'm sorry. That's not exactly what I meant."

"It's okay, I understand. The ranch isn't just my home, it's also the base for my business. You didn't get to see it last night, but one of the bigger buildings on the other side of the horse barn is where we work. There are about twenty people working out of that building or in the house."

"I'm not so sure I would enjoy having all those people around. Don't you ever just long for a simpler life?"

"That's a rare luxury these days. Once my company took off, it's been non-stop action. I always say that I'll take a week off and go sit on a beach somewhere, but it never actually happens. How about you? Being a trauma surgeon and all the drama that comes with your job, you must long for some tranquility yourself."

"I'm kind of like you. I've been in the trenches so long that it's just second nature to be surrounded by chaos, but can I tell you a secret?"

"Sure."

"Sometimes, and it's rare when it happens, sometimes the hospital is actually silent. There are no patients in trauma, no visitors around, no nurse call buttons going off, and the entire department is quiet. That's when I can finally stop and take a breath and enjoy what I've accomplished during my shift. As I get older, those are the times I long for more and more, but unfortunately, they are also getting less and less frequent. Although I love what I do, I hate that there is a need for it."

She had just told Ryan something intensely private about herself, something she had only shared once before with her father, and she had done so without prompting to a man who was virtually a stranger to her.

"Andi, I need to tell you something," he said, bringing her out of her inner thoughts.

"What's that?"

"I know it surprised you when you found out I was on the Board, but I want to be honest with you about why you're here."

"What do you mean?" she asked, suddenly on edge.

"You're here because I wanted you here. You saved the life of one of my best friends who should have died, and I wanted you in Austin."

"What are you talking about?" she asked in confusion.

"About a year ago, one of my buddies was in a motorcycle accident in Minnesota. He ended up being airlifted to the Mayo Clinic, and you were his surgeon. His family was told they did not expect him to live, but after hours in surgery, you saved his life. His name is Ron Traeger. Do you remember him?"

"You know I have operated on thousands of patients and I don't always... no, wait a minute! I do remember him. He was young... early thirties, right? He came in during the middle of the night... coded twice in the air ambulance, if I remember correctly. There was a piece of metal that pierced his heart. That was just one of the many injuries he suffered. I remember now. And you're right, he should have died."

"That's what you told his family. In fact, his wife still tells the story of his miracle recovery."

"So, he's doing well?" As with most trauma patients, she never saw the man again after being released from the hospital.

"He is, and he and his wife just had baby number three. They live in Houston now, but I see him occasionally. He still rides motorcycles, much to his wife's dismay."

"And because of that, you wanted me to work here?"

"Yes. Although we never met, Ron and his family couldn't say enough nice things about you and I was curious, so I did some research and discovered just how brilliant you are. I knew that if we were to get Level One status, we needed someone with your skills and track record here. I'll admit, when it looked like you were going to turn us down, I was pretty disappointed."

"Sorry about that. I know I kept everyone hanging for a very long time before I agreed to accept the position, but it was a big decision for me."

"Any regrets?" he asked.

"Not yet," she told him with a smile.

"So, now you know my secret and we'll have no more between us. Unless you want some more coffee, I'll get dressed and we can go riding."

. . .

Butterflies fluttered in her stomach as she followed him to the barn. It had been years since she had ridden and, being more than a bit of a perfectionist, she was afraid of looking foolish in front of Ryan. Second thoughts tinged with increasing fear slowed her steps as they neared the barn where two ranch hands were saddling the horses.

"Andi? Are you okay?" he asked when he realized she was falling behind.

"Just a little nervous." Better to admit it now.

Walking up to the chestnut horse, Ryan grabbed the halter and walked the horse slowly over to her.

"This is Sammy. Remember her from last night? She's the one that tried to eat your hair. She's the gentlest mare you'll ever meet. Why don't you give her a little pat on the nose and let her get to know you?"

As he spoke, the horse's nostrils flared. The horse shook her head before taking a few steps to stop nose level with Andi's face. Giving her head just the slightest of nods, the mare brushed her face against Andi's hair and made a soft whinny sound.

"See? She remembers you."

Encouraged by the horse's gentle demeanor, Andi reached up and gave a tentative pat on the horse's nose. Without the stall door between them, she wasn't brave enough to do much more, but at least it was something. How had she ever been brave enough as a child to feel comfortable around these massive beasts?

"Let's get you up in the saddle," Ryan said.

As Ryan guided her to the horse's left side, Andi looked with dismay at the distance from the ground to the stirrup. Being in good shape was one thing. Lifting her foot high enough to get it in the stirrup was another.

"Lift your left leg and I'll give you a boost up."

Doing as he asked, he vaulted her into the saddle. Only her quick reaction, honed from years of playing hockey, prevented her from falling off the other side, yet even with her clumsy actions, Sammy hadn't moved a muscle.

Ryan beamed up at her as he handed the reins over. "Good job. How's that feel?"

"Like I am ten feet from the ground and moments away from needing my own services," she told him honestly.

"So here are some things to remember. Sit up tall and straight. Use a squeeze of your legs to let Sammy know when you want to move. Hold the reins loosely in one hand and when you want to turn, you'll lay the reins on the side of her neck opposite from the direction you want to turn. We trained Sammy to move away from the direction of the reins touching her neck. When you want her to stop, apply gentle leg pressure and sit deeply in your seat. You can also say 'whoa,' but don't yank on the reins as that can hurt her mouth. Got all that?"

"It's sounding familiar," she admitted, "But let's not go too fast, okay?"

"We won't. We'll keep it to a slow gentle walk until you feel more comfortable and then we'll take it from there." Leaping onto his own horse, a black stallion much larger and seemingly more high-spirited than Sammy, he asked, "Ready?"

Would she ever be ready?

"I guess so."

True to his word, Ryan started off with a very slow walk, and it wasn't long before Andi found the rhythm of the horse's movements and felt more comfortable in the saddle. Concentrating on not falling off, she said little as Ryan carried the bulk of the conversation.

"This is such a great way to spend a Sunday, don't you think?" he asked without waiting for a response. "When I was a child, we'd ride the neighbor's horses often, but I never thought I would own one myself."

"I'm surprised you had horses in Canada," she told him.

"Andi!" he said with a laugh at her surprising comment. "Don't they have horses in Minnesota? Canada is right next door. I know some people think of Canada as the tundra, but it's mostly just like Minnesota."

"Touché!" she told him. "I don't know what I was thinking. Did you live on a farm?"

"I wish," he responded. "We lived in town, but ours was the last house at the city limits. My best friend Jackson lived on a farm and we rode their horses. I remember thinking how great it would be to live at his house—he could hunt anytime he wanted, fish for trout in the stream that flowed through their property and play with all the animals. As I grew up though,

I realized that more often than not, Jack was stuck on the farm doing chores when we were having fun."

"Like playing hockey?"

"Sometimes, but heck, it was Canada… everyone played hockey, even if it wasn't on an organized team. There was always a backyard rink somewhere and Jack played. He just couldn't play on our school team because of his commitments at home. It was too bad because he was a hell of a player. His work ethic would have gotten him far."

"Like you?"

"Far from it. While I love the game, practice always felt like a chore. I only did it because I knew it would make me a better player, but I hated every minute. Luckily for me, I had a natural affinity for the game. Quick reactions, speed, and agility. My first coach recognized it and helped me become successful. Fact is, I was a screw up from a very early age and if it hadn't been for Coach pushing me after my dad died, I would probably still be a screw up today."

"I doubt that. Look what you've made of yourself. Few men have that kind of success."

"Can I tell you one more secret, Andi?"

Over the last couple of days, they had shared more than a few secrets about themselves. Was that a sign of growing trust between them Andi wondered?

"Sure."

"It was pure dumb luck," he said.

"What was?"

"The software on your phone. It was a mistake. I was trying to develop a program for something else and made a mistake in it. When I discovered what I had done, I realized what the program was actually capable of. A few more hours of programming was all it took to come up with a way to stop all the spam. It was a mistake and not some genius programming on my part. I'm a fraud."

Casting a quick glance his way, she could see the pain in his eyes at his admission.

"Just because you didn't start out to develop the program doesn't make it any less valuable to people," she told him. "Did you know that an accident led to the ability to take an x-ray?"

"You're making that up," he told her.

"No, I'm not. In the late 1800s, Wilhelm Roentgen was trying to do an experiment with cathode rays when he discovered that particles of light could pass through solid objects and voila, we had x-ray capabilities. It was a complete fluke and yet think of how many lives it has saved because of his discovery. Your program might not save lives, but it is certainly improving the lives of millions of people."

"Thanks for that."

"You're welcome."

"I could also tell you the story of how sticky notes came to be if you need more proof," she said with a laugh.

"Why don't we save that story for the next time I need a pep talk?" he said with a smile. "I can see why you're such a successful doctor."

"Because I can tell such enlightening stories?"

"No, because you care so much. I saw it in the way you talked to Mark when he got hurt, and I've heard about it in the way you interact with people at the hospital. Even when I sent the cleaning crew to your house, they said you were incredibly gracious to them as you sent them away. Not everyone is that kind, you know."

"Thank you. I grew up being taught to treat everyone as if they are family. It's easy to do, well, most of the time anyway. I guess we all have one or two family members we wished we didn't have to deal with. Life is kind of like that, but I try."

Even as she was becoming uncomfortable with the attention being focused on her, she had become quite comfortable in the saddle. Maybe it really was like riding a bike.

"I think I'm ready for a bit more speed. See if you can catch me," she taunted before urging Sammy into what she had hoped would be a quick canter.

Maybe she exerted too much pressure to urge the mare on, but the horse took off at what seemed like the speed of light, leaving Ryan well behind as Andi hung on for dear life. It took a few minutes to regain her seat and adjust to the faster pace. By the time she did, Ryan had overtaken her, his horse at a full gallop that left her eating his dust. Reining in his horse, he eventually turned around and made his way back as the cloud of dirt from the dry plains of Texas settled around them.

"Good job, Andi," he said as he got closer, a look of admiration on his face. "I think you might have been underestimating your abilities. You're a natural."

"Thanks for saying that, but honestly, that was one of the dumbest things I've ever done. I don't know how I stayed upright! I'm going to need a bit more practice before trying that again."

"Anytime you want to ride, just let me know. Now, how about we head back and get something to eat? I'm starving."

. . .

Cantering into the ranch yard, she was happy to have one of the ranch hands grab Sammy's halter before helping her down to the ground. Her legs were stiff and sore and dirt covered her, but she couldn't remember a more enjoyable time. As Ryan dismounted, she led Sammy into the barn.

"Where are you going?" Ryan asked in surprise.

"To unsaddle Sammy and brush her down."

"You don't have to do that, Andi. Randy will take care of it."

"I appreciate that you have staff to help Ryan, but I believe it is the rider's responsibility to take care of her horse. It's something I used to enjoy and it will only take a half-hour. I'll meet you back at the house when I'm finished."

A series of looks passed between employer and employee, as neither man knew what to make of her declaration. Finally, Ryan also led his horse into the barn.

Having finished with Sammy before Ryan finished, Andi sat down on a hay bale and watched. Like her, he was covered in Texas grime and sweat, but he had never looked sexier.

Intent on watching him, she missed the little bundles of fur walking her way until hearing the first faint "meow." Four tiny little kittens were weaving through her legs.

"Hello babies," she said before reaching down and scooping two of them up. "Where did you come from and where is your momma?"

"She's around here somewhere," Ryan said when he realized who she was talking to. "Oh, there she is now."

A beautiful dilute calico cat had just emerged from a nearby stall and was walking slowly to Andi, ears flattened and fur beginning to fluff in warning to the strange woman who was handling her babies.

"Hello momma," she said, putting the kittens down where the mother cat could easily see them. "You're beautiful."

"Careful Andi, she's not the friendliest cat we have in the barn."

The cat stopped to sniff each of her babies before walking over and rubbing herself against Andi's legs. There was no longer any sign of aggression from her and Andi rubbed under the cat's chin before she plopped down onto the ground and exposed her belly. Having had cats her entire life, Andi knew the action meant the mother cat trusted her.

"Would you look at that," Randy said from where he had been watching the whole thing. "I've never seen Rosie take to a stranger like that before."

"Really? She seems like the sweetest cat ever," Andi said. It wasn't long before the kittens had resumed their interest and two of the tiny little felines had begun a slow crawl up her legs. If not for the jeans she was wearing, their tiny needlelike claws would have been painful and Andi reached down to release their hold on her legs before they got to her t-shirt. As she cuddled them to her chest, one purred.

"Looks like you have a couple of new friends," Ryan said as he finished his work, and Randy led the stallion away. "I take it you like cats then?"

"Love them," she responded. The kittens seemed to have made themselves at home in her arms and were just about to fall asleep. "I've always had a cat or two, but when I moved here, I had to leave my cat behind with my parents. She's sixteen and the move would have been too hard on her. I sure miss having her around. It was nice to come home to someone who loved me, even if it was only because I put food in her dish. Someday I'll get another one, or maybe two. That way, when I'm working long hours, they can entertain each other. Do you like cats?"

His answer would tell her a lot about the man. She had long felt that a man who didn't love animals wasn't to be trusted.

"I don't mind them, although I've never owned one, unless you count these barn cats. When I was growing up, we always had a dog, but I don't have one now."

"Why not?"

"Like you, I don't have enough time for a pet and it wouldn't be fair to get one and then expect my staff to take care of it. Maybe when my life settles down, I'll adopt one."

Not only did he like dogs and cats, but he was going to adopt. A man after her own heart.

"Come on, let's get something to eat," he said as he reached out to help her to her feet and she placed the kittens down for their mother to inspect and begin grooming.

"Do you suppose Mary might have another change of clothing I can borrow?" she asked as they walked back to the house. Her arms covered in a fine layer of dust, she could only imagine what her face looked like. "I'm filthy."

"I think we could find something," Ryan said, "Although I think I quite like the way you look."

"What? You mean dirty and grubby turns you on?"

As soon as the words were out of her mouth, she realized she had made a mistake. Ryan stopped in his tracks and took her hand in his own.

"Everything about you turns me on. I thought you knew that." There was no mistaking the look of desire in his eyes this time, and Andi pulled her hand back and clutched it to her chest.

"I'm sorry, I shouldn't have said that. Just friends, remember?" Was the reminder for him or, more likely, for herself?

For a moment, he looked like he was going to argue the point. Staring straight into Andi's eyes, she could see the muscles in his jaw working as he apparently debated how to respond before he lowered his eyes.

"Just friends," was all he said before he walked away, leaving her watching after him.

Why did she say that? Ever since the party ended, they had shared a wonderful time, but then she had to open her mouth with a smart comment and ruin everything. Ryan was so intense she should have known she couldn't tease him, especially when he had made it clear he wanted more than friendship from her. But what should she do now? Maybe going home was the best idea. At least then she wouldn't embarrass them both by saying stupid things; but even if that's what she wanted, and it certainly wasn't, Tom was nowhere to be found. Ryan had said his staff weren't working on Sundays. Did that apply to his bodyguard also? She could always call a cab, but being so far out of Austin that could take hours. With limited options, she finally made her way back to the bedroom, intending to shower, change into her party dress, and leave the ranch until a gentle knock on the door interrupted her. Ryan handed her a stack of clothing as soon as she opened the door.

"As requested," he said. The look on his face was hard to read. The desire that was so evident before was now gone, as was his ever-present smile. "Lunch will be ready in thirty minutes if you want to catch a shower first. See you downstairs."

He turned and walked away without a backwards glance, leaving her to wonder if she had just destroyed any chance of a friendship with him. After such a pleasant day, she discovered she wasn't ready to give up on him, even if he was giving up on her. There had to be a way they could remain friends, even if it wasn't exactly what he wanted.

She made it downstairs in the prescribed time to see a table already set for two on the back patio and Ryan delivering two plates of food to the table.

"Right on time. Lunch is served," he said, giving her a half-smile before he sat down and she joined him.

"This looks great." There was more food on the plate than she could eat, but it was a feast for the eyes with steak, grilled corn on the cob, and a mixture of grilled vegetables.

"I wasn't sure how you like your steak. It's medium rare, but I can throw it on the grill again if you like."

"No need. It looks perfect," she told him as she took the first bite. The tender meat melted in her mouth.

Neither said much as they ate, and it was making Andi uncomfortable. She was the one who had caused the tension and figured it was up to her to address it.

"Ryan, about before. What I said. I'm sorry. I didn't mean to make you uncomfortable."

"It's okay."

"Obviously, it's not because you'll barely look at me. I know you're attracted to me and if us being friends is going to be too hard for you, then maybe we should just end whatever this is right now."

"No!" he said, surprising her with the intensity of his denial. "I want us to be friends."

"If you're sure..."

"I'm sure. Just enjoy your lunch and we don't have to talk about it again."

He tried hard to liven up the conversation, but it was easy to see he hadn't completely accepted his own words. Still, he was trying, and she appreciated it. Her offer to end things with him wasn't something she was really interested in either. She was grateful he had turned it down.

Having made a substantial dent in the food on her plate, Andi leaned back in her chair, fully aware of just how tight the borrowed jeans had suddenly become across her overly full stomach.

"Lunch was great, Ryan. Thank you. And thank you for everything this weekend."

"Did you have a good time?" he asked.

"It was wonderful, but like all good things it has to end. I'll help you with dishes, but then I guess I should make my way home."

A fleeting look of disappointment crossed his face before a look of resignation replaced it.

"You don't have to do the dishes, but if you're sure you have to go, I'll go get the keys to the truck," he said before rising from his seat.

"You're going to drive me? I thought Tom…" she began.

"I gave him the day off too, so it's hitchhiking or ride with me, I'm afraid." Finally, the smile that had been missing since her careless choice of words was back.

"Thank you, but let me at least clean up. My mom would never forgive me if I didn't," she told him before clearing the table.

They put everything back in its place in the massive kitchen before Andi went upstairs to collect the clothing she had worn to the party. Ryan was waiting patiently at the bottom of the staircase when she returned.

"I hope Mary doesn't mind if I wear these clothes home. I don't relish my neighbors thinking I'm making the 'walk of shame' if I come home in my party dress," Andi said as they walked out to a pickup truck.

"They'd probably think you made some man very happy," Ryan said. After their earlier discussion, his comment surprised her. She let it pass for now.

"Actually, I'm not sure what they would think or if they would even care," she told him as he helped her into the truck before getting in himself.

"What do you mean?"

"Maybe it's just me expecting too much, but I thought the neighbors would welcome me with open arms and that hasn't been the case."

"In what way?" he asked as they headed down the road.

"Well, I've been here a couple of weeks now and not one neighbor has even spoken to me. All I've gotten is a couple of half-hearted waves. My realtor told me it was an active neighborhood with lots of couples my age and lots of kids, but I've barely seen anyone outside. I get the distinct impression they're not too pleased I'm the new neighbor."

"That makes little sense to me," he said. "Have you introduced yourself to any of them?"

"Well, no. I haven't really been home all that much."

"Well, there it is. If you haven't had the chance, that means they haven't either. I'm sure once you settle in with your life here things will change."

"Carol said I should have a party and invite all the neighbors." In fact, Carol had been insistent on it, but Andi had assumed it was just a chance for her to plan another party.

"That's not a bad idea. I could help with the party if you like."

"Thanks, but I'm still not sold on the idea. If they aren't friendly now, maybe no one will come. How would that look? I'd be a laughingstock."

"Andi, I think you're being too hard on yourself. In fact, I think you're looking for reasons not to get to know them. There's no reason they wouldn't come if you extended the invitation. When's your next weekend off?"

"At the end of the month. Why?"

"Because you're going to have a barbeque, that's why. And nope... don't even say it because I've already decided. My staff will work on the invitations in the morning. I know you're swamped with the move and the job and everything, so you won't have to do a thing except show up. I'll take care of everything."

"You don't have to do that, Ryan," she argued, before he put his hand out and put his finger on her lips.

"Nope, not another word. You're going to make friends with your neighbors."

"Would you at least let me ask my friend Carol to help? She loves planning parties."

"You mean Dave's wife Carol? Sure. I'll call her and we'll get it all set up."

Not another word was said about the party on the way home and as the miles passed, she actually thought it might be a good idea. If it turned out no one accepted the invitation, well, she would deal with that later. Pulling into her driveway, Ryan saw firsthand what she had been talking about. There were a few people out and about on the beautiful Sunday afternoon, but other than a casual glance at the truck, no one really waved or acknowledged their presence. Putting the truck in park, Ryan turned to her.

"Boy, you weren't kidding about the neighbors," he told her. "Did you play music too loud or something?"

"I swear I have done nothing to offend them and I just don't understand it. Maybe I was living in a dream world thinking that someone would knock on the door and welcome me to the neighborhood."

"Well, I think the party will be just what you need to change things around."

An awkward silence settled on them and Andi didn't know what to say until she noticed there was a light on in the house.

"That's funny," she said.

"What's that?"

"I just noticed a light on in my office. See there on the left? I don't remember turning it on."

"Maybe the housekeeper left it on?"

"I don't have one, at least not yet. It's on my to-do list."

"You probably just forgot."

That may be, but then again, she didn't even remember going into her office for the last few days.

"Yeah, I guess so," she said with more confidence than she felt. "Thanks again for everything this weekend. I really enjoyed myself and I enjoyed getting to know you."

"I'm glad you had a good time. Do you want to have lunch one day this week? Just as friends, of course."

"I would like that, but my schedule is never the same and I couldn't give you an exact time. I'd hate for you to drive all the way into the city, only to be disappointed if I have to cancel."

"Not a problem. I have an apartment in a building close to the hospital and I'll just work from there that day. How about Thursday?"

"I'll try, but if you haven't figured it out yet, I can't make any promises. That's life as a trauma surgeon."

"Understood. We'll play it by ear then. Would you like me to walk you to your door?"

"No need. Thanks again Ryan."

"See you Thursday."

CHAPTER SIX

It had been a long weekend and Andi was looking forward to an early night until she stepped out of the bath and her phone rang.

"Hello stranger."

Carol's welcome voice made her realize how much she had neglected her friend since the barbeque.

"Hello yourself."

"Where have you been? I've been calling you since early this morning," she said. "How was the fancy party?"

"Oh, sorry about that. I actually just got home a little while ago."

Dang it! Why did she say that? Carol was on the comment in a flash.

"Did you spend the night there?" she almost yelled into the phone. "Andi, that's so unlike you!"

"Okay, wait a minute," Andi cautioned. "I see where your mind is going, and it wasn't like that at all."

"What was it like?"

With as little fanfare as possible, she tried to explain about the party, her surprise at the host, and her decision to spend the night at the ranch.

"There, you see - it was all perfectly innocent and not what you think."

"I knew it. I knew there was something between you two," she exclaimed. "So, when are you seeing him again?"

"Carol, he's my boss!"

"No, technically, he's your boss's boss. There's nothing wrong with you dating the man."

"That's just semantics and you know it. We're not dating, so just get that out of your head. I told him I would be friends with him and nothing more."

"Aha, that means he wants to be more than just friends!" she said triumphantly. "You know David and I talked about him after you left the other night and it sounds like he might just be the perfect man for you. Super intelligent, kind, funny, and really driven."

"Okay, that's true... he's all of those things and more, but have you forgotten what a terrible combination that is with me? Those are the guys who all too soon figure out that the life I lead is not a good fit and we end up hating each other. No, it's better that we're just friends. I enjoy talking with him and that's all. Heck, you're probably better off finding me a guy that has no life at all and would be content to sit on his couch playing video games until I have a free half-hour to spend with him."

Although she would never be interested in a man like that, it was looking like that might be her only option for a relationship.

"Can't you just take a chance?" Carol asked. "Something tells me if you are ever going to let another man into your life, Ryan is the right one."

Why did everyone keep saying that to her? The right one?

"Nope, it's just friends, I'm afraid. And speaking of that, Ryan wants to help me make friends with my neighbors thanks to your idea."

"What do you mean?" she asked.

"Remember when I told you I have yet to meet any neighbors?"

"Again, that doesn't seem so unusual with the hours you work," she said kindly.

"It's more than that. I've seen several of them, but no one seems to acknowledge my presence even when I wave at them. When I mentioned your idea of a party, Ryan suggested hosting a barbeque and inviting all the neighbors. He said he'd take care of it all, but I'd be more comfortable with it if you and David were involved. Please, for me?"

"Of course! You know I'm never happier than when I'm planning a party."

"He said he would call you in a couple of days. Thanks so much for agreeing to this, Carol. Now that you and David will be part of it, I guess I am kind of looking forward to it."

After catching up a bit more on everything that had happened since they last saw each other, the call ended with promises to get together soon.

$$\cdot \quad \cdot \quad \cdot$$

Thinking she wouldn't see him again until their lunch at the end of the week hadn't stopped Ryan from calling each day just to say hi. The conversations were light, but once the initial pleasantries were over, their discussion easily transformed into conversations she might have enjoyed with a close friend back home. A casual "how was your day" developed into sharing the joys and disappointments of the day in detail and without actually realizing it, Ryan had become a confidante. Not about her patients certainly, but about how she was feeling and what she was experiencing each day as she adjusted to life in Texas. She began to look forward to talking to him and as soon as one call ended, she longed for more contact with him.

Not that her days weren't full. Fully immersed in work, her days were busier than ever. Working ten-hour shifts left little room for a personal life, even on the rare days when she actually got off work at the appointed time. By Thursday, the day of her planned lunch with Ryan, she couldn't get him out of her mind and lunch couldn't come soon enough. Just as it seemed she might actually join him, yet another emergency drew her into the operating room, necessitating a quick call to Ryan's cell.

"Good morning Andi! Are you hungry yet?"

"Good morning and yes, I am hungry, but I won't be able to make our lunch..." she had hesitated just a moment before the word date slipped out. It might have been an innocent slip of the tongue, but she wasn't taking any chances. "I'm sorry to cancel at the last minute, but I just got called into surgery."

"That's too bad. I hope the patient will be okay." The disappointment in his tone was plainly evident, and it made her feel guilty, a feeling she was all too familiar with.

"I'm really sorry, but I warned you this could happen. That's why I didn't want to say I could join you today."

"Don't worry about it. I understand, even if it is disappointing. Like I mentioned on Sunday, I am working out of my apartment today, so if your surgery doesn't go too long, call me. I can bring lunch to you and hey, you have to eat sometime, right?"

"Ryan, I'm sorry, but they're ready for me and I really have to go. I'll call you later, okay?"

Without even waiting for his response, she ended the call and was just about to scrub up when her cell rang again.

"Ryan, I really can't talk."

Silence on the other end caused her to pull the phone back and look at the caller ID. Another "unavailable" call.

"Who is this? I think you're calling the wrong number."

This time she could hear someone breathing, and a feeling of uneasiness washed over her. These types of calls were happening frequently now; too frequently to be mere coincidence.

"Please stop calling this number."

The dial tone echoed in her ear as the call ended, and she hoped that would be the last. Remembering Lillian's comment about the same thing happening on her office line, she made a mental note to see if IT had found anything before turning her attention back to the task at hand. She scrubbed for the surgery and her mind should have been on the patient who she could see was already being prepped on the table in the operating room, but the only picture in her head was of Ryan and the look of disappointment she just knew was on his face.

Damn it all to hell! That was exactly the reason she didn't want to get involved with someone new. Ryan might not realize it, but if they got involved, even as friends, this pattern would continue to repeat itself until one or both of them realized they couldn't take it anymore and it all blew up in their faces. Her work would always come first and any man would always feel he was second best. A single tear rolled down her cheek and disappeared behind her surgical mask. It just never got easier for her to care about a man, only to become a disappointment to him.

Straightening her back and steeling her internal resolve, she directed her full attention to the man on the operating table. The multi-vehicle accident he had barely survived that morning had really done a number on him and if she could get him stable enough to survive, an orthopedic surgeon would join her later in the OR, but he had to survive first and there was no more time to waste.

"Good morning everyone," she said as she walked into the OR and Ashley helped her into a pair of gloves.

"Your patient's name is Daniel Ward." Already Ashley had learned how important it was to Andi to recognize her patients as real people.

"Thank you Ashley. Ladies and gentlemen, let's save a life today." Pausing only to say a silent prayer for guidance, she made the first incision.

. . .

Time passes rapidly in an operating room when the work required such intense concentration, and Daniel's surgery was no different. By the time she felt confident enough that he would survive and the other surgeon came in to repair what he could of the man's shattered bones, hours had passed. Handing her patient off to the orthopedic specialist, she did her customary neck roll to relieve the tension.

"I think he's stable enough that I feel confident giving the family an update if you don't mind," she told the ortho guy.

"Feel free," Dr. Allison said. "It shouldn't take more than an hour from my end of things, although he'll need more surgery when he's recovered a bit more."

Sarah helped her remove her gloves and gown. "Great job Dr. Taylor. From the look of Mr. Ward when he first got here, I didn't think he'd make it."

"Honestly Sarah? Neither did I."

Her visit with the family was a short but happy one and as she walked to her office, the grumbling from her stomach reminded her she had yet to eat anything all day. Being a surgeon was better than any diet.

"Hi Dr. Taylor," Lillian said when she walked in. "How'd surgery go?"

"He'll live, but he'll have a lot of therapy in his future if he wants to walk again and maybe the next time he gets in a car he'll wear his seatbelt. Any messages that can't wait?"

"I've emailed you the routine ones, but Mr. Jacobs called. He asked that you call no matter what time you get out of surgery. He was quite insistent. I didn't know you knew the chairperson of the Board."

She and Lillian were becoming better acquainted and Andi had full confidence in her discretion, but she wasn't ready to spill about Ryan.

"He was the man who invited me to the fundraiser last weekend. I'll call him back after work."

"He told me you would say that, and he said that wasn't good enough and I'm supposed to make sure you call him right away. Do you want me to place the call?" She was no doubt curious about his message.

"That's okay. I'll do it."

Walking into her office, she dug the phone out of her pocket and dialed his number. He answered on the first ring.

"Ryan, it's Andi. Is everything alright?"

"It's fine, why do you...? Oh, yeah, sorry about the message, but I suspected unless I was insistent you wouldn't call back. How did surgery go?"

"It appears he will live, although he's now become yet another cautionary tale about not wearing a seatbelt. Are you still in town?" He said earlier he would head back to the ranch after lunch and with the cancellation, Andi assumed he was well on his way.

"Yup, and I want you to meet me on the south lawn of the hospital in twenty minutes."

"Whatever for?" It was way too late for lunch.

"Don't ask so many questions. Just do it okay?"

"Well, if you're going to be so bossy about it, I guess I'll see you in twenty minutes."

Andi was definitely not a fan of surprises. She wished she hadn't agreed, but now she was curious about what he was up to. After a review of the emails in her inbox, she went to meet Ryan.

"Have fun," Lillian said with a knowing smile as she walked by her desk and Andi wondered what Lillian knew that Andi didn't.

The hospital had an outside patio on the south side of the building that allowed those eating in the cafeteria a chance to get some fresh air. Thinking that Ryan would be somewhere on the patio, she headed that way. This late in the afternoon, the area was mostly empty, and she was confused when she couldn't find him until she heard him call her name. Turning towards the sound of his voice, she discovered what he was up to.

Standing about fifty yards away, muscle packed arms folded across his chest in the middle of the expanse of deep green grass, the man had a picnic lunch spread before him. Not quite believing what she was seeing, she walked slowly towards him, removing her lab coat and the stethoscope from around her neck to ease some of the late day heat. Tom lurked about twenty yards away under the shade of a large tree, looking anything but comfortable in the warm temps. The smile on Ryan's face as she got closer was electric and mirrored by her own.

"What's all this?"

"Lunch!" he proclaimed. "Well, maybe early dinner is a better description, seeing how late it is. I knew you wouldn't eat and I don't want to see you waste away. You're hungry, right? Admit it!"

"I freely admit I'm starving, but Ryan, you didn't have to do this! It would have been easier for me to grab an apple from the doctors' lounge."

"Maybe it would have been and I know I didn't have to do it, but I wanted to prove to you I understand the demands of your job and I can be flexible. Lunch was promised and a promise is a promise even if it's hours late. Come and have a seat."

"Is Tom going to join us?" she asked.

"I'm sure he would appreciate your asking about him, but he's already eaten. Just pretend he's not there."

With a little wave at Tom, she joined Ryan on the blanket, touched beyond measure he had taken into consideration the demands of her job.

Yet even though he was trying, she didn't have the heart to tell him that was how all of her relationships had started out. The guys always understood... at least at the beginning, but that understanding would wear off soon. Men always wanted their women to put them first, and she could never promise that.

"This looks fantastic," she told him as her eyes drank in the bountiful spread before them. Fresh fruit, a crisp and colorful salad topped with grilled chicken, and ice-cold lemonade—everything a girl could ask for.

"Before you say it, I have to admit I didn't make all this. My cook Jackie came in from the ranch and put it together for me. But I hauled it all over here. Please, help yourself."

"Well then, I feel really special," she told him with a laugh. "Please thank Jackie for me, will you?"

"If you come to dinner tomorrow night at the apartment, you can thank her yourself," he told her as they dished up the food. "And before you say no, I should tell you she's really looking forward to meeting you. I've told her all about you."

"Why would you do that?" she asked in surprise.

"She's from Minnesota originally. A little town near the Canadian border. That means you can't say no."

"Are you just making this up to get me to have dinner with you?" she asked suspiciously.

"Andi, you know I don't lie," he said. The light and jovial tone of his voice had turned serious. "If you don't want to have dinner, just tell me. I'll break it as gently as I can to Jackie that you don't care enough about a fellow Minnesotan to give up a couple hours of your evening to meet her."

Was he serious? For a moment, she had her doubts until the smile came back to his face.

"Fine, I'll come over, but as you discovered today, you're going to have to be flexible on the time."

"Whatever works for you."

They filled the rest of their lunch with casual conversation until her pager went off. For at least the brief time she had spent on the lawn with Ryan, she had almost forgotten about work.

"That's the ER. I'm sorry, Ryan. This has been wonderful. Thank you for it, but I have to run."

"Go. Save a life. I'll call you later tonight."

Leaving him behind, she sprinted back into the hospital and soon became caught up in a series of emergencies lasting well past the end of her shift. It was almost midnight by the time she pulled into her driveway, too tired to do much more than sit in the car with her hands on the wheel. She was dead on her feet and wanted nothing more than to go straight to bed, but for the second time in less than a week, she looked at the house and realized something was wrong. Another light was on in another room and this time she was positive she hadn't left it on.

The hairs on the back of her neck tingled. Was someone in the house? Something didn't feel right. She was scared. She specifically remembered setting the alarm that morning, mostly because she messed it up the first time and had to do it twice. Looking up and down the street for someone who might serve as backup, she wasn't surprised that every single house was already dark. Should she call the police? They'd just think she was forgetful if they arrived and found no sign of an intruder, but then again, she couldn't sit in the car all night either. Steadying her nerves, she reached for the door handle just as the cell phone in her hand rang, scaring the life out of her.

Peeking over the steering wheel, she whispered, "Hello," without looking at the screen.

"Andi, it's me," Ryan said. "Why are you whispering? Did I wake you up?"

Hearing Ryan's voice, she felt foolish for being so afraid. Obviously, she was just getting forgetful and she must have left the light on.

"No, sorry. Actually, I just pulled into the driveway. It's been a long day."

"Well, that explains why you haven't called me back. I was getting worried."

"Sorry I missed your calls earlier, but I was in surgery and then I figured it was too late to call."

"Don't worry about it," he replied. "I'm just glad you're home safe and wanted to tell you good night and now that I have, I'll see you for dinner tomorrow night. I'll text you the address."

"See you then. And Ryan? Thanks so much for lunch and for calling tonight. It means a lot to me."

"Sleep tight."

Knowing he was checking up on her gave her just enough confidence to go into the house. Grabbing her hockey stick from the front hall closet just in case someone was in the house, she went through the house room by room and, as expected, found nothing of concern. Feeling as silly as she knew she looked, she vowed to be more careful about turning off lights the next time.

. . .

A short night just added to her stress the next day when back-to-back surgeries left barely enough time for a cup of coffee throughout the day. Level One trauma center designation provided for an influx of patients that kept them busy all day. Not wanting to complain, after all that's why they hired her, she still longed for even an hour to catch up on all the paperwork she knew was accumulating on her desk. The only thing preventing a complete catastrophe in the office was Lillian. She had proven to be an exceptional assistant and Andi made a mental note to get her a raise.

"Lillian, do you know where...?"

"That report is on the top of your in-basket," she responded without letting Andi complete her sentence.

"How did you know what I was asking for?" Andi asked her with a sigh as she leaned back in her chair, rubbing her temples to ease the pounding headache that had been dogging her all day.

"You've been trying to complete that report for a week. I just figured you'd wanted to give it another go. But you only have an hour before you better get going."

"Going? Where am I going?"

"Aren't you having dinner with Mr. Jacobs tonight?"

"My goodness. I nearly forgot!" Ryan had sent his address to both her cell and the office early that morning. He wasn't taking any chances she wouldn't show up.

"He called an hour ago just to make sure you're going to make it, and I assured him I would usher you out the door on time."

"Thanks, although I'm sorry you have to babysit me. I should be able to remember my schedule."

"That's what I'm here for. If you don't mind my saying so, it seems like you and Mr. Jacobs are getting friendly. More than a few of the staff have commented about your picnic on the lawn yesterday."

Every hospital Andi had worked in had its own well-orchestrated gossip chain. The staff talking about her shouldn't have been surprising. After all, it's not like Ryan had made any attempt to keep their lunch a secret. Still, being friendly with the chairperson of the Board could be misinterpreted.

"Yeah, well, that was a surprise to me as well. I hope everyone realizes we're just friends. We share a love of hockey."

"That's kind of what I told everyone, but just between you and me, the two of you make a really nice-looking couple."

"Lillian!" she exclaimed as a blush stained her cheeks. "We're just friends. That's all. Don't go buying into whatever the rumor mill is selling." Even as the words came out of her mouth, she felt like the little boy who cried wolf.

"Just friends. Got it. Don't worry Dr. Taylor. Whatever I'm privy to in your personal life goes no further than this office. Just saying, though, he's fantastic looking!"

"Enough!" Andi said with mock anger. "Let's get back to work, okay? I have to get out of here in fifty-three minutes and don't forget to remind me."

It was difficult to concentrate on the report in front of her when she considered what Lillian had said. Why was everyone so intent on getting them together? If they were already having to defend their friendship, what position would that put her in if they became more than friends? She would need to tread carefully to protect not only her job, but her reputation as well.

. . .

With Lillian's gentle prodding, she made it to Ryan's apartment only a few minutes late. Tom answered the door.

"Dr. Taylor, welcome," he said as he opened the door fully to allow her to enter the apartment. "Mr. Jacobs will be with you in just a moment. Would you like a drink?"

As he spoke, she could hear Ryan's voice coming from another room and while she couldn't hear all of what he was saying, the word "sweetheart" jumped out at her. So, she was right. He had other women in his life. Catching herself before anger took control, she reminded herself there was nothing but friendship between them and attempted to tune Ryan's conversation out of her mind.

"Thank you, Tom, but I'm on call tonight, so I'll pass."

"Please have a seat."

Taking a seat on the sofa as requested, her gaze drifted around the apartment. Unlike his ranch home, the large apartment had a more modern flare while still decorated with family photos.

Instead of leaving her to wait alone, Tom stood patiently by the door, leaving her to wonder if he was there to protect Ryan or to prevent her from wandering away with the silver.

"Have you been with Ryan long?" she asked to break the uncomfortable silence.

"Since he moved to Austin."

What she had hoped would be a conversation starter with the man turned out to be anything but. She tried again.

"Do you like what you do?"

"Yes, ma'am."

The man was certainly polite, but obviously not much of a conversationalist. Was that different when he was alone with Ryan?

"Welcome Andi," Ryan said when he made his appearance, cell phone still in hand but with a wide smile on his face. "I hope you haven't been waiting too long."

Used to seeing him in either hockey gear, a suit, or formal attire, the jeans, button-down shirt, and cowboy boots he now sported were a surprise, and she had a hard time not staring at him. The bit of chest hair poking out of the unbuttoned neckline of his shirt and the rolled-up sleeves showing off well-muscled forearms ignited a slow burn of desire in her body and she had to look away.

"Actually, I just arrived," she told him as she looked once again around the apartment. "Your apartment is beautiful."

"But?" he said, apparently waiting for more.

"But what?"

"But it's not a home, is it?" That's exactly what she had been thinking before he walked in.

"Well, let's just say it's not exactly my style," she said diplomatically.

"It's okay. I never want you to feel you have to lie to protect my feelings. It's not a home and I know it. Mostly I just use it instead of having to go to a hotel. It's a good place to have business meetings when there's not enough time to go to the ranch. It serves its purpose. Tom, let's get the lady a drink."

Not wanting to get Tom into trouble, she explained about being on call before Tom left.

"All right then. Jackie tells me dinner will be ready in half an hour. I thought we'd sit on the terrace until the other guests arrive, if that's okay with you."

"Thank you. That would be nice, but I thought it was just the two of us tonight?"

"That was the original plan, but then I spoke to your friend Carol about the party and asked her and Dave to join us. I hope that's okay with you."

It was more than okay and she told him so as they wandered out onto the terrace.

"So, how was your day?"

Maybe not being able to get the word "sweetheart" out of her mind, her answers were shorter than normal.

"Busy."

"I'll bet. Everett tells me that the ER has doubled its patient load since you arrived."

"That's what I've been told."

"Andi, is something wrong? Have I upset you?" he asked in response to her clipped replies. "I'm sorry. I was on a call with my sister when you arrived. I didn't intend to keep you waiting."

So that explained the sweetheart comment. With no justification for being jealous, she was relieved that it wasn't another woman.

"No, I'm sorry, it's nothing. I'm just tired, I guess. It has been a very long day." Without realizing she was doing so, she rubbed her neck and twisted her head from side to side... a sign she recognized in herself as stress.

Before she could protest, Ryan moved behind her to begin a slow and almost sensual massage of her neck. It felt wonderful, but the intimacy of his action was making her very uncomfortable and twisting away from him, she stood up to walk to the balcony railing.

"I'm sorry," he said behind her. "It just looked like you were in a bit of pain and I thought I could help."

"That's okay. I guess it's more of a habit than any actual pain. I'm fine."

Carol and David's arrival saved her from having to discuss her reaction further as they exchanged greetings. With drinks delivered to the newcomers, the couples sat on the terrace together. It didn't take Carol long to bring up the party and as she and Ryan made their plans, David and Andi moved to the railing to better enjoy the view of downtown Austin.

"I have to say I'm pleasantly surprised, Andi," David said as he sipped his drink.

"About what?"

"Carol told me about your friendship with Ryan. I'm happy for you. He's a good man."

"Care to explain?" she asked.

"What?" he said in mock surprise.

"The way you said friendship. It sounded like it should have had air quotes around it. We are just friends, no matter what Carol told you."

"Oh, no. That's exactly what she told me," he hurried to clarify. "I know men are supposed to be totally clueless about these things, but I've known you long enough to know you like him... as more than a friend, I mean. I can see it in the way your eyes never leave him. Aha! There you see! Even now you were looking at him."

Guilty as charged. David had always been very perceptive.

"That means nothing. He is our host after all, but I'll admit it... he's very easy on the eyes."

David erupted into a full-on laugh at her comment, causing Ryan to look their way before turning back to his discussion with Carol.

"It's okay Andi, your secret's safe with me, but remember what I told you the other day. You haven't met the right one yet. Ryan might be that one."

"Sir, Jackie says your meal is ready." Tom was so quiet Andi barely realized he was nearby, but it was a welcome distraction from the conversation with David.

"Great. Thanks, Tom. I hope you're hungry everyone because you are in for a treat. Jackie's a fantastic cook."

Gentleman that he was, Ryan pulled out a chair for Andi and Carol gave a pointed look to her husband to do the same, which left them all chuckling. They all looked up as an attractive young woman walked into the room to place colorful salads on the table.

"Everyone, this is my personal chef, Jackie Morgan. Jackie, this is Mr. and Mrs. Madsen and Dr. Andrea Taylor."

"Dr. Taylor, welcome to Texas," the woman said excitedly as they shook hands and she nodded a greeting at Carol and David.

Happy to meet someone from home, Andi greeted her with her own smile. "It's wonderful to meet you, Jackie. Ryan told me you're originally from Minnesota."

"Just barely. I'm from Angle Inlet in the Lake of the Woods. Have you heard of it?" she asked.

"Isn't that right at the border with Canada?"

Her face lit up.

"Yes! I'm surprised you knew that. Few people do. In fact, to get there, you actually have to go into Canada first. It's the only place in the country like that."

"So what brought you to Texas?" It wasn't just idle conversation. Andi was dying to know how a girl from such a small community ended up all the way in Austin.

"I'm ashamed to say, but I followed my boyfriend here. He wanted to be a cowboy and when we got here, he realized he had made a mistake. He moved back to Minnesota, but I stayed, got a job in a restaurant as a sous chef and now I work for Mr. Jacobs."

"And there's no better chef in the city," Ryan proclaimed.

"Thank you, sir. Well, I don't want to hold up your meal. It was a pleasure meeting you all."

Although she was younger than Andi by more than a few years, Jackie's excitement at meeting a fellow Minnesotan suggested she was eager for reminders of home. Would that be Andi in a few more months?

Ryan was spot on in his assessment of Jackie's cooking skills. The food was delicious, and they ate until they could hold no more.

"Oh, darn it," Carol said as she looked at the phone in her hand. "Honey, we have to go. Carter is running a temp."

"Do you want me to come and check him over?" Andi offered.

"That's okay, I'm sure it's just a cold. He had a bit of the sniffles earlier. You stay here and enjoy your evening," she said with a wink that only Andi could see before they left for home.

While it wasn't unusual for a child to suddenly be under the weather, Andi wondered if perhaps the excuse was another carefully orchestrated matchmaking attempt.

"That was wonderful, Ryan, but I ate so much I can hardly move. It's a good thing Jackie doesn't work for me or I would be huge!"

"I know what you mean," he told her as they moved back into the spacious living room and took seats on either end of the sofa. "That's part of the reason I work out every day."

There didn't appear to be an ounce of excess weight on the man, so she knew he wasn't exaggerating about his workouts.

"I usually work out every morning before work, but since I got here that just hasn't happened. About the only exercise I'm getting these days is running the stairs at the hospital several times a day. I haven't even been able to take advantage of my membership in the Hockey Association."

"Why don't we go to the rink now?" he suggested.

"You're kidding right?"

"Why not? They're open late and at this time of the night, there should be few skaters."

"But I don't have any of my gear with me." The idea of lacing up a pair of skates was enticing.

"We don't have to play hockey, we can just skate and they have skates available to rent there. What do you say?"

It wasn't hard to convince her, and in short order, Tom had chauffeured them to the arena. In stark contrast to the last time she had been in the building, the arena was now quiet and desolate.

"Are you sure they're open?" she asked as they walked up to the front doors. There wasn't a single car in the parking lot and the interior of the building looked dark.

"I'm sure," he insisted before a young man with the arena logo emblazoned on his shirt opened the door.

"Mr. Jacobs, welcome," he said as he opened the door to let them pass. Lights came on all over the lobby as they walked in.

"Pete, how are you tonight?" Ryan asked as he shook the young man's hand. "This is Dr. Andrea Taylor."

"From the Gophers, right?" the man said, to her surprise. "My Dad and I saw you play several times. Didn't you also play on the Olympic team?"

Without realizing it, he had hit on a sore spot.

"Actually, I didn't. I was lucky enough to receive an invitation to be on the team, but medical school got in the way."

"Mr. Jacobs said you were the one who saved Mark's life a few weeks back. It was lucky for him you were here that morning. Listen, I don't want to hold you up. Rink number one is all ready for you both and I've left a selection of skates on the bench for you. If you can't find a pair that fits, let me know and I'll bring some more out. Enjoy your evening folks."

As he walked away, it dawned on Andi that there was more to this brief trip to the rink than Ryan had let on. Obviously, they had opened just for Ryan.

"So, they're open late, are they?" she asked with a raised eyebrow. "Did you set all this up just for me?"

"Guilty as charged," he admitted, looking more than sheepish. "Are you upset by my little surprise?"

How could she be?

"Of course not, but what would you have done if I hadn't agreed to come?"

"I was hoping I wouldn't have to deal with that. Thanks for being a good sport about this, Andi. Come on, let's hit the ice."

Taking her hand in his, he led them to the players' benches where Pete had left a selection of skates. Finding a pair in her size, she changed and took her first step on to the virgin ice. That was always her favorite moment at the rink; after the Zamboni had just finished resurfacing and the ice was smooth as glass. It felt like you could glide forever and she circled the ice before stopping once again at the bench to see what was taking Ryan so long. Skates on his feet, he stood at the boards, watching her with a look on his face that was hard to interpret.

"What's taking you so long slowpoke?" she teased before skating backwards away from him. "Did you have too much to eat tonight?"

Leaping over the boards in response to her taunts, he chased her around the rink until they were both winded. Slowing down, they skated slowly around the rink while they caught their breath.

"Do you do this often?"

"Do what?"

"Bring girls here after hours."

"You mean like on a date?" he asked with a laugh.

Not meaning to imply that they were on a date, she clarified.

"A date or just as friends," she said without looking at him.

"To answer your question, no... I don't bring girls here. You're probably the only woman I know who even knows how to skate. Why do you ask?"

Why had she asked?

"Just curious about how a man with more money than God entertains a date, I guess. Do you fly them to Paris for dinner in your private jet or buy out a concert hall for a private show?"

"First, I don't have a private jet, and second, I have never taken a woman to a private concert. Is that really what you think my life is like?"

"I don't know. I really know little about you at all. What do you like to do on a date?"

"Well, when I'm first getting to know a woman, I like to spend time with her one on one so we can talk and learn more about each other. Dinner at a fancy restaurant... in Austin, not Paris. Maybe a movie or a walk. And then, once we know more about each other, we can go rock climbing or spend a weekend together at the gulf or with friends. My dates are a lot like every other guy I suspect. How about you? What do you like to do on a date?"

"Honestly, it's been so long I barely remember," she admitted. "Most of my relationships get no further than the second or third date."

"Why is that?" he asked as they continued their leisurely skate around the rink.

"Me, I guess... or my job. It usually gets in the way and once the guy realizes I end up canceling every other date because of work, that's the last I see of him."

"Huh. Maybe you're just dating the wrong guys. Any man who can't understand how important your job is doesn't seem to be worth your time."

"That's kind of what David told me," she said in surprise. "He said I just haven't found the right guy yet."

"He's a smart man. You should listen to him."

Easier said than done, she thought. As they continued around the rink, each lost in their own thoughts, Andi wished for just a moment that Ryan was that right guy.

After an hour together on the ice, it was time to go. Neither said much as Tom drove them back to Ryan's apartment.

"Do you want to come up for a nightcap?" Ryan asked as he offered his hand to help her out of the car.

"Sorry, still on call," she reminded him. "I better head home. Thanks for a wonderful evening and please thank Jackie for the terrific meal, will you? Tell her I'd like to share some Minnesota stories the next time I see her."

"I will and she'd love that. I think she's homesick. Can you make it home okay by yourself? I can ask Tom to take you." Tom was still waiting in the shadows and she knew Ryan had been right; she was becoming used to having him around.

"Ryan, I'm fine. But thanks for the offer and thanks again for tonight."

She could see him watching as she drove away. It had been a lovely evening; one she hoped they might repeat.

CHAPTER SEVEN

"Dr. Taylor?" came Lillian's voice over the phone.

"Yes?" she asked absentmindedly as she tried to complete yet another report. The unending paperwork was really getting to her.

"There's a messenger here with something for you. Can you come out here?"

"Can't you just sign for it? I'm swamped with paperwork."

"Actually no. I think you better come out here yourself."

Something in the tone of her voice caught Andi's attention, and she pushed herself away from the mess on her desk to find out what was going on.

"Lill..." The word stuck in her throat at the sight of an animal crate tied with a large red bow, holding two very cute and very familiar kittens. Hearing their tiny, scared meows, she hurried over to gather them into her arms as Lillian signed for the delivery. They were the kittens she had fallen in love with at Ryan's ranch.

"Who would send you live animals?" Lillian asked as she tentatively reached out to pet them.

"Who indeed?" she said as the kittens nestled into her arms and began to purr. "Wasn't there a note?"

"Oh yeah, sorry," Lillian said as she grabbed the note attached to the crate and passed it over. "What does it say?"

"It says they missed me and that all the supplies I need for them are waiting for me at home."

"What does that mean? They missed you?"

"I've met these little guys before. Their mom belongs to a friend of mine and when I saw them, I mentioned I missed having a cat. I guess they're mine now."

"I never wanted a cat. They always seemed so sneaky to me, but these guys are just adorable," Lillian admitted.

"I think the paperwork on my desk can wait until tomorrow. If you have nothing pressing, I think I'll take these guy's home."

"Nothing that can't wait, but I think you're forgetting something important, Dr. Taylor," Lillian said with a smile.

"What's that?"

"What are you going to name them?"

They reminded her so much of her favorite cats growing up she had no hesitation in naming them. "This little gray one will be Casey and the orange tabby will be Charlie."

She was barely in the car before Ryan called.

"So?" he said. She could hear the smile in his voice.

"You are the best friend ever!" she told him excitedly. "I can't thank you enough."

"You're very welcome. I'm sure Rosie is going to miss her babies, but I can't think of a better home for them. Mind if I stop over tonight and see how they're settling in?"

"You don't even have to ask. I'm just on my way home now so come anytime. Lillian brought me a casserole today and we can heat that up for dinner."

"Great. I'll see you in an hour."

True to his word, Ryan arrived just as she finished setting up the kittens' litter box in the laundry room while they tussled on the floor under her feet. It had been a very long time since she had a kitten in the house and their antics were already making her laugh.

At the ringing of the doorbell, she carefully closed the kitchen door behind her to ensure they didn't make a dash for the great outdoors.

"Come on in," she said in welcome.

Ryan came bearing an armload of cat toys.

"Don't you think you've given me enough for one day?" she said with a laugh, catching a few toys that spilled out of his arms.

"These aren't for you," he said as he placed the pile on the hall table. "They're for my god kittens."

"What?" she asked with a laugh.

"I fully expect to be named godfather to those two and don't you forget it!" he told her with as serious a face as he could muster. "So, how are they settling in?"

"Come see for yourself, but tread carefully because they are little and fast!"

Casey darted between her legs, chasing his brother as both had somehow escaped the confines of the kitchen.

"I can see now why you're so fond of cats," Ryan admitted. "Dogs are fun, but these guys never stop going."

"That's what you think," she said. "Just give them a few more minutes and they will be sound asleep. That's the life of a cat... brief spurts of intense activity and then they sleep for hours."

"Look, you're right," he said, pointing out that both kittens had dropped to the floor in exhaustion.

Scooping them up, Andi placed them gently in their new basket near the fireplace and watched protectively over them like any new mother.

"Ryan, I think they are just about the nicest gift anyone has given me. Thank you so much!" Without even thinking about what she was doing, she kissed his cheek before pulling back and lowering her gaze. "You're a great friend," she told him to reaffirm they were nothing more than that. Thank goodness the timer on the oven went off and she could change the subject.

"Casserole's done," she said before hurrying into the kitchen. "Should we eat in here tonight?"

Over dinner of a creamy chicken casserole, salad, and an inexpensive bottle of white wine, they talked like the friends they had already become until Andi was too tired to keep her eyes open. Still, she didn't want the evening to end. She and Ryan were complete opposites in so many ways, but in ways that really mattered, she was discovering they were in perfect harmony. It also didn't hurt that he made her laugh more than anyone she had ever known.

"My Mom called today and said I have a new nephew," he told her as they moved to the family room. "My brother Kevin and his wife had their baby today."

"That's wonderful! You don't seem very excited."

"Oh, no, I am, but when family stuff happens and I'm so far away, it can be tough."

"Why don't you fly home for a visit? I'm sure they would love to see you. Doesn't Mary have a semester break coming up soon? The two of you could go." She had yet to meet Mary, but Ryan often spoke of how much his sister missed her family.

"I suppose that would be a good idea and Mary would love it, but I can't really get away right now and, of course, your party is coming up soon. I couldn't miss that."

"You can come up with all the excuses you want, Mr. Jacobs, but I know you miss them. You're the boss, so I know you can make the time if you really want."

"Maybe you're right. I'll think about it. But what about you? Didn't you tell me your parents wanted to come down for a visit? When is that happening?"

"That's a good question. I think I'll give my folks a call tomorrow and invite them down now that my schedule at work is more predictable."

Truthfully, she had been thinking the same thing for a couple of weeks now, but hesitated because her mother would jump to conclusions about Ryan. For that reason only, she hadn't mentioned his name to them.

"Well, I better get Tom home," he said resignedly.

"Do you want to have lunch tomorrow?" she asked as they walked to the door.

"Sorry, I can't. I have to fly to Dallas for a meeting. I won't be back until Saturday. How about we spend the day together?"

"Perfect. Travel safely and I'll see you when you get back."

The most natural thing in the world would have been for them to kiss. For just a moment she thought he might be about to do that, but then he backed away, offering only a smile before walking out the door and leaving her longing for the touch of his lips on her own. She had seen the desire in his eyes yet again and knew she wasn't the only one having these feelings, but he had made no move to touch her.

As far as she knew, Ryan wasn't seeing anyone. How could he with the amount of time he spent with her? But as a strong, viral man in the prime of his life, would that continue to be the case while she kept him at arm's length even as her feelings for him were developing into more than just friendship? Would she be able to handle her own feelings when he finally started dating someone else? She had boxed herself into a corner and, at least for now, there didn't seem to be a happy ending in sight.

· · ·

True to her word, she gave her parents a call the next morning.

"Hi Mom. I've missed you so much."

It had been a couple of weeks since the family had last spoken and hearing her mother's voice, a wave of loneliness swept over Andi.

"Hello, sweetheart. We've missed you too! So, tell me what's been going on with you."

"Just super busy with work. I'm sorry I haven't called. How are you both? I'd love to see you."

"We're fine, but you called at just the right time. Your father and I have just decided it is time we come and see your life in Texas for ourselves. If it's all right with you, we'd like to fly down next week."

That meant they would be here for her party with the neighbors.

"Of course you can come, and your timing is perfect. I finally invited the neighbors over for a barbeque and I could use a couple of friendly faces around me, especially if no one shows up."

She had fully apprised her parents of the situation with the neighbors and once she admitted to them what was, or rather what wasn't going on, they had agreed that it was unusual.

"That's a wonderful idea, Andi, but what are you going to feed them? You certainly can't just offer chips and dip!"

"Mom, I appreciate you want me to learn how to cook, but I've already arranged for the food. Ryan's personal chef is going to do all the cooking, and she's wonderful. And, get this, she's from northern Minnesota!"

"That's lovely, dear, but I have just one question... who is Ryan?"

Dang it all. Andi had long ago realized that sharing anything with her mother about her relationships was an open invitation to send out wedding invitations but she could imagine her parent's reaction to learning he was chairperson of the hospital board.

"He's a friend," she admitted after more than a moment's hesitation. "I met him playing hockey."

"So will Dad and I get to meet him when we're in town?" her mother asked sweetly.

"He'll be at the party." As much as her mother wanted to meet Ryan, it wasn't hard to figure out he would want to meet them.

"What does he do for a living?" The seemingly innocent question was one thing, but again Andi knew it would only be the first of many as her mother grilled her about any potential suitor. Better to just get it over with.

"He's an entrepreneur. He owns a tech company. Originally from Canada. Has two brothers and a younger sister and no, he's not married." Her tone was more abrupt than she had intended, but she had been through this many times before.

"Andi, you don't have to be so short with me. I was just asking a simple question."

"Yes Mom, I know and I'm sorry, but I've got to run to a staff meeting. Why don't you text me your flight details and I'll pick you up from the airport if I can or send a car to you if I can't get away? And Mom?"

"Yes, dear?"

"I can't wait to see you both. Love you, but I've got to go."

.   .   .

Short-handed at the hospital as staff left for long delayed vacations, Andi was putting in even longer hours. Things got even busier when Ryan and Carol dragged her into the planning for the barbeque. To her immense surprise, most every invitation had been accepted by the neighbors and it appeared over a hundred people would attend the party.

"See, I told you folks would come," Ryan gloated as they enjoyed a glass of wine on the back patio after seeing the latest action thriller at the local movie theater.

Doing things in public with Ryan had been an eye-opening experience for Andi. More often than not, complete strangers approached him for a selfie, an autograph, or just to talk to the man who was famous in Austin for his technological advances. His fifteen minutes of fame was definitely lasting much longer than most. He was recognized almost everywhere he went. Pushed to the fringes of the crowds that often surrounded him, Andi watched in fascination as he interacted with complete strangers, knowing that she could never be as comfortable in the same situation.

Tonight had been no different. A handful of people had set upon him the moment they stepped out of the car. Out of necessity, Ryan had learned it was easiest to spend time with his admirers and then politely ask for them to respect his privacy. He had employed the same tactic as they entered the theater. Surprisingly, to her at least, the crowd complied. They weren't bothered for the rest of the evening.

"I admit you were right," she said in defeat. It had been months since she moved into the house and the neighbors were still standoffish. Considering that behavior, it was a surprise they would be attending.

"Hold on a minute! I know why they accepted. It's because of you. They want to meet you."

"Don't be silly," he insisted. "My name wasn't on the invitation."

"That's true, but they had to have seen you coming and going from my house. They're probably curious about you. Yep, that's it," she said smugly.

"Can't you, for just a moment, admit that maybe they really want to meet you?" he asked with a smile.

"Sure, that makes sense," she said. Putting her glass down, she leaned forward in the chair with both hands in front of her. "Let's see... on one hand we have a world famous, to die for handsome millionaire and on the other, a stranger from Minnesota."

Moving her hands like she was balancing a set of weights, she tried to make her point. "Which one would you rather meet?"

"So, you think I'm to die for handsome, do you?" he asked with a smirk.

"Really? That's what you got out of what I was saying?" she said in mock frustration. Their ongoing banter was one thing she most liked about being with him. "I am thrilled that people are coming, but the whole thing is just a mystery to me. At least you'll be there with me and Carol and David and my folks. Say, speaking of them, can I ask you a favor?"

"Of course."

"Is there any way you can send a car to pick them up at the airport? I would love to do it myself, but being short-handed at work, there's no way I can get off. They'll be here Wednesday afternoon."

"I can do better than that. I'll pick them up myself," he told her.

"No, it's okay. You don't have to do that. I know you're busy." What would her parents think if Ryan himself showed up in her place?

"Consider it done. Just text me their flight information and I'll collect them. But unless you're going to invite me to spend the night, I better start back to the ranch. Tom gets grumpy if he doesn't get his eight hours of sleep."

Deciding that discretion was the better part of valor, she let his comment about spending the night pass before walking him to the door, where they exchanged hugs before saying goodnight. Watching him drive away, she realized the thought of sharing a bed with Ryan was becoming harder to resist, but things were going so well between them, and his friendship was becoming so important to her, she didn't want to risk losing it by starting something she knew would end badly between them. Still, each time those chocolate eyes stared into her own or he smiled at her in the way she now recognized he reserved for her alone, she could feel her resolve chip away. How much longer could she withstand his charm?

. . .

The day of her parents' arrival, she was on pins and needles. Ryan had insisted on picking them up at the airport and even though their flight had landed hours ago, she had heard nothing from any of them. Called into another lengthy surgery just as she was about to leave for the day, she ended up pulling into her driveway well after dark. The house was lit up from top to bottom and Ryan's car occupied the driveway spot next to her own. With everything else he had going on in his life, had he really stayed the entire time? A feeling of guilt washed over her and she dawdled for a bit in the car before finally heading inside.

Juggling her belongings to free a hand so she could enter the door code, Tom surprised her by opening the door for her.

"Welcome home Dr. Taylor," he told said with his usual stoicism. "Everyone's in the kitchen."

"Thanks Tom."

Placing her briefcase and purse down on the hall table, laughter erupted from the kitchen and she hurried to join them, stopping in the doorway to watch for just a moment unobserved. Seated at the kitchen table, with a glass of wine in front of her mother, beers for her dad and Ryan, the three of them appeared the best of friends. The smell of Italian food lingered in the air and her stomach growled. Finally, Ryan looked up and noticed her.

"Andi, there you are," he said with a smile as he rose from the table to give her a quick hug. "Why didn't you tell me how funny your parents are?"

Funny? Was he really talking about her parents?

"Hello sweetheart," her dad said as he offered a kiss on the cheek and enveloped her in his arms. "We'd just about given up on seeing you tonight."

"I'm so sorry," she apologized before greeting her mother. "I got called into an emergency just as I was walking out the door."

"You don't get home this late every night, do you, honey? Have you eaten? You look like you've lost weight. Ryan saved you some pasta. Let me heat that up for you."

"Mom, you don't have to wait on me," Andi told her with more than a touch of guilt.

"Kristine, let me do that. You two sit down and catch up," Ryan said, before jumping into action.

So now he and her mother were on a first name basis? What Twilight Zone was this?

"Thanks Ryan. I'm so sorry everyone. I had planned to take you out for a nice dinner... say, wait a minute. Where did the pasta come from? Mom, did you cook? You didn't have to do that."

"Unless you have learned how to cook since you got here, Andi, I'm pretty sure your mother was planning on cooking for us," her dad said with a laugh before he saw the hurt look directed back at him. "Sorry honey, that wasn't a dig at you. We're just so excited to be here with you and we don't want you to have to wait on us hand and foot."

"A lovely young woman named Jackie delivered the food Andi," her mother clarified. "And did you know she's from Minnesota? You should really meet her. She's so nice and such a talented chef. Did you know she works for Ryan? And that man in the hallway, Tom? He's Ryan's bodyguard." The last pronouncement came in a stage whisper.

"Yes Mom, I know, in fact..." What was the point? She had been about to say she had already told her about Jackie, but it didn't matter. She was just so happy to see them both that none of it mattered.

By the time Andi finished her late dinner, she had set aside all her guilt and was finally beginning to relax and enjoy the evening when Ryan announced it was time for him to go.

"Jerry? Kristine? It was a pleasure finally meeting you both. I'll pick you up tomorrow at eight for that golf date." Shaking her father's hand and giving her mother a quick peck on the cheek, Andi could only stand and watch in amazement at how easily he had charmed them both. They said their goodbyes, and she closed the door behind Ryan.

"That was a nice evening, but if you ladies don't mind, I'm going to head up to bed," her dad said.

"Dad, your room is..." she said before he cut her off.

"I know dear. Ryan already took our luggage up. See you in the morning."

Wow! Ryan really had covered for her.

"Honey, I don't know why you didn't tell us about Ryan before. He's wonderful!"

"Mom, don't go there," she cautioned as she walked back out to the kitchen to clean up a bit. "He's just a friend."

"He told us you would say that, but even if you won't admit it, I see the way you look at him. You like him." Holding Casey and Charlie in her arms, she wouldn't look her daughter in the eye.

"Of course I like him. He's a wonderful man, but he's still just a friend. And I might as well tell you right now... he's also technically my boss. He's the chair of the hospital board."

"We know. He told us. Isn't it wonderful that he is so successful and still has time to be on the board of the hospital? He said that he is the one who pushed for them to hire you. Something about a friend you operated on."

"Hold it! He told you he's my boss, but you think it's okay for me to be more than just a friend with the man?" she asked incredulously.

"Ryan said he's not your boss. He can't fire you, so that means he's not your boss, so it's okay if you and he..."

"Mother! Did he really say that? Did you actually talk to him about the two of us being more than friends?"

"Andrea, please don't take that tone with me," she said as she put the kittens down. "We didn't bring it up. He did. In fact, I'm just going to tell you. He told us he intends to marry you."

Andi dropped the wine glass she had been washing. The sound of it shattering echoed through the kitchen as Casey and Charlie ran from the room in fear. Her mother's words couldn't have come as more of a shock.

"Oh dear. Honey, did you cut yourself?" her mother asked as she hurried over to the sink to see the damage. Thankfully, there were no cuts.

"Say that again," Andi asked. "He said he is going to marry me? Is he out of his mind?"

"Actually, he appeared quite lucid, but I take it the two of you have never talked about it?"

"No, of course not. I told you. We're just friends, nothing more. Mom, you know how it is with me and men. Work always gets in the way and the guy always ends up getting hurt or, worse yet, hating me. I like Ryan enough that I don't want that. All we're ever going to be is friends. I thought he had accepted that."

Her friendship with Ryan had easily become one of the most important in her life, but knowing how he really felt, maybe things needed to end with him. A single tear rolled down her cheek as others threatened to follow before her mom gathered Andi into her arms.

"Oh sweetheart, maybe I shouldn't have told you what he said. Please don't be upset. I know what you've been through in the past and I don't want you to get hurt, but there's just something about Ryan. Maybe he is finally the right one for you. Couldn't you open your heart a little and take a chance again?"

Overcome with sadness, Andi wiped the tears away.

"I can't do that to him. He is so wonderful, and he deserves a woman who will make him the center of her world. That just will never be me."

"You're tired, and it's been a long day. Things will look better in the morning, I promise. Come on, let's go up to bed."

"You're right. I love you Mom and I'm so glad you and Dad are here. You head up and I'll be up after I turn off all the lights and set the alarm."

Her mom headed upstairs, leaving Andi to consider what Ryan had told her parents. Had he really still had this in the back of his mind all this time? How could she not have seen it? And just what was she going to do about it? Too tired to think logically, she went up to bed with Casey and Charlie hot on her heels.

. . .

After a mostly sleepless night spent tossing and turning that disturbed the kittens just as much as Andi herself, she got up early the next morning, but not quite early enough to beat her parents. Walking into the kitchen, she found her father already reading the paper while her mom was busy at the stove fixing breakfast. It was a scene she had witnessed every morning growing up.

"Morning, Andi," her mom said from her place at the stove.

"Good morning honey," her dad said as he set the paper aside, "Did you sleep well, kitten?" Hearing his pet name brought back a host of childhood memories. Although his endearment had always meant the world to her, once her friends at school learned of it, she was teased mercilessly.

"Yes, thanks," she lied. "I'm surprised you're both up so early."

"The joy of getting older is you don't need as much sleep," her father admitted.

"What would you like for breakfast? I couldn't find much in your fridge... we'll have to go grocery shopping later, I suppose.... but I found eggs."

"Sorry Mom, nothing for me. I'll just grab some coffee, then I have to be on my way. Can you feed Casey and Charlie for me?"

"They've already eaten," Mom assured her as they played together in a patch of sunshine on the floor.

"Did I hear right last night? You guys are going golfing with Ryan?"

Golfing was a sport her parents had taken up as a couple after retirement. From all accounts, they weren't very good, but it was something they enjoyed doing together.

"That's right. And then he's taking us to see his ranch," Dad said. "Did you know he owns PrivaTech?"

"I know, Dad," she said with a smile before reaching down to pet the kittens. Ryan's spam filter app was her father's favorite software. "Well, I better get going or I'll be late. Call me if you need anything and tonight we're going out for dinner. My treat. I should be home by six. Love you guys."

• • •

Going about her day, Andi couldn't help but wonder what more revelations Ryan was dropping on her parents as he entertained them in her absence. Even in the cold light of day, she hadn't been able to figure out what to do about his marriage declaration. He had to have known that telling her parents would mean they would repeat it to her, but it apparently didn't matter to him, and she wondered what their next interaction would bring. It was unusual, but after weeks of daily contact, he hadn't called or texted since picking up her folks from the airport. Just what was he up to?

Finally, just as she was about to leave for the day, her phone rang.

"Hi Ryan. Are you tired of playing tour guide yet?"

"Not at all. Your parents are wonderful. Are you just about done for the day?"

"I am and was just about to leave to pick them up for dinner. Why do you ask?"

"They're still with me, actually, and we're in the limo outside the hospital."

"Why? What's going on?" she asked.

"Instead of a fancy dinner, how do you feel about a little hockey?"

"What are you talking about? My mom and dad love hockey, but they're getting a little old to put on skates."

"I'm not talking about us playing hockey. I thought we could all enjoy watching a game."

"You mean the Dallas Stars?" she asked in confusion.

"No, I mean the Austin Tigers. They're one of the Dallas farm teams and they play here in Austin, well, really, just outside of the city in Aspen Park. So, what do you say? Want to join us?"

"You bet! I'll be right down."

The more she thought about Ryan's idea, the more excited she became. It had been ages since she had seen a professional hockey game in person.

She wasn't the only one excited about the evening. Joining them all in the limo, it was easy to see her parents were fast becoming accustomed to the attention and amenities provided when traveling with Ryan. She hoped he wasn't just trying to show off.

The limo pulled up to a state-of-the-art arena with thousands of seats filled with fans decked out in the team's logo. Heavy traffic caused the ride to take longer than expected and with the game just about to start, there was no time to stop at a concession stand for even a hot dog before one of the stadium employees was directing the group towards their seats. Instead of heading down the main concourse, it surprised Andi when the usher opened the door to a large private suite. Her parents immediately found seats down front as the game started. Leave it to Ryan to go all out.

"So, you just got tickets last minute?" she said, turning to Ryan as he took off his sport coat and loosened his tie.

"I never said that," he said with a smile.

"Then how did we end up here?"

"I have to have something fun to do with my money. I'm a part-owner of the team. The suite just comes with it." The cheeky smile on his face was her undoing, and she couldn't be angry at him. With her parents already engrossed in the game, they might as well have been alone.

"Thank you, Ryan," she told him, touching his arm lightly in emphasis.

"For this? It's nothing," he said humbly.

"No, for everything. For picking up Mom and Dad, for spending the day with them, for Casey and Charlie, for, well... everything. Your friendship is very important to me."

"Are you saying I'm very important to you?" he asked. Suddenly, the banter was replaced with the intense look she was becoming all too familiar with, and she became flustered.

"Of course you are. All my friends are," she stammered. "Let's watch the game."

As happy as she was to be in an arena watching hockey, her mind was going a mile a minute and the game barely registered. His presence next to her, so close his leg touched her own, made her forget everything except the look in his eyes and the flicker of hurt that registered there when she relegated his friendship to that of all the others in her life. She was treading dangerous waters with the man and it appeared she had forgotten how to swim.

The suite came fully stocked with a wonderful selection of foods and while everyone else ate in between periods, Andi stood in a corner watching their interaction. Judging by the way her mother continually touched Ryan's arm and hung on his every word, she was already smitten. Her father seemed torn between his loyalty to Andi and his desire to get to know Ryan better. Yet something in the way he and Ryan were getting along made her suspect he was already looking at Ryan as the son he had always longed for. Even if Ryan had never told her parents about wanting to marry her, she knew they would have still reacted the same way to him. He just had that effect on everyone.

By the end of the game she could tell the day had wiped her parents out. It had been a long and very active day for them and while they were extremely healthy for their age, they weren't used to such a full day. Saying their goodnights as soon as they got home, they headed upstairs trailed by the kittens, leaving her alone with Ryan while Tom waited in the car.

"Would you like a beer or a glass of wine?" Andi offered.

"If you don't mind, I'd love a cup of coffee," Ryan suggested. "I have to be up for a while yet for a scheduled overseas conference call in a couple of hours."

"Don't you ever slow down?" she asked with a laugh. She made coffee while Ryan took a seat at the breakfast bar.

"What would be the fun in that?" he said in reply. "Your parents are terrific."

"I know they really like you too," she told him. "I think my mom has a bit of a crush on you."

"Hum... nice to know at least one of the Taylor women does," he teased.

"Can I ask you a question?" Somewhere in the last twenty-four hours, she had made the decision to address what he told her parents.

"Of course."

"Why did you tell my parents you're going to marry me? You can't just kid around about stuff like that," she insisted.

"I'm not kidding."

"Ryan, stop it. I've said it repeatedly. We're just friends. If you can't accept that, then this has to end right here, right now."

The words were barely out of her mouth before he flew from his seat and took her into his arms. His lips descended for a passionate kiss she could not resist as she melted against him and her arms wrapped around him of their own volition.

"You were saying," he said with a smirk as the kiss ended.

A flash of anger at the look of victory on his face made her push him away before realizing they weren't alone.

"Ah, sorry to interrupt," her dad said in embarrassment. "Just came for a glass of water, but never mind. Continue doing what you were doing." Giving Andi a quick wink, he turned and went back upstairs, no doubt to fill his wife in on what he had seen.

Ryan reached for her again, but this time she evaded his grasp.

"I think you better go," she told him, unable to look him in the eyes.

"Andi, please..."

"No, please go."

"All right, but I'll call you in the morning," he insisted as he picked up his jacket.

"Goodnight Ryan."

The front door closed softly and tears fell down her cheeks. Why did she bring up the subject with him? They could have continued on as they were, just friends, and eventually Ryan would have moved on to someone else. But she had opened the can of worms and look how it had turned out.

Things were now awkward between them and the party was only a couple of days away. For a smart woman, she could make some poor decisions and tonight it might have just cost her a friend.

· · ·

Another night of tossing and turning showed on her face when she came down the next morning.

"Morning sweetheart. Do you feel all right? You look like you haven't slept at all."

"It was a short night mom, but I got up this morning and realized my car is still at the hospital. I guess I'll have to call a cab."

"Your car is in the driveway," her dad said as he walked into the kitchen with the newspaper in one hand and the kittens in the other. "Ryan just dropped it off... actually, his bodyguard did. I hope you don't mind, but when the man stopped by earlier this morning, I gave him your keys and now they are on the hallway table. Is everything all right with you two?"

"It's fine," she lied before taking the kittens from him and burying her face in their fur so he wouldn't see she was lying to him yet again. He had always been the human lie detector in their family and she felt bad for telling the fib, but she didn't want to discuss what her father might have seen last night.

"How about pancakes?" her mother suggested when it became apparent she had nothing more to say on the subject.

"Now that I don't have to take a cab, that would be great. Thanks Mom. What are you two doing today? If you drop me off at the hospital, you can take my car and do some sightseeing," she suggested.

"We don't have time," her mom said while her dad continued to read the paper. "Carol and Ryan are coming over to get ready for the party."

After how last night ended, Andi suspected those plans would change. "I think Ryan has a lot to do today and he probably won't make it." Better to put it out there now so they wouldn't be so disappointed when he didn't show up.

"Oh, he'll be here, right Jerry?" her mother insisted, leading Andi to wonder if her father had kept what he saw the night before to himself.

. . .

A busy workday became even more so as her few free moments had been interrupted by texts from Carol and her mother with endless questions about the party. While they had officially removed all planning from Andi, it was obvious they felt obligated to keep her in the planning loop. Still, she knew them well enough to figure out they would go ahead with whatever they wanted, regardless of what Andi said. There was no mention of Ryan in any of the discussions, and she hadn't heard from him all day, even though he had said he would call. It was probably for the best. Maybe she could salvage their friendship if she allowed him some space to soothe his wounded pride.

By the time she arrived home, it was to a completely different house. Furniture that had somehow magically appeared had supplemented her own meager furnishings. The house finally looked like a home. Carol must have spent hours at a rental place picking everything out just so the guests would have a place to sit.

The kitchen was also a whirlwind of activity. Every available surface was full of food, either already on trays or in piles of ingredients waiting to be turned into a delectable dish. Jackie had certainly gone the extra mile for the party.

"Wow, you guys have been busy," Andi exclaimed as she walked into the kitchen and reached down to grab Casey and Charlie before they jumped up onto the kitchen table. Scanning the room for the one face she wanted to see more than the others, her heart sank with disappointment. Ryan was nowhere to be found and while she desperately wanted to ask if he had made an appearance, in the end she said nothing.

"Dr. Taylor," Jackie said as she wiped her hands on her apron. "It's so nice to see you again. Thank you for letting me help with the party."

"Please, call me Andi, and I think I should thank you. There's no way I could have done any of this."

"She knows you can't cook," Carol said with a laugh before Andi's mom joined in.

"Don't worry about it. That's what keeps me in my job," Jackie said kindly. "Let me show you what we're preparing."

Before she could do so, her father and David walked into the kitchen.

"Did you save a life today?" her dad asked.

"That's what they pay me for," she told him. "Everyone, I can't thank you enough for this. I wasn't expecting something so grand. You've literally saved this party."

"Don't forget Mr. Jacobs," Jackie corrected.

"And Ryan, of course. If you give me a minute to change clothes, I'll be right back down to help."

"Honey, there's nothing else to do," Mom insisted. "But go get cleaned up. Ryan is taking everyone out for dinner."

"But..."

"But nothing. He'll be here in less than an hour to pick us all up. He said we're going to the best steakhouse in Texas."

The decision made for her and, seeing the excitement on their faces, she didn't protest further. Taking the kittens, she went upstairs to change as the work continued in the kitchen. The thought of spending the evening together with Ryan, especially knowing that the first time they saw each other after last night's kiss would be with an audience, made her anxious. Nevertheless, going out for dinner made obvious sense since the kitchen was full of party preparations.

What to wear? She had already learned that a Texas steakhouse could be full of cowboys and working-class people dressed in jeans and t-shirts or it could be formal attire. Unable to decide, she finally settled on one of her favorite dresses and a pair of her highest heels. They would never do for a long-term outing, but wearing them made her feel not only substantially taller, but confident and strong; both attributes she would need to face Ryan.

Casey and Charlie, who had been contentedly napping in the middle of the bed, raised their heads at the sound of the doorbell.

"Well, you two... how do I look?" she asked the kittens before risking a quick glance out the window to see Tom already stationed at the side of the limo. Did it have to be a limo? She had to wonder if Ryan was doing it simply to impress her parents, but then again, Ryan didn't have a vain bone in his body and with the number of people going out to dinner, it made perfect sense.

"Andi, Ryan's here."

Descending the stairs, all conversation stopped as each pair of eyes looked up at her in surprise. It appeared she was the only one dressed up. How could she not have realized that would be the case? It's not like Carol, David, and Jackie had shown up this morning in formal attire.

"I guess I'm a little overdressed," she said in embarrassment when she got to the bottom step. "Will we be too late if I pop back upstairs and change?"

Ryan made his way through the crowd and leaned in to whisper into her ear. "You look beautiful," he said before pulling away. "You don't have to change if you don't want."

"Are you sure?" she asked. "It would just take me a minute."

"Andi, you look beautiful and I wouldn't change a thing," her father said before taking her arm in his. "I'm starving, so let's go."

Father and daughter held back for a minute as everyone else made their way out to the car. He obviously had something to say.

"Are you okay with this, kitten?" he asked.

"Dad, about last night... it wasn't what you think," she told him.

"You're just friends. I get it," he said before giving her arm a squeeze. "You sit by me tonight and everything will be okay."

"Thanks Dad."

"Anything for you, my darling daughter. Now come on. I really am starving. Your mother wouldn't let us taste a thing."

With her father at her side all evening, she relaxed. Ryan was happily entertaining his end of the table while she and her father got to know Jackie better. Surprised that they had included her in the dinner invitation, it took

Jackie a while to feel like she was part of the group, but once the Minnesota stories started, she relaxed.

It was late by the time they made it back to the house with full bellies and faces that hurt from a night of laughing.

"Tomorrow morning back here bright and early," Carol announced before everyone went their separate ways. "First guests should arrive by three and we have a lot of work to do."

Little did everyone else know what they were in for tomorrow, Andi thought, but she was ever so grateful for the help. "Thank you again everyone for all your help. See you in the morning."

Her parents went into the house and Jackie got into the limo as Carol and David drove away, leaving the two friends standing alone together in the driveway.

"Finally, we're alone," Ryan pointed out as he stood mere inches from her. "I'm sorry for last night. I shouldn't have kissed you."

"No, you shouldn't have," she responded with little emotion. Letting herself get worked up about it again wouldn't help either of them. "I've been completely upfront about what's between us since the moment we became friends, haven't I? You've become really important to me, but all we're ever going to be is friends. You have to put this idea of us being more than that aside, or I can't spend time with you anymore. I just don't know how much clearer I can be."

"I understand," he said softly.

"Do you really? Because I can't go through this again."

"I understand, and it won't happen again. Just friends," he assured her. "Well, I guess we better get back to the apartment. Jackie will be here first thing tomorrow, and I'll get here when I can. My overseas deal is falling apart and I have to salvage what I can."

Still suspecting that most of her neighbors had agreed to come to the party simply to meet Ryan, she hoped he could make it or there would be a lot of disappointed people.

"Thanks again for everything," she said lamely as he walked to the limo. With a last wave, he headed home.

· · ·

If Andi thought Friday's activity was chaotic, it was nothing compared to Saturday morning. After a quick breakfast of toast and coffee, the others arrived and soon the house was abuzz with preparations. Carol was firmly in charge and the rest of them learned life was easier if they just did as they were told. The hours flew by with the last detail attended to just minutes before the first guest arrived. The only thing missing was Ryan.

"Hello and welcome. I'm Andi," she said as she welcomed each group of guests until the house and backyard were full to the brim with neighbors.

Working her way through the crowds offering drinks and appetizers, she tried valiantly to direct the focus of conversation away from herself and just learn more about the new neighbors. It worked pretty well at first, but then the questions about her background started.

"Andi, you're from Minnesota, right?" Jack asked, his wife Peggy close by his side as others joined the discussion. The couple and their two young children lived next door.

"I am." Not surprised to find out they knew she hailed from the north, she wondered what else they knew.

"So how do you like Austin?" Peggy asked.

"It's nice. Although I haven't really had time to see much of it."

"I'm surprised you bought this house," Jack said. "Surely someone like you would have opted for a house in one of the gated communities."

"What do you mean, someone like me?" What exactly was he implying? Suddenly, the group fidgeted nervously.

"Well, ah..." Jack began. "I didn't mean that negatively. But when you're a world-class surgeon and pals with the owner of PrivaTech, it isn't hard to figure out that this neighborhood is not exactly your style."

The group nodded their agreement with the statement.

"Yeah," one child said, "You're not really as stuck up as my mom said you were."

Andi looked in amazement at the child and then at the slowly reddening faces of the surrounding adults.

"What are you talking about?" she asked in surprise. "Where would you get that idea?"

"I'm so sorry, Andi, but it was your realtor," Peggy told her. "He told us you were world famous and that you probably wouldn't want to interact with us. He said he'd never had a snobbier client. But you're not like that at all!"

"Who are you talking about? My realtor was a woman."

"No, it definitely was a man," Jack said. "He came around to all of our houses before you moved in and told us all about you... how you were the top surgeon at the Mayo Clinic and only dealt with celebrities like Mr. Jacobs and how we should just leave you alone because you really don't like dealing with what he called 'little' people. None of us could figure out why you would even buy this house if that's how you felt."

So that explained the weeks and weeks of being ignored by the neighbors. Someone from the realtor's office had been spreading lies about her. Why would someone be so hurtful?

"I don't know who that man was, but he lied to you all. I am a surgeon and I did work at the Mayo Clinic before coming here, but I am a nice person who enjoys being friends with my neighbors. To be perfectly honest, I couldn't figure out why none of you had even said hello and what I had done to offend you all. Can we put all that nonsense behind us and be friends?" she asked the group.

"Dr. Taylor... Andi..." Jack began, while encouraging everyone to raise their glasses. "This is long overdue and we're all very sorry for it, but welcome to the neighborhood!"

Finally, the ice was broken and she relaxed. Between the good food that never seemed to end and free-flowing drinks, everyone, herself included, seemed to enjoy themselves. Too bad Ryan wasn't there to witness it. It was already dark and since he still hadn't arrived; she wondered if maybe he wouldn't show up at all.

"Andi, look, there he is," Peggy said.

Glancing in the direction the woman was pointing, she expected to see Ryan, but her blood ran cold. For just the briefest of moments, she thought she was looking at Richard Kelly, the man who had stalked her back at

Mayo. As quickly as he appeared, however, the man was gone. Obviously, her mind was playing tricks on her.

"I'm sorry?" she asked. "Who am I supposed to be looking at?"

"It was that man who came to our door before you moved in. The realtor. He was right over there by Jack and the other men," she told me.

"Which one?"

"Rats. I don't see him anymore, but I'm pretty sure it was him," she said hesitantly. "Maybe I was wrong."

"What did he look like?"

"He looks a bit like Tony from three doors down... brown hair, medium height, medium build. He might be in his forties, but it's hard to tell."

Richard Kelly had blond hair, a fairly distinctive scar on his forearm, and was well over six feet tall. It couldn't have been him. Anyway, she could have been describing half the men in Texas.

"Whoever the man was, he definitely did not receive an invitation to the party," Andi assured her. "Now, how about another drink?"

Having promised herself long ago that she wouldn't waste one more second worrying about Richard Kelly, it was annoying that her thoughts immediately went to him. She had already spent too much time living with the fear that he would pop up again somewhere. Anyway, there was no way he had followed her to Texas. Still, something was nagging at her and she could feel herself tense thinking about him again.

Leaning against the patio door watching the activity in her backyard, Andi had to admit the party had been a good idea, and she vowed to tell Ryan the same thing if he ever arrived. Even though it had taken an army of family and friends to put the event on, she was grateful he had insisted on it and that she had finally cleared up the misunderstanding that had kept her neighbors away for so long.

"Looks like your party is a success," Ryan whispered into her ear, causing her to jump. It was like she had conjured him up with her thoughts. "Sorry I'm so late."

"I know you've got a lot on your plate right now. I'm just glad you could make it at all. Everything work out with your business deal?" she asked him as they stood side by side.

"I might have to travel a bit to meet with the investors, but I think it will work out," he said before helping himself to a beer. "How's the party going? Did you find out why they were ignoring you?"

"I did, and it was the strangest thing." With as little fanfare as possible, she relayed to him the story of the man who had contacted all the neighbors before she moved in. "Why do you think someone would do that?" she asked.

"Not a clue," he admitted. "But maybe you need to call your realtor on Monday and ask a few questions."

"That's a good idea," she said before Jack and some of the other men realized Ryan had arrived. Within minutes of his arrival he was surrounded by neighbors who all wanted to meet the famous Ryan Jacobs. Leaving him to his fans, Andi made her way into the kitchen where Jackie, Carol, David, and her parents were finally taking a break.

"Looks like the party was a hit, Andi," Carol offered.

"Thanks to you guys," she said graciously as she joined them at the table.

"I see Ryan finally arrived," her father said as they noticed the commotion outside the door. "He sure draws a crowd, doesn't he?"

Everyone could see the group that surrounded him.

"Maybe I shouldn't say this about my boss," Jackie offered, "but it never seems to faze him. I've never seen him turn down an autograph request or a request for a picture. He's always gracious and humble no matter if he's talking with the President of the United States or the President of the PTA."

"She's right," David said. "In fact, I knew Ryan for months before I even realized who he was and what he's achieved. He's a genuinely nice guy to everyone."

Discussion continued around her about Ryan's attributes while Andi watched him interact with the neighbors. Jackie was right, of course. He was one of the nicest, most down-to-earth men she had ever met, and certainly the most handsome. So why was she keeping him at arm's length?

"I suppose I better go rescue him," she said, getting up slowly from the table.

"We'll get started on cleanup."

"You don't have to do that, Mom," she said. They had already done so much. "Leave it all and I'll take care of it in the morning."

"No can do Andi. We're full-service party planners," Carol said with a laugh. "With all of us pitching in clean-up will take no time. You go say goodnight to your guests and leave this to us."

Knowing she wouldn't be able to talk them out of it, Andi wandered outside to join Ryan and his fan club with an offering of food for him.

"Sorry to break up your time with Mr. Jacobs," she said as she worked her way into the crowd, "but I know he's been waiting all day for some barbeque."

Casting a grateful look her way, he said his goodbyes before finding a seat on the patio and eating while she said her own goodbyes.

When the last person had left, Andi walked back around the house and collapsed into a chair across the table from Ryan and closed her eyes. She was beat, but even so could feel the intensity of Ryan's stare and she slowly opened her eyes to look at him.

"What?" she said tiredly.

"Was it worth it?" he asked.

"The party? Definitely. Thank you for pushing me into it."

"You didn't really take all that much convincing, but I'm glad it turned out well. Judging by the mess in this backyard, it was quite the crowd."

"That it was, but like I predicted, I'm sure most of them were here to meet you." As he tried to protest, she held her hand up to stop him. "Nope... don't even try to deny it. I saw how those folks flocked around you the moment they realized you were here. I'm pretty sure most of them would have left hours ago if it weren't for the possibility of meeting you."

"Maybe you're right," he admitted, "but that doesn't mean they also didn't want to meet you. They seem genuinely impressed with you."

"That's nice," she said. "How's the food?"

"Excellent, as always, but why are you asking me? Are you telling me you didn't eat again today?"

"No... well, not since breakfast anyway. Once the party started, I was too busy to eat."

"Shame on you," he said before pulling a chair closer to his own. "Come over here and have some of mine."

She didn't argue, although the intimacy of sharing a plate of food with the man should have made her think twice. Grabbing another fork from the containers in the middle of the table, she helped herself. By the time her stomach was full, she had eaten nearly everything on Ryan's plate and cast a guilty look his way.

"Sorry, I guess I was hungry. Do you want me to get you some more?"

"No thanks. How come I never realized before how much such a little woman can eat?" he said with a laugh. "You've got sauce here..." he said as he raised his napkin to the corner of her mouth. She froze at his touch.

Maybe she had drunk too much or was overly tired, but staring into those hazel eyes, what she wanted more than anything was for him to kiss her again, and she leaned towards him as he did the same.

"Andi, where do you put your big roaster?" Carol shouted from the kitchen.

Pulling away from Ryan, she wasn't sure whether to be grateful for the interruption. The look of disappointment on Ryan's face left no doubt how he felt about it.

"Andi, did you hear me?" Carol asked again. This time, she was standing in the doorway with a large pan in her hands.

"Ah, I'll be right in," Andi told her, her eyes never leaving Ryan's.

"Ryan, I..." she started, but realized she didn't know what to say and her voice trailed off.

"You better go in," he said softly.

"I'm sorry," was all she could offer before walking away.

"Did I interrupt something?" Carol asked as Andi walked by her.

"It doesn't matter," she said sadly.

. . .

In far less time than it took to get the party ready, cleanup was over and they had distributed leftovers to the group. After a long couple of days, everyone was too tired to sit around and rehash the party and her parents headed upstairs to bed as soon as Jackie, Carol, and David left for home. Once again, she was alone with Ryan, while Tom stood guard outside the front door.

After what nearly happened on the patio, she hadn't expected Ryan to hang around either, but he seemed content to find a spot on the sofa waiting for her to join him. Dead on her feet but too keyed up by the success of the party to have any interest in sleep, Andi sat on the other end of the couch and turned to look at him.

"You look tired," she said to break the ice.

"I could say the same about you," he said with a wry grin before taking a long pull from his beer.

"I admit it. Today was a lot of fun, but I'm glad it's over. At least now, though, I think I've made some friends in the neighborhood thanks to you."

"I'm happy to admit the party was my idea," he said, "but making friends was all down to you. You're pretty easy to like."

How did they always get right back to this point? Not one to deny the attraction she felt for the man, she should have been more careful.

"Thanks. Even so, I think it was you they came for."

"Shouldn't we just say what's really on our minds?" he asked suddenly.

"What?" She knew exactly what he was going to say, but was she ready for this conversation again?

"Back there before Carol interrupted us. You were going to kiss me, weren't you?" he said as he moved closer.

There was no sense in denying it. "Yes."

"But you want us to just be friends, right?"

He moved closer yet again.

"We are just friends," she said as definitely as she could, her eyes never leaving his face.

"And friends don't kiss."

He moved closer until their bodies were touching.

"No... they don't," she said weakly.

Ever so slowly, Ryan leaned in until his lips were on hers and her breath caught in her chest. When she offered no resistance, his kiss became deeper and more passionate and she melted under his touch. Time passed in a haze as she let the sensations he stirred within her wash over her body, coming back to reality only when he pulled away. The sudden chill on her lips was jarring, and she longed to feel the warmth of him again.

"Good night, friend," he whispered. One last peck on the cheek and he stood and walked out the door, leaving her filled with unrequited desire.

She moved to the window and watched him get into the car without a backwards glance before Tom drove away.

What had just happened? Was Ryan trying to make a point? If he was trying to point out she wasn't following the rules she had insisted on, he had done a good job. That kiss and the unspoken promise of what more there could be between them would be hard to forget.

CHAPTER EIGHT

The rest of her parents' visit had flown by and the house became lonely without them. As she had predicted, it had been hard for Andi to get away from the hospital to entertain them, yet that hadn't stopped Ryan from chauffeuring them around town to see the famous sites. It was more than a touch ironic that while her folks had spent plenty of time with Ryan, Andi had spent little time with him at all. Worse yet, there were no phone calls, texts, or emails either. Careful questions directed at her parents before they had left for home showed Ryan wasn't even asking about her. It seemed he had shut her out of his life.

She was the one who had established the ground rules of their friendship, and she was the one who ended up hurt and alone. The only thing making it easier was the new friendships with neighbors who now freely exchanged greetings with her. That at least made Ryan's absence easier to bear until one of them would mention they hadn't seen him around. It wasn't a lie to excuse his absence by saying they were both busy, but it also wasn't the truth.

"Morning, Andi. Beautiful day isn't it?" Peggy offered from across the hedge separating their two properties.

Andi was leaving for work even earlier than normal and it surprised her to see her neighbor up already. It was a gorgeous morning, but yet again, it would be a scorcher. Already Andi was sweating. She placed her briefcase and purse on the front seat of the car before walking next door, where Peggy was watering her flower garden.

"Good morning Peggy. You're up early," she said with a smile. It was barely six. "It seems like I've hardly seen you since the party. How are things?"

"Not too bad, but I thought I better get out and water before the sun comes up and it gets too hot. Our AC went out last night."

"That's too bad. Do you think you can get it fixed today? You're all welcome to spend the night at my house if it doesn't. I've got plenty of room for your family."

A week ago, she never would have made the offer, but now it seemed the neighborly thing to do.

"That's okay, we should be fine. But can I get the name of your repair guy? It might be easier to call him rather than to find someone we don't know."

"What are you talking about? What repair guy?" she asked in confusion.

"The guy who was at your house doing work. Carl was his name, if I remember correctly."

"I'm sorry, Peggy, but you must be mistaken. I've had no need for repairs since I moved in."

"Maybe I'm not remembering right," Peggy said as she turned off the water. "Let me think. It was a couple of weeks back. You had already left for work, I think. It was early, but not too early, and I saw this guy coming out of your house in coveralls carrying some tools before getting into a white van. It said, 'Carl the Handyman' or something like that on the side of the van."

"And he was coming out of my house? Are you sure about that?"

Suddenly, all of her senses were on high alert. Had a stranger been in the house?

"You seem confused about all this. Maybe I was wrong. Now that I think about it, I didn't actually see him coming out of the house. I saw him walking away from the front door, though. Yeah, that's it. He was just walking away. We exchanged waves, and he got into the van and drove away. He probably was at the wrong house. Jeepers Andi, I'm sorry. I didn't mean to scare you. You have an alarm system, right?"

"I do, and from the sound of it, that's a good thing. Well, I better get to work. Early surgery this morning. Remember, you can use my spare beds until you get your AC fixed. Just leave a message for me at the hospital if you need a place to stay tonight."

Hearing a strange man had been at her door caused more than a bit of anxiety. She tried to think logically. Most likely it was a simple mistake, and the man was indeed at the wrong address. Their subdivision was full of similar sounding street names and Peggy was probably right... wrong house, wrong address. Nevertheless, remembering to turn on the alarm had just become even more important.

.   .   .

"Good morning Dr. Taylor," was Lillian's cheerful greeting as she walked into the office. "How was your weekend?"

"Fine thanks, and yours?" Since beginning to work for Andi and now having regular hours, Lillian and her husband had developed an active social life. She was in early so she could leave early for the ballet that evening.

"We spent the weekend at the gulf eating seafood and soaking up some sunshine. It was wonderful. You and Mr. Jacobs should think about going there. I can give you the name of the B&B we stayed at."

A wave of sadness washed over Andi at her suggestion. Ryan continued to keep his distance and Andi, being too proud and more than a bit hurt by his absence, had not picked up the phone to call him. It appeared the friendship that meant so much to her was at an end.

"Thanks, but unnecessary," Andi said, trying to hide the tears welling in her eyes.

Lillian was too perceptive to miss the fact that Ryan wasn't calling the office anymore, and she offered a look of sympathy in return.

"Okay, well, if you change your mind, let me know. Ashley called from surgery. She didn't explain, but she said they had to push back your first surgery by an hour."

Since attempting to arrive early, the delay was unfortunate, but not all that uncommon.

"I guess I'll just catch up on some paperwork then. When you get a minute, can you bring me a cup of coffee, please?"

"You got it."

"Oh, I almost forgot," Lillian said through the open door. "IT says there's nothing wrong with your phone. The calls must be all wrong numbers."

That piqued Andi's attention. The hang-up calls had plagued her at the most inconvenient times throughout the day and into the night. If it had just been her office phone, she would have assumed the callers were trying to reach her predecessor, but whomever it was had been calling her cell and her home phone. This was no mere coincidence, and goosebumps stood out on her arms.

"This is getting really annoying," Andi said. "Let's do this for a while. If you get a call that says 'unavailable' on the caller ID, let it go to voicemail."

"Are you sure?" Lillian asked in surprise. From the beginning Andi had insisted Lillian answer all calls.

"At least for a while. If it's important, the caller will leave a message. If it's someone just playing around, which is where I'm leaning, maybe they'll tire of their games when there isn't a real person on the other end. We have more important things to worry about and this way you won't have to deal with them."

"If you're sure...?"

"I am."

Even if they didn't answer every call, it's not like she would miss Ryan. They were no longer in touch, and this drastic change had put a damper on everything in her life. His silence spoke volumes. It was obvious he had moved on with his life, even if she wasn't exactly sure why. It reminded her of the pain suffered by the men in her life when she ended things. At least she had had the good grace to end things face to face. How did people overcome this type of hurt?

If she wanted to move on, which she fully admitted she did not want, it was proving nearly impossible. While Ryan might not be physically present in her life anymore, the hospital provided constant reminders. As chair of the hospital board and one of the hospital's biggest donors, his name was everywhere. But it wasn't just the hospital either. Casey and Charlie, growing into young adult cats now, were constant reminders of him and every time she opened her phone, the PrivaTech app stared her in the face.

Was coming to Texas the mistake she had so feared? Her job was going well, lives were being saved, but without Ryan she discovered she wasn't happy anymore and after many sleepless nights, she finally admitted to herself she had been falling in love with the man. However, as with so many other things in her life, most notably the Olympic bid, the timing was wrong and now she had lost him. Whatever had been between them was over.

The hour she should have spent working on paperwork disappeared as she mused over the situation with Ryan.

"Dr. Taylor? Ashley's on the phone. She said they're ready for you now," Lillian called from her office.

If the first delay was any indication, it would be a topsy-turvy day, but it might be just what she needed to take her mind off Ryan. The morning's delay only served to make the day's already packed schedule even more difficult. Gathering her stethoscope and putting her lab coat on, Andi headed out.

"I'll be right down, but don't expect to see much of me the rest of the day. If I don't see you, have fun tonight."

"Don't worry about a thing here and I'll tell you all about it tomorrow!"

. . .

Those couple of hours in the morning ended up being the highlight of Andi's day. Like Murphy's law, everything that could go wrong did and before the afternoon was out, she had lost her first patient.

They had drilled into their heads from the first day of med school—don't get attached to patients - and it had never been a problem for her, but this time was different. Although she had never regained consciousness since arriving at the hospital, the patient who died had been a five-year-old girl. The odds of her making it through surgery had been almost nil. Seeing that sweet face, Andi hoped this one time the patient could beat the odds. Yet, in the end, nothing Andi did could save the child and the loss on top of Ryan's absence was heart breaking.

Each time she lost a patient, a little piece of her soul seemed to go with them. She knew she couldn't save them all, but that's what medicine was for—to save lives. When a patient actually died, she couldn't help but internalize her feelings. To process her sadness, she had always needed time alone. Heading to her office, she intended to do just that.

Lillian had already left for the day, and both offices were dark. Unlocking the hallway door there was just enough late day light for Andi to find her way through to her own office where she peeled off both stethoscope and lab coat and threw them on the couch before dropping unceremoniously into her desk chair and swinging around to stare out the window at downtown Austin. Lights were already going off in buildings near the hospital and traffic was picking up as people made their way home.

She too should have been on her way home, but a wave of loneliness strong enough to bring tears to her eyes washed over her. All she wanted was to hear Ryan's assurance that the little girl's death hadn't been her fault. Family and friends were just a phone call away, but it was Ryan she wanted and could never have. He was the one person who could make her feel better, and she had thrown away any chance she had of that happening.

Wrapping her arms tightly across her body did nothing more than emphasize how truly alone she was.

Lost in her sadness, the ringing of the desk phone caused her to jump. As she had previously discussed with Lillian, she had been careful to check caller ID before answering calls, but this time the display said 'Ryan' and her mood changed instantly.

"Ryan? I'm so glad you called." The smile on her face was electric in the darkened room, yet the only sound on the other end was heavy breathing. Was he ill? Had he been in an accident?

"Ryan, what's wrong?" she asked. "Talk to me! Are you hurt? Why aren't you saying anything?"

"Hello doctor," came a deep gravelly voice that definitely wasn't Ryan.

"Who is this?" she spat out.

"Don't you remember me?" the man asked. "I remember how much you wanted me and what I wanted to do to you."

If the heavy breathing hadn't been enough to cause her skin to crawl, the words of Richard Kelly certainly were. Slamming the phone down with enough force to cause everything on the desk to jump, Andi buried her face in her hands and shivered uncontrollably before hurrying to lock the office door. Was he in the building? How did he get her direct number and why did it say Ryan's name on the caller ID?

Pacing the room, she worked to make sense of it all. The caller ID had said Ryan and not his full name like it usually did; similar enough to cause her to let her guard down and answer the phone. Hadn't she read something about spammers being able to spoof other people's numbers? Had Richard figured out how to do that? Did he know about her relationship with Ryan? Obviously so if he chose that name to get her to answer the phone. How in the hell did he find her, but more importantly, where was he right now?

All the strange things that had been happening since her arrival in Texas finally made sense. The lights on in the house, the strange repairman at the door, all the incessant hang-up calls. It had to be Richard, but could she prove it?

Going over everything that had happened in the past few months, she realized how very careful he must have been. Nothing that had been happening could be specifically tied to Richard and if she went to the police, they might just think she was being hysterical. To her knowledge, they had filed no charges after Richard's actions in Minnesota, and that most likely meant no paper trail either. Without concrete evidence, what could the police do?

Realistically, there seemed to be nothing to do for the moment, but in the morning, she would definitely get hospital security involved. Tempted to spend the night locked in her office, Andi paced the limited confines of the small space before her heartbeat returned to a more normal rhythm. Casey and Charlie were alone at home and would need to be fed. She had to go home, but was she brave enough to leave the hospital?

Richard was just trying to scare her. He had done nothing in the past to cause her physical harm which made it safe to go home. Still shaken by the call, she asked hospital security to escort her to her vehicle. Safely inside with the doors locked, she risked a quick look around the parking structure before putting the car in gear and driving home. For maybe the first time since moving to Texas, she parked the car in the narrow open space in the garage that had just recently been created by her unpacking. She made sure the garage door was down all the way before getting out of her vehicle and going into the house.

Securely closing the house door to the garage and locking it from the inside, she waited in the dark, listening for sounds that might show someone was in the house. Her heart raced in her chest and her ears strained for even the smallest out-of-place sound. After what seemed a lifetime, her heartbeat returned to normal, and she switched on the kitchen lights. Richard might have the ability to fake a name on caller ID, but the security alarm was still functioning, and she was safe enough.

The fear she had felt ever since realizing Richard was on the other end of the line suddenly became overwhelming and she sank to the floor with tears welling in her eyes. Ryan was gone, Richard was back, and the beautiful little girl had lost her life. She just wanted to crawl into bed and shut the world out by pulling the covers over her head.

Ryan had become the one person she turned to for comfort and now, more than ever before, she longed for him and the love and friendship he offered. As much as she tried to be strong and independent, when it came right down to it, she needed him in her life. What was it that David had said? Right man at the right time? Could Ryan have been that man for her?

By the time the tears dried up, Casey and Charlie began to weave through her legs.

"Hi guys. Boy, am I glad to see you."

An hour of playing with the kittens lifted her sadness, and she picked up the phone, looking for a friend.

"Hi David, it's Andi. Is Carol home?"

"Hey Andi. Sorry, but she's in her yoga class. Anything I can help with?"

"Thanks, but I just wanted to chat. Nothing specific."

"She usually goes out for a drink after class with the other ladies, but should be home around eleven. Should I have her call you when she gets home?" he offered.

"That's okay. I'll call her tomorrow instead." That should have been the end of the call, but she couldn't help herself. "So, have you seen Ryan lately?" she asked nonchalantly.

"Why are you asking me that?" he said in surprise. "Aren't you guys joined at the hip? Andi, what's going on? Did you two have a fight?" How could she have forgotten how perceptive David was?

"Not exactly, but I haven't heard from him in a couple of weeks."

"What do you mean, not exactly? Oh Andi, you didn't dump him, did you?" Now he sounded just like his wife.

"No, this time it's me."

"I know I'm not Carol, but do you want to talk about it?" he offered.

It was embarrassing to discuss her relationship with Ryan with her friend's husband, but she knew full well that if she had been talking to Carol, she would have eventually told David everything.

"Let me ask you this... say you were single and friends with a woman and she kissed you passionately and then just walked out and you didn't hear from her again. What would it mean?"

"Did you kiss Ryan like that?" he asked. She could almost see him smiling, thinking that he had bested Carol.

"No!" she said emphatically. "He kissed me. The night of the party, after everyone else had left. He kissed me and then got up without a word, patted me on the head and walked out the door and I haven't heard from him since. What am I supposed to think?"

"Did you call him?"

"Well, no."

"Why not?"

Was it because she was too proud or too stupid? Why hadn't she picked up the phone?

"Because... well, just because!"

"Look, I know Ryan pretty well, and there has to be an explanation. He's a pretty straightforward guy, and he doesn't play games. If he's been MIA, there must be a reason. He makes no secret that he's really into you and even if you are holding him at arm's length, no guy who feels like that would just walk away without a fight, least of all Ryan. Pick up the phone and call him. Even if it doesn't turn out the way you want, at least you can stop wondering."

Everything he was saying made sense.

"How did you get to be so smart?"

"My wife's an excellent teacher!" he said with a chuckle. "Any other problems I can solve for you tonight?"

For a moment, she considered telling him about her suspicions about Richard Kelly, but as wise as he was, even David couldn't solve that problem, if indeed there was a problem.

"I think you've done enough good for one night, Obi Wan Kenobi. Tell Carol I'll call her tomorrow, and thanks."

"Any time."

. . .

"Wow, somebody has an admirer!"

Looking up from the surgical notes she was entering after another horrific day, Lillian's comment didn't register at first. Another patient lost, but this one never even made it to the operating room. With such severe injuries, they could not get him stable enough to move him to the OR.

"These just arrived for you and I'm so jealous." She was carrying a massive bouquet.

Ryan! Did she dare hope that this was his way of apologizing for dumping her? Taking David's advice, she had placed a call to Ryan's cell phone as soon as she woke up, but it went straight to voicemail.

Lillian placed the large vase carefully on the one corner of Andi's desk that wasn't covered with paperwork.

"Who are they from?" she asked with a wink.

"I don't know. Let me look at the card."

"I already looked. There isn't one, and I even asked the delivery man. He said there wasn't one. They're from Mr. Jacobs right?"

"No, well, at least I don't think they are."

"Yeah right."

"Seriously, I don't know who they're from. Could you call the florist and see who ordered them, please?"

"Let me see what I can find out, but someone sure has exquisite taste. Not one of these flowers is in season now."

"Lillian? Please?" Andi asked, hoping to end the conversation.

Ryan was the only person who would have sent her flowers.

As if she had conjured him out of thin air, her phone rang. She checked caller ID, relieved to see Ryan's full name this time. She took a deep breath, letting it ring a few more times before answering.

"Hello," she said cautiously, still a bit worried about being fooled again.

"Hi Andi." How odd that he addressed her as if they had just seen each other yesterday.

"Ryan, hello," she said as calmly as she could. "I'm surprised to hear from you."

"I'm just calling to see..."

Andi cut him off before he could continue.

"Yes, I got your flowers, but why..."

"What are you talking about? I didn't send you flowers," he said emphatically.

"You didn't?"

"No. Not that it's not a good idea, but no, I didn't. So, who's your secret admirer?" he teased.

"I just assumed..." she said weakly. Just hearing his voice again dissipated her anger.

"You assumed I sent you flowers. That tells me a lot about how you think of me. Aha! You think of me as more than a friend!"

"No! I didn't say that and stop trying to change the subject. I jumped to a conclusion is all."

"What did the card say?"

"That's the thing... there wasn't one. Lillian even asked the delivery man in case he left it in the truck, but he said there never was one. I've asked her to call the florist to find out who... oh wait, here she is now. What did you find out?" she said, switching the conversation to Lillian.

"Not much. The owner of the shop said she didn't know. It was a man, but she couldn't really remember what he looked like and he paid cash. She distinctly remembers asking him several times if he wanted a card and all he said was, 'she'll know it's from me.'"

"Thanks for trying. Would you close the door on the way out?" she asked as a nagging fear ate at her stomach. "Ryan? Did you hear that? Come on, admit it was you," she pleaded.

"Andi, I'm happy to take credit when credit is due, but I swear it wasn't me. It appears you have a secret admirer."

"Don't say that!" she pleaded. "I mean, please... this isn't funny. If you didn't send the flowers, then why are you calling me after ignoring me for the last two weeks?"

"I'm sorry. I wasn't trying to make light of it, and I wasn't ignoring you. It was hard finding a time to call you from Japan."

"You were in Japan?" she asked in surprise.

"Yes, didn't you get my message? I asked my assistant to call you and let you know I had to travel to Japan for a couple of weeks. Remember that business deal the day of the party? Turns out the investors would only deal with me in person. I just got back this morning. I'm so sorry and can't imagine what you must have been thinking. Does it help to know that you were always on my mind while I was gone?"

If her mind wasn't already going a thousand miles an hour about the flowers, she would have recognized the smile in his voice, but the flowers in front of her posed a bigger problem.

"Are you being straight with me? You didn't send me flowers. What in hell is going on here?"

As hard as she tried to keep her emotions in check, she still couldn't keep the tears from welling in her eyes and her voice from shaking.

"Hey, are you okay? There's something else going on, isn't there?"

"I've had an awful couple of days is all, and I just want to go home and soak in a hot bath." A weak excuse for sure, but it was the best she could offer.

"Why don't you let me take you out for a meal and then you can make it an early night?"

"Thanks, but I really just want to go home."

"What kind of friend would I be if I let you do that knowing you're so unhappy? How about this? You go home, I'll stop and pick up some Chinese and meet you at your house. We can eat and then I'll even run a bath for you. I've given Tom the night off, so it will be just the two of us."

The thought of Ryan running her a bath caused her cheeks to turn a delicate shade of pink. Maybe if she had been feeling better, she would have had some snappy comeback, but she was too tired to argue about it.

"Fine."

"Wow," he said. "That was easier than I expected. You head home and I'll meet you there in half an hour."

. . .

After saying good night to Lillian, she drove home, wishing that she had turned down Ryan's offer. Exhausted and incredibly sad as life's disappointments piled up, she just wanted to crawl into bed, but she also wanted desperately to see him and knowing he wouldn't be far behind, she collected her things from the passenger seat and walked up to the front door, key in hand. What she saw stopped her dead in her tracks.

Lying on the ground in front of the door was her mail—arranged in the shape of an upside down cross. Her blood ran cold as fear overwhelmed her. Back in Minnesota, she had once come home to the same scenario, and she knew without a doubt Richard Kelly had been at the house.

Trembling in fear, clutching her purse to her chest, Andi stared at the ground, expecting him to jump out of the bushes at any moment and wishing desperately she had a weapon. Staring at the pile of mail while trying to remember what the police had told her about how to protect herself, she didn't hear Ryan pull into the driveway and walk up behind her.

"Something wrong?" he asked before laying a gentle hand on her shoulder and receiving a scream of fright in response as Andi's bags dropped to the ground and she backed away from him.

"Andi, it's me, Ryan! What's wrong?"

"Ryan? Oh my God, it's you," she said, finally comprehending he posed no threat to her.

Every breath was coming in short bursts and her heart threatened to beat out of her chest, but seeing the worried look on his face, she tried to calm herself.

"Uh, it's nothing. It's been a really long day, and I came home to find that," she told him before pointing to the ground in front of them. Her dropped bags had served only to scatter the mail and now the pieces just looked like someone had accidentally spilled them to the ground.

"You dropped your mail? That's no big deal," he said, giving her a curious look as he stooped to pick up the envelopes. "Don't worry about it. I'll bring it in. Why don't you go inside and I'll be right behind you."

"You don't understand..." she tried to tell him before he cut her off.

"It's okay. I know you've had a bad day. Why don't you go inside, have that bath, and we can eat when you're done? I'll tell you all about Japan. Come on now. I'll keep the food warm. Go on in."

It had been a long day and for a second she wondered if she had imagined everything with Richard Kelly. It had to be kids in the neighborhood playing tricks on her with the mail. However, that didn't explain everything else that had been going on, did it?

With no other choice, she let Ryan take the keys from her hand, unlock the door, and shepherd her into the house. Dumping her belongings on the hall table, she dragged herself upstairs to the bathroom while Ryan watched with a confused and concerned look on his face.

She moved as if in a fog, replaying the sight of the carefully arranged mail in her mind repeatedly. Finally, with the hot water filling the tub and the gentle scent of her favorite bath oils filling the room, she stripped off her clothes and slipped into the tub, letting the warm water envelope her up to her neck. She placed a warm cloth over her eyes to shut out everything that had happened. Only Ryan being somewhere downstairs prevented her from panicking as images of Richard Kelly flashed through her mind. A gentle knock on the door roused her a bit.

"Andi, I thought you might like a glass of wine. Can I come in? I promise to keep my eyes closed."

"Thank you," she said tiredly. "Come in, but don't peek."

True to his word, he kept his eyes closed as he walked through the door before bumping into the towel warmer.

"Damn it all to hell!" he said as he doubled over in pain, nearly dropping the glass of wine. His eyes flew open and lingered on Andi for just a moment before he turned his head away. "Damn, I'm sorry Andi. I saw nothing, I promise. Here's your wine."

Turning away from her, he held the glass out in her general direction, but not quite close enough for her to reach. She rose from the bath just enough to grab it from him before realizing that with his eyes now open, the mirror on the back of the door provided an unobstructed view of her very naked body. She dropped back into the tub as water splashed over the side.

"Thanks. I'll be down in a few more minutes," she told him, hoping he hadn't seen what she thought he could.

"Take your time. I've got dinner warming in the oven and I can make a few calls until you're ready to eat."

Knowing that he had seen her naked should have angered her, but with everything else going on in her life, it just didn't seem that important, and she sank back into the comforting cocoon of the scented water.

By the time the water cooled, she was calmer and in her mind had already concocted rational explanations for everything that had been happening except for the flowers. Yet even that could be explained if she thought hard enough about it. A grateful patient? Carol? Mom and Dad? Even with her mother's aversion to cut flowers, it wasn't out of the realm of possibility that her parents had sent the flowers.

Clad in a pair of shorts and a t-shirt, still-wet hair arranged in a single heavy braid cascading down her back, she joined Ryan in the kitchen. Seated at the breakfast bar, he was still on a call and motioned it would be just a minute. She pulled the Chinese food out of the oven and poured herself another glass of wine.

"Sorry about that," he told her as he finished his call, stopping to stare at her with the intense look he often directed her way. This time, it caused her to stop what she was doing and stare back.

"Why are you looking at me like that?" Reaching nervously up to smooth her hair back, she could feel a flush beginning to build in her chest.

"Do you have any idea how beautiful you are?" he asked, his voice deeper and gruffer than normal.

Standing before him-no makeup, wet hair, and dressed like a college girl, she felt anything but attractive. With everything that had happened recently, the only thing she was feeling was vulnerable.

"Ryan, please."

"No really. I don't want to make you uncomfortable, but when it comes right down to it, you're a stunning woman, Andi."

His passion as he spoke brought tears to her eyes. To hear something so nice after such a horrible day was more than she could bear, and she burst into tears.

"Oh Andi, don't cry. Please don't cry."

Hating herself for being one of those women who can't control their emotions, she also couldn't stop the tears from falling and Ryan gathered her into his arms, rubbing his hand slowly up and down her back until the tears subsided. For that singular moment in time, she never wanted him to let go, and she clung tightly to him. Neither of them said a word as she cried until she could cry no more.

"I'm sorry," she said finally before pulling away and taking a seat while dabbing a tissue at the few remaining tears.

"Don't be sorry," he said kindly. "Sometimes we all need a good cry. Now why don't you tell me what's really going on?"

"It's okay. I'm better."

"Come on, Andi. I know you too well to believe that. Let me help you."

"You can't. I've lost two patients in two days. The first one was a little girl who was only five."

"I'm so sorry."

"We aren't supposed to get attached to patients, every doctor knows that, but this child was so tiny and she had the most angelic face. I let myself believe that despite all of her horrible injuries, I could save her."

"I'm sure you did your best," he said encouragingly.

"Maybe, but I was being arrogant and let myself believe I could save her, even though we all knew she would die. But I've made miracles happen before, so why not this time? You should have seen her mother's reaction when I told her. Her entire world fell apart in that one second and I caused that."

"No, you didn't. You gave the little girl a chance that she wouldn't have had otherwise. I know you. You did everything in your power to save her, but Andi, you're not God. You don't have the power to decide who lives and who dies."

The bluntness of his statement was startling, and she whipped her head up to look at him, realizing he was exactly right.

"I'm sorry to be so direct, but all anyone can expect of you, all you can expect of yourself, is to do your very best. The rest of it is out of your hands."

"You're right," she said sadly, "but that doesn't make it hurt any less."

Reaching over to hug her once more, he agreed. "No, it doesn't, but that's what makes you such a good doctor, right?"

"I guess. Tell me some good news. What did you do in Japan?"

As Ryan talked, she tried hard to pay attention, but Richard Kelly wasn't far from her mind. He was out there somewhere, stalking her, waiting for a chance to... waiting for a chance to what? What exactly did he want from her? The only thing that would make the situation better was to share her fears.

"It's early yet. Want to watch a movie?" Ryan asked as he helped clean up the kitchen after dinner.

"If you don't mind, I'd rather just talk. Maybe I should have told you earlier, but there's something else you need to know."

"Sure," he said before grabbing their wine glasses and the half-empty bottle from dinner and joining her on the sofa in the family room.

"You probably think my reaction at the door was weird, right?"

"Sure, but you're shaken. It's understandable."

"Maybe, but it had nothing to do with my patients," she told him. "I think someone has been stalking me. No, it's more than that. I know he is."

Ryan's demeanor changed instantly. He put down his glass and turned towards her.

"Has someone threatened you?" he demanded. The look on his face was pure fury.

"No, not really, but you need to know the entire story. Before I came to Texas, I had an issue with a patient. He was obsessed with me and even though we never discovered how he did it, he was everywhere I went outside of the hospital. Dinner with friends, a movie, even church on Sunday morning. He was everywhere I went. He did nothing to hurt me physically, but it creeped me out so badly I eventually went to my bosses and told them about it. They got the Police involved and after they paid the man a visit, I didn't see him again and I thought it was over. In fact, I hadn't seen him for months before I moved here."

"Are you telling me you've seen him here?"

"No, but a lot of strange things have been happening since I got here."

"Why didn't you tell me this before? For God's sake, Andi!" Ryan's anger was even more obvious when he got up and started pacing around the room. "Who is this guy and what's been happening?"

"His name is Richard Kelly. At first, I thought it was nothing. Just being forgetful. Lights being on in the house when I come home, things moved out of place from where I thought I had left them. One day, I came home from work to find Casey and Charlie locked in my laundry room."

"I used to have a dog that accidentally closed the door and ended up stuck in a room before."

"You don't get it. They didn't lock themselves in. Someone had actually pushed the lock on the door. How could a cat do that? Ryan, I think he's been in my house!" Finally admitting it out loud sent a wave of panic through her body and for a moment, she couldn't breathe. "And the man who went to all the neighbors and told the lies about me, it could be him."

"That wasn't much of a description," he suggested. "Heck, it describes half of the men I know."

"I agree," she told him, "But Peggy from next door said she saw him at my party. She was sure it was him and even though I only got a quick look, I immediately thought it was him until I convinced myself it was impossible. How could he possibly know I was here?"

"I suppose anyone with the most basic computer knowledge could find out. You have a medical license in Texas and that's public information. And you have gotten more than your share of publicity since arriving here."

"Thanks," she said sarcastically. "That's not really helping."

"I'm sorry, but that is the world we live in."

"And Peggy told me she had seen a repairman coming out of my house a couple of weeks ago. She said they waved at each other before he got into a van and drove away."

"What's wrong with that?"

"Ryan, I didn't hire an electrician, or a maintenance worker, or any kind of repair guy. There was no reason for this man to be at my house. Then today, flowers with no card. He sent me flowers once before, back at Mayo."

"The flowers could be from anyone," Ryan offered as her fears ratcheted up and her words came faster.

"As much as I would like to think that, after seeing the mail that way, I know it was him."

"What do you mean by the mail? Sure, they tossed it to the ground, but that could have just been kids playing around."

"No, you don't understand. Before I dropped my bag on it, someone had arranged the mail like a cross. An upside down cross just like one I came home to back in Minnesota. You can't tell me the mailman did that and kids wouldn't do that sort of thing either. And it's all the phone calls. Dozens of them to my home phone and my cell. The caller always hangs up, but I can always hear someone breathing on the other end. At first, I thought they were wrong numbers, but then it started happening at the office too. Lillian would send the call through, and when I answered, they hung up. The caller ID always said 'unavailable', so we stopped answering those calls and let them go to voicemail. Then a couple of days ago, he called again. This time it said 'Ryan' on the caller ID and I thought it was you, but as soon as I heard the voice, I knew it was him. He said something creepy and then I hung up on him."

"Did he threaten you?" he asked with barely controlled rage as his hands curled into fists at his sides.

"Not really. I mean, he only talked for a few seconds before I hung up on him, but he scared me."

With the story finally out, she should have felt a measure of relief, but having said the words aloud, her body shook in fear before Ryan gathered her into his powerful arms.

"It's going to be okay, Andi. I won't let anything happen to you," Ryan said assuredly. "You'll come and stay at the ranch for a while until we catch this guy."

"Ryan, I can't do that... I'm on call at the hospital and I can't be an hour away. I have to stay here."

As he considered her rejection of his offer to stay with him, she could see the muscles in his jaw working. He wasn't someone that was used to hearing no.

"All right, I understand that, but I'm going to stay here tonight, and tomorrow I'll bring in Tom and the rest of my security team and we'll go over the house top to bottom, changing all the locks and checking your security system. Tom will stay with you round the clock and we'll find this guy and put an end to his tormenting you."

Ryan's confident tone should have been infectious, but she couldn't shake the feeling that things with Richard were going to get much worse before they caught him. Burying her head in Ryan's shoulder, she prayed he could figure it out before that happened.

"Come on. It's been a long day for you. Let's get you to bed."

His tenderness was her undoing and like a child, she allowed herself to be walked up to bed, slipping off her shorts as Ryan tucked the bed linens tight around her. As he turned to leave the room, she reached out for his hand, causing him to turn back.

"Please, I don't want to be alone tonight. Will you please stay with me?"

Any other man would have taken that as an invitation to share her bed, but Ryan simply slipped off his shoes before lying next to her on top of the bed linens and pulling her in closer.

"I'm not going anywhere," he told her. Placing a soft kiss on her forehead, he whispered into her ear. "Sleep tight, little one."

· · ·

The sunlight streaming in through the windows jolted her out of bed when she opened her eyes the next morning. A quick look at the bedside clock showed she had seriously overslept and Ryan was nowhere to be found.

With no time for a shower, she threw open her closet to grab a clean set of clothes for work when Ryan walked in with a breakfast tray and a grin.

"Good morning sleepy head. I wasn't sure you'd be up yet."

"Why didn't you wake me? I'm so late!"

"Andi, calm down. I already called the hospital and told them you won't be in today."

"What? Why would you do that?" As much as she appreciated everything he had done for her last night, how dare he call the hospital?

"I'm not taking any chances with your safety until we find this Richard guy," he said as he placed the tray carefully on the end of the bed.

"But I have to go to work... I have patients..."

"Dr. Miller is covering for you. I spoke to him directly, and he's happy to do it. Don't worry, you can go in tomorrow, but today we have to get some things sorted to make sure you're safe."

"Like what?" she asked. What he was saying made sense. She only wished Ryan had consulted her before he told everyone she wouldn't be coming in. What must the staff have thought to get a call from Ryan on her behalf?

"Well, for starters, Tom is already here. He's downstairs, and he's already got a crew in going over the house. They'll change all the locks, check the security system, and install some cameras."

She could hear strange voices in the hallway.

"The camera feed will go to the ranch where my staff will monitor it 24-7 and I'll have access to it on my phone at all times.

"I'm not so sure I want you to watch everything I do in my home," she said. As much as she trusted Ryan, it seemed too personal and an invasion of her privacy.

"Don't worry, we won't have any cameras in the bathrooms or your bedroom, but the rest of the house has full coverage. That way, if this guy is getting in the house, we'll be able to find out how and stop him. I wouldn't do it if I didn't think it was necessary, Andi. You never know what these nut cases are capable of, and I'm not taking any chances with you. If it turns out you really don't want it, we can take them out again."

"I'm sorry, Ryan, but maybe I overreacted. It's a combination of being overly tired and losing the little girl. Maybe I'm blowing this all out of proportion."

"No, I don't think so. While you were asleep last night, I called in some favors and found out more about Richard Kelly. He's not someone to be taken lightly, I'm afraid."

"What do you mean?"

"Richard's been in prison. In fact, he got out just a few months before you met him."

"Why was he in prison?" She wasn't sure she really wanted to know the answer to the question, and his hesitation spoke volumes.

"Seems he likes to force himself on women and when they don't cooperate, he beats them up pretty bad. But that's not all. He was a sharpshooter in the Army before they gave him a dishonorable discharge, and he's known to have a large cache of weapons. The detective I talked to in Minnesota knew a lot about the man and he told me they were quite concerned when he started following you around. When he unexpectedly disappeared, they figured he had moved on to another victim. Andi, this guy is a psycho and I'm not taking any chances with your safety."

If she needed anything more to frighten her about Richard Kelly, the new information was more than enough.

"There's one more thing," Ryan said as he reached into the pocket of his slacks. "I want you to wear this."

In his hand was a beautiful turquoise pendant necklace.

"I can't accept that," she said, waving off his gift.

"It's not what you think," he said before sitting next to her on the bed and reaching to secure the pendant around her neck. "This contains the personal safety sensor my company has been working on. We haven't worked all the bugs out yet, but it will provide enough information about your body's metrics that I can tell when you feel unsafe. Even though Tom will be with you most of the time, he can't always be there and this will be just another weapon we can use against Kelly."

"Okay."

"Leave it on. Don't even take it off in the shower. Once I activate it, if you take it off, it will immediately trigger a response from us, okay?"

"Are you sure this is necessary?" she asked.

"Andi, don't you know how important you have become to me? I couldn't live with myself if something happened to you. Just promise me you won't take it off."

As if she needed any more convincing, the fear in his eyes provided all the incentive she needed.

"I promise. Thank you."

"Now I better get downstairs and see how things are going while you get dressed. Eat something and I'll see you soon."

Ignoring the toast and coffee he had brought up, she heard him speak to Tom before she headed to the bathroom. As she stared into the mirror, it was the face of a stranger looking back. Having shed more tears yesterday than she had the entire previous year, she looked as bedraggled as she felt. She wrapped her fingers tightly around the pendant and prayed Ryan's technology, prototype or not, would help keep her safe. Ryan's presence and the work of his team in the house gave her hope they would find Richard before she became his next victim.

. . .

The security team had worked all day, but eventually the house emptied of Ryan's staff, leaving just the two of them and the ever-present Tom who was currently unpacking in one of the guest rooms near Andi's.

"What would you like to do tonight?" Ryan asked when they could finally relax together in the family room.

"Why don't you just go home? I've pulled you away from your work enough for one day, and Tom's here in case Richard appears."

After a year of not even thinking of the man, he was once again on her mind. Still, if he had been watching the house, he would have seen all the activity and most likely had second thoughts about trying to get to her.

"Don't worry about me. Now that we've been through the house and have the cameras up and the locks changed, I'm not too concerned he can get to you. Let's try to get back to normal. How about we go out for dinner?"

"I'm not hungry," she admitted. "But you know what I would like? I'd like to go for a run. Will you join me?"

Ryan had never said he was a runner, but she needed to get outside, exert a little energy, and enjoy the freedom of running.

"After everything that has gone on today, I'm surprised you want to exercise," Ryan told her. "You must be a glutton for punishment, but if it would make you feel better, I'll go along for the ride. I've got workout gear in my trunk. But you have to promise to keep the pace slower than you're used to, so Tom and I can keep up."

"Tom?" she asked with a raised eyebrow.

"Yes Andi... Tom is coming with. Where you go, he goes. That's his job," he scolded.

"Okay, I'll try to remember. Let me go up and change."

"I'll meet you back downstairs in fifteen."

While Ryan went out to his car for his change of clothing, Andi ran up the stairs, knocked on Tom's door, and informed him of the plan before heading to her bedroom to change. Tying her running shoes, she glanced out the window at the setting sun. Was Richard Kelly out there some place watching her at this very moment? What about the women who had already been his victims? It took little to imagine their terror as he raped them and then tried to kill them with his fists. Was she next on the list?

"Andi? You ready?" Ryan yelled up the stairs.

Knowing he was in her corner was the only reason she felt safe enough to leave the house.

CHAPTER NINE

"Morning Andi. Feeling better?" Dr. Miller asked the next morning. It took a moment to realize that Ryan had most likely used illness as her excuse for missing work.

"Yes, I am thanks and thanks for covering for me. I hope I didn't ruin any plans you might have had for your day off."

"Just working on my honey-do list at home. Trust me, I much preferred being at work."

Seeing his eyes focus on something behind her, she felt a moment of fear until realizing he was looking at Tom.

"Can I help you, sir?"

"Dr. Miller, this is Tom. He's going to be shadowing me for a few days." Having already decided to share what was going on in her life with as few people as possible, she offered no further explanation.

"Oh, pleased to meet you, Doctor," he said as he offered his hand to Tom.

"He's not a doctor," Andi corrected. "He's interested in learning how things work around here and Dr. Thompson has given us the go-ahead for him to be with me."

They had decided the cover story after Ryan had contacted Dr. Thompson the day before to fill him in on the situation. He had graciously agreed to allow Tom access to the hospital while in Andi's company. While he wouldn't be in the operating room, he could stand guard in the scrub room with full view and easy access if needed.

Dr. Miller opened his mouth to say something more but stopped when Andi, trailed by Tom, turned to walk away without further explanation and he hurried to catch up.

"Yesterday was a quiet day anyway, so you didn't miss much. Dare we hope that we have two in a row?"

"I think any chance of that just went out the window," she said with a tired smile. Surgeons were a superstitious lot and both she and Dr. Miller realized too late his comment had just jinxed them. "Haven't you learned not to tempt fate?"

No sooner had the words left her mouth than both their pagers went off. "See? I'm off to the ER. See you later."

Stopping only to drop her bag in the office, Andi hurried down to the ER, with Tom trailing closely behind. Having seen how well he handled the run the day before, she had no qualms about taking the stairs, and he was barely winded by the time they reached the emergency department. Amid the emergency personnel dressed in various shades of scrubs and lab coats, his suit coat looked out-of-place, but without the jacket, his gun would have been plainly visible. After all the drama from the previous few days, Andi wasn't eager to start any more.

Brian's wish for a quiet day was dashed as a flood of shooting victims from a nearby mall arrived at the ER. After ensuring her first patient of the day was stable enough for surgery, she and Tom hurried to the operating room.

"I hope you're not squeamish Tom, because this is going to be one messy surgery."

"I served in the Gulf War, Dr. Taylor, so I've seen it all," he assured her.

Entering the scrub room, she showed him where to stand as she scrubbed while watching the rest of her team already prepping the patient in the other room.

Reaching up to take her necklace off, he stopped her. "Remember Dr. Taylor, the necklace stays on."

"Sorry," she said, realizing what she had been about to do. "Just habit I guess. If you need anything while I'm in surgery, press the button over there for the intercom. Otherwise, I'll join you when I'm finished."

"Good luck, Doctor," he offered before she stepped into the comforting confines of the OR.

Hours later, the last stitch was being put in and she stepped away from the table. For that period at least, she hadn't wasted one moment's thought on Richard Kelly and it felt great.

"Great job everyone," she told the team before reaching up to untie her gown as Ashley came to assist.

"Thanks Dr. Taylor. Now can you tell us who the guy is who's been standing in the scrub room since you got here?" Ashley asked.

"His name is Tom, and he's going to be observing me for a while. Just pretend he's not here."

"Are we in some kind of trouble? Usually, the only time observers are here is when they think we've made a mistake." Every pair of eyes in the room was on Andi.

"This has nothing to do with any of you. Everything's okay, I promise. Now I better get cleaned up and update the family."

Tom wasted no time joining her as she left to talk to the family, and she had to ask him to keep his distance as she entered the waiting room. Like all families, the waiting parents exhibited a mixture of fear, grief, and impatience. Their daughter had been at work in the mall when the shooter came in and her parents hadn't yet seen her.

"Mr. and Mrs. Meyer?" Andi said as she extended her hand to each of them and they both stood.

"How's Katie?" the woman asked hurriedly. Tear stains still lined her cheeks.

"She should be fine. The bullet did some internal damage, and I had to remove her spleen, but she should live a long and healthy life without it. She was a very lucky girl. If that bullet had been just an inch to the right, she might not have made it."

"Thank you Doctor," her father said before casting a worried glance at Tom who stood bigger than life blocking the entrance to the room. "Can we see her now?"

"One of my nurses will come and get you when she's ready for visitors. It shouldn't be too much longer. Is there anything else you'd like to ask? If not, I'll check up on Katie a little later. Try not to worry, okay?"

Accepting hugs from each of them, she started back to her office to complete her surgical notes.

"It must feel pretty good to give news like that to the family," Tom said. Now that it was just the two of them, they walked side by side.

"It just about makes up for the times when I have to give the other news. I'll never get used to that."

"Why do you do this?"

"You mean surgery?"

"Yeah, why not just be a family doctor... put in a few stitches, fix a broken bone here and there? It seems so much easier and you'd still be helping people."

That's the same question her mother had asked when Andi had announced her decision to be a surgeon.

"I could ask you the same thing," she responded. "Why is someone a bodyguard when the risk of getting hurt is so much higher than, say, being a mall cop? There's something about the challenge and the sense of fulfillment I get when I do my job and do it well. Knowing that I literally hold someone's life in the palm of my hand every day is a rush like nothing else. Even when I can't save someone, I get through it by knowing I did the best I could. It's always hard to lose a patient, but as Ryan reminded me just yesterday, we don't control who lives or dies. Here's my office. Let me introduce you to my assistant."

Lillian would need more of an explanation and, rather than alarm her by giving too much information, she let Tom do the talking. As she expected, his professional demeanor made the news of the potential threat easier for Lillian to accept.

"So, am I in danger too?" she asked when he finished. Her eyes were as big as saucers, which under the circumstance was to be expected. If Andi hadn't already had time to process it, she would have reacted the same.

"No ma'am, we don't think so," Tom told her. "Other than the phone calls, all previous contact with Kelly has been outside of the hospital. We don't see any reason he would change his behavior this time. Still, to be safe, hospital security has received a copy of the man's photograph and we have briefed them on the situation. He won't get past the front doors, much less make it all the way up here."

"Please don't be worried Lillian. Tom is excellent at his job and he or one of his associates will be with us until the situation is resolved. I have every faith in his abilities to keep us safe. Until then, I have to ask you to keep this between us. You know how things are these days with shootings every other day. People are scared and if the hospital staff thought there was a crazy man on the loose, who knows what would happen? So, can we just keep it between us?"

"Of course, Doctor." The woman had already proven she could keep confidences.

"Tom, if you don't mind, I think when I'm in the office you can have a seat out here with Lillian."

"After I do a sweep of your office, that would be fine."

"Lillian, can you please make sure Tom has whatever he needs, starting with some strong coffee?"

"Yes doctor," she said before busying herself making a fresh pot of coffee.

With that sorted and Tom having assured the safety of the inner office, Andi closed the door gently behind her before exhaling slowly. News of Tom's presence would make it around the hospital in short order, eliminating the need for her to make any more excuses for his presence, and hopefully, things would get back to normal.

Pulling her cell out, it did not surprise her to find several messages from Ryan.

"Hi."

"How'd your surgery go?" he asked. She could hear papers rustling in the background and imagined him sitting at his desk at the ranch.

"How'd you know? Oh, I forgot. You can track me now, can't you?"

The sensor she was wearing provided a GPS signal to Ryan's phone.

"Not that I am watching your every move, but yes, I know where you are, give or take fifty feet. How are you getting along with Tom?"

"It's going better than expected, although I really hate lying to everyone. As far as most of them know, he's just observing me for a few days. It will be for just a few days, right?"

"Honestly, that depends on Kelly. Until we locate him, I don't know what to think. I don't want to frighten you more than you already are, but the police think that the fact that he followed you to another state is a good indicator that you're more than just a passing fancy to him. Even if he doesn't contact you again, I have a dozen private detectives tracking him down. Nothing is going to happen to you, I promise."

"Don't you sometimes wish you had never met me?"

"Why would you say that?"

"It seems like ever since we met, I've caused you nothing but trouble."

"Andrea!" he retorted. He had never called her by her full name before, and she knew she had struck a nerve. "Don't you ever say that. Meeting you was the best moment of my life. In fact..."

He didn't finish his sentence, but he didn't have to. She knew the man was falling in love with her, but any further discussion about what he didn't say became moot when her pager went off.

"Oops, I'm being paged to the ER again. I'll call you tonight when I get home," she said, reaching for her lab coat and stethoscope.

"I'm already in the city this afternoon for a meeting. How about I stop over? I'll bring food."

"I should be home by seven. Come anytime. See you then."

Lucky for Andi, Tom was quick on his feet and they flew down to the ER before heading back to the surgical floor. This time he got nary a look from the team and they spent the rest of the day going in and out of surgery before finally heading home.

The house was dark, and the neighborhood was quiet, but Tom wasn't taking any chances. He pulled the vehicle into the garage and waited until the door had closed securely before opening the car door.

"Let me go in first and look around. I'll come and get you when I'm sure it's safe. Until then, stay in the car and keep the doors locked," he instructed before letting himself into the house.

That he did so with gun drawn, albeit pressed securely to his thigh, should have hammered home the potential danger, but the cloak and dagger stuff would have been laughable in any other situation. Andi did as instructed before Tom came back out and allowed her to enter.

"All clear, doctor," he said as she walked by him and he secured the door behind her.

"Thank you Tom. I should let you know Mr. Jacobs will join us this evening. He should be here any minute. You're welcome to join us for dinner."

"Thank you, but if you don't mind, I'll just make myself a sandwich once he gets here and go up to my room. I'm sure you two would like to be alone."

Unsure what Tom might have thought was between his boss and her, she didn't pursue the issue.

"We've got a team stationed in the neighborhood overnight, so you should be secure for the evening. I'm just upstairs if you need me."

"Thank you. Help yourself to whatever you like in the kitchen. I want you to know how much I appreciate your help today."

"You're very welcome. What time would you like to leave for the hospital in the morning?" he asked.

"If we leave about six, that would work for me. I'm going to go upstairs and freshen up. Will you let Ryan in for me?"

"Certainly."

After a quick shower and a change of clothes, Andi came back down to find Ryan in the kitchen, filling Casey and Charlie's food and water dishes as they played with the mountain of toys in their favorite corner of the room. Tom nodded politely as he walked by with a large sandwich and a drink and headed up to his room for the night.

"Hi there," Ryan said. "You look nice." Before she could respond, he had pulled her into his arms for a lingering hug, and she felt her body relax into his. "You smell nice too."

Hearing his compliments made her happy, but she was exhausted and surprised by how tense she had felt all day. Ignoring his look of disappointment, she pulled away to sit at the table.

"Thanks for bringing food. I'm famished. I asked Tom to join us, but he turned me down."

"That's the response you'll always get from him. He has this thing about not getting too attached to his charges. That way, if something..."

"... if something happens to them, to me, he won't feel so badly. That's what you were going to say, right?" she asked as tears gathered in her eyes.

"Yes. I'm sorry Andi. That was insensitive of me," he said as he sat across the table and took her hand in his own. "You're going to be okay. We'll get this guy soon and it will all be over. I don't want you to worry."

"Thank you. I know you're doing your best and I appreciate it, but when I'm tired and let my mind go to what could happen, it's overwhelming. When I just thought he was a normal run-of-the-mill crazy back in Minnesota, it was annoying, but not too concerning. Now, knowing what he's done to other women? It's a whole different ballgame and I just want it to be over. I want my life back."

Ryan came around the table and pulled her into his arms again. Just days before, Andi had thought their friendship was over and now it had again become the most important thing in her life.

"I know you don't like it when I say stuff like this to you, but you are the single most important person in my life and the thought of something happening to you... well... I just won't let that happen. You know I would never lie to you and I promise you I will get this guy."

Using his fingers to raise her tear-stained face to look into her eyes, he lowered his lips and kissed her gently. For the first time, she didn't push him away.

"I love you, Andi."

Overcome with emotion, she buried her face in his shoulder, content in knowing that this incredibly strong and generous man was going to make everything right again.

"Come on, little one," he said finally. "Let's eat before it all gets cold."

With the house secured, a team of guards patrolling outside, Tom upstairs, and Ryan at her side, she could relax for the first time all day even though she couldn't help but steal an occasional glance at the darkness outside. Was Richard somewhere watching at this very moment? Each time she let herself drift away in worry, Ryan was quick to pull her attention back to him as they sat together in front of the fire, content to hold each other without speaking.

"Ouch!" he cried suddenly as Charlie launched himself from a chair onto Ryan's shoulder. For such a tiny thing, the cat had a tremendous athletic ability.

Releasing Charlie's grip on Ryan's shirt and checking to make sure there was no sign of blood, she apologized for her earlier reaction.

"Don't be. I kind of like it when you need me to be the strong one. It's nice to be needed every once in a while."

"And about the other thing..."

"You mean my telling you I love you?" he asked.

"Ryan, I..."

"It's okay Andi. I know you're worried about hurting me, but I'm a big boy and you're worth the risk." Turning to face her on the couch, he put Charlie back on the floor before taking her hands in his.

"We can't choose who we fall in love with and maybe in a perfect world the woman I loved would be at my side all day every day, but I fell in love with you... every part of you. Being a surgeon is who you are and I wouldn't ask you to change that. Everything in life has trade-offs and I know loving you will mean we won't always be able to be together when we'd like. If that's the price I have to pay to be with you, I'm willing to pay it."

"That's what my ex-boyfriends always said. They were willing to put up with my schedule at first, but then it became too much and they end up hating me. I care for you too much to have you hate me, Ryan."

It was true. She did care for him too much. In fact, she was in love with him, which made it that much harder to think how miserable she would eventually make him.

"You can't waste your time worrying about what might happen in the future. Look at couples who have been married for ten, twenty, or even thirty years who get a divorce. The odds were against them from the beginning, but they took the chance and probably had many years of happiness together before it fell apart. Why would you give up the chance at what could be the best thing that's ever happened to you? Please don't throw your life away on what-ifs. Please don't throw away what I feel for you because you're too scared of what may or may not happen. Andi, I'm asking you to just take a chance and let yourself experience the possibilities. Sometimes we have to stop letting our heads control what we're feeling and let our heart speak for us."

Reaching up to caress his cheek, feeling the muscles working along his jawline, Andi traced her fingers along his full red lips as the intensity of his stare never wavered from her own.

"Ok," she said softly before leaning in to fulfill her need to feel his lips against her own. After a few minutes of enjoying his kiss, he pulled away.

"Is something wrong?" she asked in surprise.

"No. To be honest, I'd like nothing more than to make love to you right here and right now, but I want to make sure I'm not just getting you at a weak moment. You've had a hard time lately, so how about we take things slow for now?"

Her desire for the man had finally been unleashed, and now he was pulling back?

"Trust me," he said knowingly as he stood. "I know what I'm doing. Before I change my mind, I better go. I love you and I'll call you in the morning. Lock the door behind me and be safe, little one."

Kissing the top of her head, he walked out the door, leaving Andi speechless on the couch.

What had just happened? After all this time, she had offered herself to him and been rejected. What new hell was this?

Letting herself think of Ryan as more than just a friend should have been a turning point in their relationship, at least to Andi's way of thinking. However, each time they were together after that night, Ryan barely touched her. A quick kiss here or there was all he offered, and she wondered what she had missed in their earlier conversations. With few exceptions, they continued to spend the greater part of each day together to where she suggested Ryan move into her house, hoping their relationship might become more intimate if he did.

"It just makes sense. You spend so much time here anyway and if we were both in the same place, think how much money it would save on bodyguards," she insisted as they discussed it.

Once Tom was assigned to protect her, a new bodyguard had begun to shadow Ryan.

"It's not a question of money, Andi. I would give every dime I have to keep you safe. You're just not ready for us to live together. But even if you were, if I was here, we'd never flush Kelly out."

"You're saying you won't move in because I'm bait?" she asked angrily.

"That's not it at all and you know it," he insisted. "It's been weeks now and even though I have a team of men working around the clock, we still don't know where he is."

"That's probably because he has given up," she said. She didn't feel like she was still in danger, but more likely, she was just becoming accustomed to living in fear.

"Now that we're talking about Richard yet again, I've been meaning to talk to you about this. It's getting harder and harder to justify Tom's presence at the hospital. Security already knows not to let Richard in the hospital if he shows up, so isn't it about time Tom said goodbye to being with me round the clock?"

"Andi, I don't think..."

"Wait a minute," she said, holding up her hand to silence him. "I'm not saying no bodyguard at all, I'm just saying not at the hospital and not in the house with me. He can still drop me off in the morning and pick me up at night, but you've already proven that the house is Fort Knox. Can you just pull back a bit and we'll see how it goes? If something weird happens, we can always go back to how it is now, but I need some breathing room. And..." she said seductively as she walked her fingers up his chest, "I wouldn't mind it if you and I could finally be alone."

Make-out sessions in front of the fire were great, but each time she made it clear she was ready to move up to the bedroom, he had pushed her away and it was getting more and more frustrating for her.

"Your womanly charms, as enticing as they may be, will not work on me. I already told you I want things between us to go slowly," he said as he moved her hands away from his chest.

Slow?! He was like a glacier!

"But if you really insist, I think we can lighten up on Tom a bit as long as you continue to wear the sensor. It's working pretty well. I'll talk to him before I leave and tomorrow he'll be with you only when you're in transit or away from the house or hospital. But the first sign of anything out of the ordinary and he moves back in, okay?"

It wasn't what she really wanted, but at least it was something.

"It's a deal."

. . .

"Dr. Taylor? Mr. Jacobs is in my office. He'd like to see you," Lillian said as she walked into Andi's office the next morning. It was the first time since they had met that Ryan had visited her at her office.

"Show him in please," she said before checking her reflection in the window behind her.

"This is a first. Have you come to invite me to lunch?"

"Unfortunately, no," Ryan said before depositing a soft kiss on her cheek. "I had a board meeting here in the hospital and have to run to another meeting in a few minutes, but wanted to ask you for a favor."

"Of course. How can I help?"

"I got a call from Mary this morning. She's coming to the ranch for the weekend and wants to meet you."

"Meet me?" Andi asked in surprise. Although she had been in Texas for months, she had yet to meet Ryan's sister.

"Yes silly. How would you feel about spending the weekend at the ranch so she can get to know you?"

"Do you think that's such a good idea with Richard still out there somewhere?" Although there had been no sign of the man, she didn't want to put anyone else in danger.

"Actually, I think it's a wonderful idea. We have more security at the ranch and Richard couldn't get within miles of you there. Not only would it give Tom a break for the weekend, but I think you could use a break, too."

Reaching up to caress the side of her face, the warmth of his hand and the love in his eyes were enough to convince Andi.

"If you're sure..."

"I am, and Mary is going to love you. You can make a quick stop at your house after work, and Tom will drive you to the ranch."

"What about Casey and Charlie?" She didn't feel comfortable asking a neighbor to take care of them.

"Bring them with, of course. I have to run, but I'll see you later tonight at the ranch. Love you, little one." A quick kiss and he was gone again.

His term of endearment was actually growing on her, but not nearly as much as he was.

· · ·

It was well after dark by the time they made it to the ranch, and judging from the many texts Ryan had sent before they arrived, Mary was more than eager to meet her. Expecting he was exaggerating her interest, Mary's exuberant greeting as Andi stepped out of the car lived up to the hype.

"Dr. Taylor, it's so great to meet you," she said before enveloping Andi in a hug, her slight frame belying the strength behind that hug. "Ryan has talked about you so much, I feel like I already know you."

"Hi Mary. It's nice to meet you also and please, call me Andi. So, you're the little sister Ryan is so immensely proud of. He told me how brilliant you are, but he didn't say how beautiful you are."

She was indeed stunning and probably had college men drooling at her doorstep. She looked nothing like Ryan, but as the only girl in the family, that was probably a good thing. Dark copper colored hair flowed around her shoulders and deep brown eyes that seemed to take in everything around her captivated Andi's attention, but it was her welcoming smile that brought her face alive.

"Thank you for that, but Ryan talks about how beautiful you are and he sure wasn't lying. Oh my gosh, are there cats in that crate? I love cats!"

Mary had been talking a mile a minute when she finally spotted Tom with the cat carrier. Casey and Charlie's faces peeked out inquisitively, and she immediately went to inspect the pair as Ryan made his way to Andi's side and pulled her into his arms.

"Finally! I was thinking you had changed your mind," he whispered into her ear.

"Not a chance," she whispered back. "I missed you."

The look of desire in his eyes told her he felt the same.

"Hope you're hungry. Jackie's been cooking all day," he said as he took her bag and they made their way into the house.

Mary had claimed the cat carrier as her own and they were barely in the house before she had opened the latch to let Casey and Charlie out. Expecting them to be a little wary in unfamiliar surroundings, everyone laughed when they bounded right out and began running around as if they had never left the ranch. Andi, knowing Ryan wasn't used to having cats in his house, suggested it might be better to restrict Casey and Charlie to her room for the weekend.

"You don't have to do that, Andi. I've gotten used to being the victim of those two holy terrors. Let them run free," Ryan said.

"Don't worry Andi, I won't let them out of my sight," Mary assured her. "Do you want me to show you to your room?"

"Upstairs and to the left in the north wing, correct?"

It was where she had stayed the last time she visited the ranch. Even though it had only been a few months, it seemed ever so long ago.

"I've got you in the south wing this time," Ryan clarified as she looked back at him in surprise. The south wing was where Ryan's bedroom was, as Andi well knew. "Tom, will you take Andi's things up for her, please?"

"Dinner is ready when you are, Mr. Jacobs," Jackie said as she walked into the room. "Dr. Taylor, hello. It's a pleasure to see you again."

"And you also Jackie, but I thought we agreed you would call me Andi," she said warmly. "I hope we can find time this weekend to catch up."

"I'd like that also," Jackie admitted before addressing her boss. "Whenever you're ready, sir."

"Ladies? Are you ready to eat?" he asked before directing them into the dining room.

Andi's first tour of the ranch had included a brief walkthrough of the dining room, but with the massive table set for only the three of them, the room looked cavernous and much too grand for a family dinner. Maybe it was the mood set by the candlelight, or the easy friendship that was developing between Mary and herself, but she felt like she was home.

Ryan seemed content at first to be a spectator as Mary relayed stories of her life at college and Andi, mindful that not everyone enjoyed a good surgical story, gave a watered-down version of her work week. For such a young woman, Mary surprised her by showing an intense empathy for the patients Andi worked with and on more than one occasion as she spoke, Andi saw tears in her eyes. Ryan often showed the same compassion for others; something Andi quite liked about him.

"All that on top of dealing with this Richard Kelly person? Wow! How do you handle that much stress?" Mary asked.

Surprised he would have shared information about Richard with his sister, Andi raised an eyebrow in Ryan's direction.

"I hope you don't mind that I told her what's going on. She's had a little on-the-job training developing the sensor and since you are the test case for it, I couldn't really keep it from her."

"I don't really mind, but I can't help but worry that what I'm going through is putting everyone around me in danger," she told them as she subconsciously reached up to wrap her fingers around the pendant. "But back to your question, Mary. Stress is part of being a surgeon. There is no getting away from that when you're dealing with people's lives, but you're right. Having a stalker intensifies that stress. Thanks to Ryan, and Tom of course, it's getting easier to sleep at night even if we haven't found him yet."

Reaching across the table, she grabbed Ryan's hand, giving a squeeze while trying to hold back her tears. "I'm really lucky to have your brother in my life."

Ryan leaned over and kissed her on the lips and as they pulled back, Mary's face lit up with excitement.

"Oh my God, you guys are so cute together!" she said excitedly. "I wish Mom could see you right now."

"Mary..." Ryan said with caution. "Enough."

"Andi, do you know how long we've been waiting for this?" she said before casting her brother a wary glance.

"I'm sorry?" Andi asked in confusion. "Waiting for what?"

"Not what. Who! We've been waiting for you!"

"Mary, that's enough," Ryan said a bit more emphatically.

"As handsome as my brother is and as kind as he is, we didn't think he would ever get serious about a woman and now here you are."

"For God's sake, Mary, she doesn't need to know this."

Now Andi's curiosity was piqued. Thinking she knew most everything about Ryan, his more than apparent discomfort proved her wrong.

As if Ryan hadn't even spoken, Mary continued.

"You see, Andi, Ryan always told us he didn't want to waste his time on women who weren't the right one. He has never been serious about anyone before and he always said he would know her, the 'right one' I mean, when he saw her. That he's had a relationship with you for some time now and you're here at the ranch means you must be the right one! Don't you see?!"

She looked from Ryan to Andi and back again for confirmation. "Admit it Ryan! I'm right, aren't I?"

"I think you've said enough for now, Mary. Why don't you go find the cats?" he said in mock anger. He was trying very hard not to smile.

"I will, but only because I know you want to be alone with Andi. Let's go riding tomorrow morning, okay? You do ride, don't you?" she asked Andi as she stood from the table.

"Barely, but I would love to go riding," Andi assured her.

"Sorry about that," Ryan said as Mary left, calling for the kittens as she did so. "She's one of the smartest girls I know, but sometimes I forget she's still technically a teenager. Come on, let's get some fresh air."

Taking her hand, they walked out to the patio, sitting side by side in front of the fire pit before settling in to look up at the stars.

"Is Mary right?" Andi asked quietly. "Am I the right one for you?"

"Of course you are. I told you that at the start," he admitted without hesitation. "Remember what I said to you at Carol and Dave's party? I'm going to marry you. It's taking longer to convince you of that, but it's still true."

"But how could you have known? You barely knew me back then."

"It doesn't make much sense, does it? I just knew the very first time I looked into your eyes. You were kneeling at Mark's side, covered in his blood, and there was something in the way you looked around at us all before your gaze lingered on me for just a moment. You probably don't even remember it, but I'll never forget what I felt that moment I looked at you."

In all honesty, she didn't remember what he was talking about. For her, it was that moment in the hallway outside of Mark's room when Ryan had first asked her to dinner. Without admitting it then, he had stolen a little piece of her heart that night and every time since he took a bit more.

"David told me he thought you might be the right one for me as well."

"Oh, he did, did he?" Ryan said, before turning to face her directly. "And is he right?"

The look of hope on his face was unmistakable.

"I think so," she said before Ryan leaned in for a kiss filled with passion that left them both breathless and wanting more.

"My God, you are beautiful," he said. The deep huskiness of his voice wasn't the only response his body was having.

"Ryan?"

"Yes, little one?"

"We've waited long enough, don't you think?"

Her body was on fire and tonight, finally, she hoped they could be together.

Without another word, he pulled her to her feet, and they walked arm in arm up to his bedroom. As he closed the door softly behind them, Andi noticed her suitcase was already in the room and she turned to look at him.

"What would you have done if the night had gone differently?" she asked as she slowly unbuttoned his shirt.

"It was never an option," he said with a grin.

Moving her slowly backwards until the bed blocked her path, they undressed each other, savoring each new discovery and luxuriating in their ability to be together.

Being with Ryan was like nothing she had experienced as he made love to her with a level of care and tenderness that moved her beyond measure. Through some innate sense, he seemed to know where and how to touch her to bring forth the most intense pleasure she had ever experienced, and she knew she would never get enough of him. Together, they sealed the love she had so firmly resisted and after hours of lovemaking, she was finally at peace.

"I love you, Andi," he said finally, his voice a mere whisper in her ear before he drifted off to sleep.

Ryan slept soundly by her side while Andi luxuriated in the security provided by his powerful arms holding her close. It had taken months for them to get to this place and, as frustrated as she had been when he rejected her advances, she was glad they had waited. Great sex was one thing... and it had indeed been great... but making love with someone that meant so very much to her had taken the experience to a whole new level.

Unexpectedly, the thought came that she could happily spend the rest of her life with Ryan; something she had never dared consider with any other man in her life. Did that mean that he truly was the right one? More than anything, she wished it to be so and finally closed her eyes and slept deeper than she had in years.

CHAPTER TEN

A persistent knocking woke them the next morning, and she opened her eyes to see Ryan smiling at her.

"Good morning, my love," he whispered as he moved a stray hair from her face. "Sleep well?"

"Better than ever," she admitted. "But who's knocking on the door at this hour?"

"Mary," he said. "She's been calling your name quietly for about five minutes. Did I mention to you that although she's brilliant, she doesn't seem to understand personal boundaries? I was hoping for another way to start our day," he said with a wink before pulling her close for a passionate kiss.

"Andi?" came Mary's soft voice yet again. "Are you up yet?"

"What would happen if we just ignored her?" Andi whispered, snuggling deeper into his arms.

"I've been trying that for nineteen years... doesn't work, so you might as well answer her."

"Good morning Mary," Andi called out.

The door burst open as Andi pulled the sheets closer to her chin. That they were naked under the bedclothes didn't seem to dawn on Mary as she plopped down on the foot of the bed, trailed closely by Casey and Charlie, who crawled between them looking for some attention.

"I thought we were going riding this morning," Mary said, smiling from ear to ear. "Morning Ryan."

"Mary, do you know what time it is?" Ryan asked.

"Of course I do," she insisted. "And it's well past the time you usually get up. Jackie's making breakfast already, so come on, get up!"

Her enthusiasm for the day was infectious. Andi couldn't help but laugh.

"All right, give me a half hour to shower and dress and I'll be down. You," Andi said, poking Ryan playfully in the chest, "can go back to sleep. I'm sure you're pretty tired out."

"Goodbye Mary," Ryan said, nodding towards the door with what appeared to be a stern look on his face. Mary, finally realizing she was intruding, returned his stern look with a smile that had stretched even bigger.

"Do you want me to take the cats with me?" she asked. Without waiting for an answer, she scooped them both up and was out the door.

"How the girl could be so smart and so clueless at the same time is beyond me," he said before pinning Andi beneath him. "Let's say we put that half-hour to good use!"

Time management had always been a strong suit for Ryan and, true to his word, they made the most of their time. A five-minute shower, no makeup, and hair piled on top of her head was all Andi could squeeze in after they had made love and she hurried to join Mary downstairs for a quick breakfast.

"Geez, Andi, I'm sorry," Mary apologized when Andi walked into the kitchen. "I'm so used to Ryan being alone, I just never thought... well, sorry."

"Don't worry about it. Thanks for taking care of Casey and Charlie for me. I hope they weren't too much bother."

"I think they missed you last night, but eventually, they settled down. Maybe now that Ryan has gotten used to having cats in the house, he'll let me get one."

An unusual silence descended between them. Although she had only known Mary for one day, she could tell something was on her mind.

"Is something wrong?"

"Do you think you and Ryan will get married?" she asked out of the blue. "I mean, you're going to be around for a long time, right?"

How should she answer that? It was obvious how Ryan would answer her, and Andi would love to tell her they would be together forever, but she still didn't know. Pondering her answer, Mary stared at her and Andi suspected there was another, less obvious, reason for her question.

"Why do you ask?"

"Well, you know I'm from Canada, right? And I'm just here for school?"

"Yes."

"I'm the only family Ryan has here, and when I'm away at school, I think he's pretty lonely. He hasn't come right out and said it, but I think he expects me to stay here in Texas with him after I graduate."

"And you don't want to?"

"It would be okay. I mean, Texas is pretty nice and I have a lot of friends here now, but what I really want is to go back home to Canada and start an engineering firm."

"And you think Ryan would be upset if you did?" she asked in surprise.

"Well... yeah. But if you were here, I think he wouldn't mind so much if I went back home."

"Mary, you know him better than I do, but the one thing I know about him is that he only wants what's best for the people he loves. I'm sure he would miss you, but he would never stand in your way whether I'm part of his life or not. Have you told him that's what you want to do?"

"Well no. I didn't want to hurt him before I have to."

Age difference aside, it appeared she and Mary were a lot alike; neither one of them wanted to hurt Ryan. Before she knew it, she was giving Mary the same advice David had given her.

"Give him a chance. Tell him how you feel and give him a chance to prove you wrong. I think you're underestimating your brother and not only will he not be upset, but he'll probably help set up your company back home," Andi assured her.

"Do you really think so?" she asked hopefully.

"I'm pretty sure of it. And as to your initial question... I hope to be around for a very long time."

Rising from the table, the women exchanged hugs before Casey jumped up onto the table and knocked over a nearly empty coffee cup. Andi hurried to clean up the mess.

"Sorry Jackie," she said with a smile as Jackie rushed over to help. "I guess these troublemakers haven't learned their manners yet. I'll put them upstairs until we get back from our ride."

"Don't bother," she said. "I'm quite enjoying them. Will you be back by lunch, or should I pack something for you?"

"No, we'll be back. When Ryan comes down, will you tell him I said goodbye?"

He had been in the shower when she came downstairs and it surprised her he hadn't come down for breakfast yet.

"I will. Have a great ride you two."

. . .

By the time they got to the stables, she found she was becoming a little more excited at trying her riding skills again. Randy, the hand who had helped the first time she and Ryan went riding, had just finished saddling Sammy. Mary's ride stood patiently waiting nearby. Just as Randy was about to give her a leg up, Ryan and Tom came running at them full steam.

"Thank God you haven't left yet," Ryan said breathlessly. The fear in his voice was tangible.

"We were just about to," Andi told him. "What's wrong?"

"Randy, take the horses back into the barn. The ride is cancelled," he said firmly.

"Whatever for?" she asked in surprise. It was unlike Ryan to be so brusque. Mary started to argue before Ryan held his hand up to silence her.

"No arguments."

Randy led the horses back into the barn as Mary stormed back to the house. Ryan grabbed Andi's elbow before she jerked away.

"Ryan, what the hell is going on?" she retorted. His behavior was frightening.

"Let's go back to the house," he said, a little less forcefully. "Please Andi."

"No. Not until you tell me what's going on. Why are you behaving this way?" Hands on her hips, they stared each other down for several minutes before she saw his shoulders slump in resignation.

"I don't want to scare you..."

"You're doing a pretty poor job of it then. What is God's name is going on?"

"It's Richard Kelly." The hairs on her arms stood up and a chill washed over her. "We found him."

"And?"

"He finally used a credit card to buy gas."

"And?" she asked again. Finding him should have been good news, but based on Ryan's hesitation, she suspected it was anything but.

"And it was at a station only thirty miles away. The good news is local law enforcement is closing in on him as we speak.

"There's more, isn't there?" Something in the way he was speaking made her suspect he hadn't told her everything. "What is it?"

Ryan exchanged glances with Tom before speaking again.

"The clerk at the convenience store said she could see weapons in the back of his SUV. Rifles with scopes. That's not unusual in Texas, but remember I told you he was a sharpshooter in the military? That's why you can't go riding. He could be anywhere and with his military skills, he could get to you from up to a mile away. Please, let's go in the house."

This time she didn't argue, and they hurried inside, where Ryan gathered his entire staff in the living room to explain the new information and the security procedures he and Tom were putting in place. None of them missed the fact that Ryan and all the guards were now armed.

"Mary, you're going to go back to school immediately, and we're sending a bodyguard with you. The Sheriff is sending a squad to take you both to the airport."

For the first time all weekend, Mary didn't argue with him. She looked terrified and, trailed by a bodyguard, she left to pack. That she hadn't argued with her brother spoke volumes.

"We're doubling the number of guards around the ranch until they have Kelly in custody. Until then, we'll keep all the blinds drawn in the house and everyone will shelter in place right here. No one goes outside unless it's absolutely necessary. Is that understood?"

Everyone nodded their understanding and a few of the female staff cried while casting accusatory glances at Andi. She couldn't blame them. She had brought this down on all of them.

"Andi, a bodyguard will be with you at all times until we have him in custody."

"Ok," she said meekly. Mary wasn't the only one too frightened to argue.

"I guess that's all for now. I'll let you know as soon as I know more. Thanks everyone."

As the group dispersed and the blinds were drawn, it didn't take long to feel a siege mentality sink in. Everyone clustered in small groups talking quietly together and every little sound in the house caused them to jump. The knock on the door when the Travis County Sheriff's Deputy arrived caused more than one cry of fear.

"Call us as soon as you're home safely," Ryan told Mary. They hugged as if it might be the last time they would see each other and Andi's heart broke at the heartache she had caused.

"Be careful, Mary," Andi said, the tears in her own eyes mirrored in Mary's. "Once this is all over, we should spend a weekend together, okay?" All she could muster was a weak attempt at a smile.

"Ryan will protect you, Andi. I'm sure of it." Her expression of confidence in her brother gave Andi a glimmer of hope.

Ryan and Tom seemed awfully sure sending Mary away was the best option to keep her safe. Nevertheless, Andi said a prayer as they drove away.

After Mary left, Ryan went back to his office, leaving Andi in Tom's protection and she paced back and forth nervously, too keyed up to sit still for long. Each time the phone rang, she braced for more bad news and her anxiety level increased with each passing hour. Jackie offered sandwiches and coffee while they waited, but the hours of waiting for any kind of news about Richard were unbearable. Even Casey and Charlie's antics couldn't bring a smile to the room and eventually they too succumbed to the somber mood to cuddle in her arms, blissfully unaware of the danger. Looking around the room at people who were virtual strangers to her, Andi felt guiltier than ever. If it weren't for her, none of them would be in harm's way right now.

Finally, close to midnight, Ryan emerged from his office.

"It's over," he said victoriously as she raced into his arms. "They have him in custody and it's over. They're holding him on some outstanding warrants from Minnesota, but he can't hurt you anymore."

Tom left to spread the word that the restrictions had been lifted and she could hear cries of relief echo throughout the house.

"He should be in custody for hopefully a good long time."

"You're sure?" she asked, barely able to comprehend that the danger was now over.

"Got it straight from the Sheriff," he said with a smile before leaning down to kiss her gently on the lips. "You're safe now, little one."

"Thank you," she said tearfully. "I don't even want to think what could have happened if I didn't have you in my life."

"What was it David told you? Right man at the right time?" he said with a smile. "If this doesn't prove it to you, I don't know what will."

"I think I'm convinced," she assured him.

"It's been a long day. Let's go to bed."

He didn't need to ask twice. After saying goodnight to everyone and making sure the house was locked up tight, they headed up to bed.

They had replaced their passion from the night before with a need to comfort each other after the stressful day. They moved in tandem, speaking with whispered endearments as their love culminated in an explosion of sensation that left her in tears.

"Don't cry," Ryan urged. "You're safe now and I won't ever let anything happen to you."

"It's not that," she assured him. "It's just that I almost pushed you away forever and I can't imagine how lonely my life would be without you. You're the best thing that has ever happened to me. I love you Ryan."

"It's about time you realized it!" he said with a smile as her eyes closed and she fell fast asleep.

CHAPTER ELEVEN

"There's something I need to ask you, and you can say no," Ryan said over brunch the next morning. The entire household had slept in, turning breakfast into brunch.

"What's that?" she said absentmindedly, watching Jackie play with the kittens while she sipped her coffee.

"The Tigers want to honor you for saving Mark's life. They've scheduled a pre-game ceremony at the end of next week. With everything that was going on with Kelly, I didn't think it was such a good idea, so I didn't bring it up before, but now that Kelly's out of the picture, what do you say?"

"Sure, whatever you want," she said, still not really paying attention.

"Andi, I'm moving back to Canada."

"What do you mean you're moving to Canada?" she finally asked in surprise.

"Okay, I'm kidding, but you weren't paying attention to me. I asked you if you'd like to be honored by the Tigers for saving Mark's life. I know how you feel about publicity, but I think this is a fantastic thing for you and the hospital. Mark and his family have already agreed to it."

"I suppose they could persuade me. You'll be there too, right?"

"Yes, but I won't be on the ice with you. After the ceremony, we'll watch the game in the suite. I'll invite Mark and some other members of the Sunday morning team to join us in the suite, if that's okay with you."

"What would I have to do? I don't have to make a speech, do I?"

The whole thing seemed kind of silly to her, but it seemed important to the others involved.

"No speech if you don't want. Just stand there, smile as pretty as you always do, and accept the award."

"All right. Now what are we going to do the rest of the day? I'm on nights next week and don't have to be at the hospital until late tomorrow, so we have the whole day together."

"Any chance I could persuade you to give me some help with the personal sensor? I could use a doctor's perspective on the body metrics."

"I'd love that. Since this has been hanging around my neck for so long now, I'd love a chance to see what you've been seeing."

"You know you can take it off now that Kelly's in custody," he reminded her.

"I know and I thought about that this morning, but I've grown kind of attached to it. It's a reminder that you're always watching over me and I quite like that. Is it okay if I keep it for a while yet?"

"I don't see why not. We have a couple of other ones we're using in our testing. I'm going to head over to the lab now and when you're ready, come on over."

"All by myself?" she teased with a smile.

"All by yourself."

Tom had been part of the fabric of her life for so long now, and while she had long ago become accustomed to his presence, the thought of going somewhere without him nearby was both exhilarating and odd at the same time. That Ryan was allowing her out of the house unchaperoned proved the nightmare was over and finally, she had her life back. There wasn't a better feeling in the world, and she made her way to Ryan's lab with a spring in her step that had been missing for far too long.

The horse barn was the furthest they had gotten on the tour of the ranch the night of the party, but she knew the lab and Ryan's offices were housed in the enormous adjacent building. Greeted with smiles from PrivaTech employees, it was a far cry from the fearful and accusatory looks the day before. She followed the signs to the lab.

"Andi, come on back," Ryan mouthed from behind a glass partition. About a dozen people spread throughout the large lab barely looked up from their computers when she walked by. Banks of computer monitors exhibiting programming code filled the room, but to Andi's untrained eye, it all looked like gibberish.

"Andi, this is Matt, one of our brightest programmers. He's been working with me to get the sensor you're wearing ready for real life testing."

Matt looked to be all of about sixteen and he made her feel ancient.

"Dr. Taylor," he said, extending his hand with a confused look on his face. "I see you're still wearing the sensor. I thought..."

"Andi has agreed to keep wearing the sensor to give us more feedback to work on," Ryan explained. "She's not in any danger anymore."

"Oh, that's great. Maybe you can help us with some indicators we're still having trouble with."

"That's what I'm here for," she told him with a smile. "Why don't you show me how it works?"

For the next two hours, Matt and Ryan did their best to explain how the equipment picked up on different indicators from the sensor. While she didn't totally understand the computer end of things, it wasn't long before she had a good grasp of what they were trying to achieve and she provided some sound advice to narrow the trigger points. Looking at a chart on the monitor in front of her, she noticed four points where the sensor had triggered on the subject.

"Take this sensor, for instance, and look at this high point that triggered a response. That one makes sense, but then you have several more points hours later that went through the roof. I don't expect this subject was in any actual danger, so what was the difference? Maybe you could filter out some readings by tightening up your trigger points."

Looking up from the monitor, she noticed Matt blushing furiously and Ryan with a guilty look on his face.

"What? What am I missing?"

"Matt, could you give us a minute?" Ryan asked as Matt left the room.

"Did I say something stupid?" she asked in confusion.

"Not at all. In fact, you have a surprising insight into where we're going with this. It's just that... well..." he stammered.

"What?"

"Andi, the test subject you're looking at, is you," he finally pointed out. She had indeed missed her name up in the top corner of the monitor.

"And?" she asked, still confused by their reaction.

"Those three indicators were when we were... uh... making love," he finally admitted as her face turned a deep shade of crimson.

"Does everyone here know?" she whispered.

"No, but Matt probably suspects. That's why he was so embarrassed by your comment."

"Well then, I can see why the sensor's not ready for sale yet," she said with a laugh. "So, this higher reading, that would be when you told me Kelly was in the area, right?"

"Exactly. You might remember I had my phone in my hand when I was telling you that. The sensor was triggering all kinds of warnings at that point as you processed what I had told you and your anxiety levels increased."

"That's where you should start your monitoring," she told him, pointing to the screen. "When the fight-or-flight level kicks in. I don't know about men, but for women, or for me, there are a lot of things that can trigger heightened reactions, and I think you aren't taking that into account. You'll get too many false positive readings if you don't move the trigger point higher. Many everyday situations could trigger increases in what you're keying on that you would be constantly responding to situations that were normal like standing in front of a room of people giving a speech. Dealing with a loved one who is seriously ill. Asking your boss for a raise."

"I see what you mean," he said as he studied the monitor, considering what she had suggested.

"The people who will buy this device would most likely already have a reason to fear for their safety. It's a marvelous piece of jewelry and all, but no one is going to buy it just because of that. Your customers are going to be people who are already in a stressful situation. Unless I'm missing something, you need to start higher."

Turning away from the screen, Ryan pulled her into his arms as those around them tried but failed to hide their amusement at the display of affection.

"You just saved us months of work," he said before planting a kiss on her lips. "We've been looking at this all wrong and have spent months trying to solve this problem, and you came up with it in just minutes. You're brilliant."

"There's just one more thing," she said sheepishly.

"What's that?"

"The pendant is beautiful and all, but not really practical, especially for men. Have you thought about putting the sensor on a watch or a bracelet? Or maybe a tiny little patch worn behind the ear that hair could hide? Or, how about…"

"All excellent ideas for sure and when we get that far, I will consult with you on the design," he said with a laugh. "But for now, I think I've worked you hard enough. Let's get some lunch."

. . .

They spent the rest of the weekend and well into Monday enjoying the tranquility that comes after such a stressful period. She and Ryan took the ride she had hoped to enjoy with Mary and it finally seemed as if all was right in their world allowing them to take full advantage of the relative privacy of the ranch to learn more about each other until it was time to go back to work.

Being able to go to work without a bodyguard made her feel like a butterfly slowly emerging from its chrysalis, and she didn't hesitate to test her wings. Parking in the furthest corner of the parking ramp, something that never happened when Kelly was at large, she strolled leisurely into work and enjoyed the mild evening, even stopping at the coffee kiosk for a quick cup before her pager went off.

"First night shift, Dr. Taylor?" the intern at her side asked as she dumped her things at the nurse's station and gowned up. A multi-vehicle accident had just arrived.

"Yes, Dr. Connor, but not the last by a long shot. What have you got?" she asked the ER staff as she walked into the cubicle.

"James Michaels, a thirty-two-year-old male, no seat belt, went through the windshield, shredding his chest. Coded more than once in the ambulance, but for now, at least we have a pulse. He's intubated and fluids are in. I've got my hand clamped on his pulmonary artery, but I don't know how much longer that's going to work."

"This guy might not make it to the OR, but let's try people. Move!" she ordered.

With no time to waste, they rushed the patient up to surgery, where Andi scrubbed and studied the films being held up in front of her. Everywhere she looked, there was damage. All of which could end the man's life, but she would do her damnedest to make sure that didn't happen.

"Ladies and gentlemen, let's save a life today."

They had heard her repeat the same mantra before each operation, but to not say it was to tempt fate and for a case that would already be an uphill battle, not saying it was never an option. Accepting the scalpel from her nurse, she made the first incision.

· · ·

Surgery over, the difficult discussion with Mr. Michaels' family done, it was now up to the patient. He had made it through surgery but was still just clinging to life. It would be a very long night in the ICU.

"I guess it's true what they say about you," Dr. Connor said.

Turning to look at the intern, she raised her eyebrow. The gossips continued to work overtime talking about her and her relationship with Ryan, but still she couldn't imagine what this young doctor was talking about.

"That guy..."

"Mr. Michaels, you mean," Andi said pointedly.

"Yes, sorry. Mr. Michaels. He should be dead and yet somehow you saved him. Everyone told me what a miracle worker you are and now I believe them," she gushed.

"I'm not a miracle worker and Mr. Michaels has a very long way to go before we can be sure he's going to make it. That means you're going to be at his bedside in the ICU until I tell you otherwise. If anything changes with his stats, and I mean anything, page me immediately."

Striding away from her, Andi's tone was harsher than it needed to be, but the intern needed a wake-up call. Just because the patient made it through surgery didn't mean he was out of the woods. The sooner she learned that tough lesson, the better.

The ringing of her cell phone interrupted the quick cup of coffee she had been hoping for.

"What are you doing up so late?" she asked Ryan, the smile on her face bright enough to light up the dim corridor. It was well after midnight and only a few hours since he had dropped her off at her house.

"Missing you and wishing you were here with me in bed," he said smoothly. "How is your first night shift going?"

"Busier than ever. I was just heading back to my office for a cup of coffee, so your timing is perfect. How was your day?"

"Pretty good, thanks to you."

"What do you mean?" she asked, expecting him to say something about them spending the morning together in bed.

"That advice you gave about the sensor is really moving us forward. Matt and I spent most of the evening fine tuning the metrics as you suggested. I think we are definitely on to something thanks to you, and so I was thinking you deserve a reward."

"So, what are we talking about here? A gold medal... you know I could have had one of those once," she said with a laugh. "Or maybe a date with my favorite man?"

"Maybe we should have our first date," he responded. "This relationship hasn't exactly gone according to the norm, has it? What do you think about breakfast together tomorrow morning? You get off at seven, right?"

"Theoretically," she reminded him. "And I'd love to have breakfast with you. Want to meet at the hospital?"

"I was thinking more like your house. I'll cook eggs and then tuck you into bed."

"And will you be joining me?" she asked seductively.

"You've been so helpful I think that could be arranged," he assured her. She could hear the huskiness in his voice and knew he was feeling the same desire that had suddenly washed over her.

"I can't wait," she told him as her pager went off. A quick look told her it was Mr. Michaels in the ICU.

"Ryan, I have to go. The patient I just operated on is crashing. Love you."

Without waiting for a response, she ran to the ICU where every alarm in the room was sending out warnings and a nurse was performing CPR.

"What happened?" she demanded as a nurse helped her into a gown and gloves.

"He was doing fine and then suddenly went into v-fib," the intern stammered. The look on her face was one of pure devastation.

"Get the crash cart," Andi instructed before taking over the compressions. "Charge to two hundred. Clear." As the jolt of electricity went through Mr. Michaels, his whole body convulsed before settling back onto the bed. No response.

"Charge to three hundred," she said again. "Clear." One more jolt of electricity and she held her breath, waiting to see if his battered body would respond. Just as she was about to call it, the monitor showed a normal sinus rhythm. His heart rate was weak, but getting stronger.

"Dr. Taylor, I don't know what I missed," the intern said nervously as everyone relaxed. "I never left the room."

"That's why he's in the ICU," she said now more calmly. "I told you before that he was just hanging on by a thread and he's still not out of the woods. We've done everything we can, but now it's up to him. If he makes it through the next couple of days, he might have a chance. Is his family still here?"

"Yes doctor," one of the ICU nurses answered.

"I better give them an update. You," she said, looking directly at the intern, "don't leave his side. Is that understood?"

"Yes, doctor," she said sheepishly. After what had just happened, Andi knew she would follow her orders.

The family had been waiting for hours, determined to stay at the hospital until their loved one was out of the ICU, and seeing Andi's face in the doorway in the middle of the night was less than comforting. Hearing about the most recent episode caused a wave of tears and as much as they wanted assurances he would live, Andi just couldn't give it.

"His heart stopped, but we could get it going again."

"So he's going to be okay?" Mr. Michaels' very young and very pregnant wife asked hopefully.

"I don't want to give you any false hopes. Honestly, I just don't know. He's made it this far. That tells me he's a fighter, but his body went through hell in the accident and I can't make any promises. My best guess is if he makes it through the next couple of days, he's got a good chance, but he has to get there first."

As the family gathered in the middle of the room to surround Mrs. Michaels with hugs, she knew even they wouldn't be enough to protect the woman from the challenges and heartbreak that may yet materialize.

"Isn't there something else you can do for him? More surgery or something?" his brother asked.

"He's too weak to survive another surgery right now. About the only thing left to do at this point is to pray," she said honestly. Heads immediately bowed down around the room. "I'll be here through the night and we are monitoring him at all times. I'm sorry I don't have better news for you, but if something changes, I'll be back. Maybe you should go home and try to get some rest."

"I can't leave Jim alone," his wife insisted, although she looked like she was about to collapse herself.

"I understand, but make sure you get something to eat and drink. Your husband is going to need you as much as you need him, and his recovery is going to take a long time. You need to take care of yourself."

"We'll make sure she does," his brother vowed. "Thank you, Dr. Taylor."

For a shift that had started out busier than ever, the rest of the night was relatively uneventful and she sat at Mr. Michaels' bedside. Dr. Connor seemed grateful for the break, but thirty minutes later, she returned and pulled up a chair. Together, they sat vigil through the night. By morning the patient's vitals had improved and while that was a good sign, experience wouldn't allow Andi to get her hopes up. She knew it was up to the patient and whatever higher power they might all believe in. If he had the will to survive and could keep on fighting, he just might make it.

Dr. Miller arrived shortly before seven and, after a thorough review of her cases, she left her patients in his care and headed home to Ryan.

. . .

"Hi honey, I'm home," she said happily when she walked in the front door.

She had always wanted to say that, but figured she would never get the chance. Casey and Charlie were the first to welcome her, and she reached down to scoop them up.

"Hi guys," she told them as they brushed their furry faces against her cheek. "Where's Ryan?"

"Good morning, my love." Ryan had appeared from the kitchen with an apron tied firmly around his waist, and the sight of him stirred more than one emotion within her. Taking her into his arms, he planted a long, passionate kiss on her lips. "I missed you last night."

"And I missed you, but coming home to this might just make up for it," she whispered as she ran her fingertips over his lips. "Have you been cooking?"

"Thank God Jackie saved me the embarrassment," he said with a laugh. "She sent an egg dish that I just had to put in the oven. It's just about ready."

Putting the cats down, they walked arm in arm into the kitchen before Ryan asked about Mr. Michaels.

"He made it through the night and that's a good sign, but it's still touch and go," she admitted before taking a seat at one of the place settings at the kitchen table.

"Would you like some coffee or maybe some juice?" he asked before donning a pair of oven mitts and taking the breakfast dish out of the oven.

"Juice would be great. If I have any more coffee, I'll never sleep," she admitted.

Moments after he placed a full breakfast in front of her, Ryan watched in amusement as she wolfed her food down in a very unladylike manner.

"Sorry, but this is really fantastic, and I was starving," she told him when she had noticed the look on his face.

"It's good to see you eat a full meal again," he admitted.

During the weeks of worry about where Richard Kelly might be, she had lost several pounds that she didn't have to lose. That Ryan realized it told her just how well he knew her.

"Well, that's all going to change now. In fact, I'll have to be careful that I don't pack on the pounds. Working nights won't give me time to work out, and I certainly won't be able to hit the rink any time soon."

"Hum, I think we can find other ways to keep you in shape," Ryan said before pulling her to him for a kiss. "Let's get you to bed."

"I thought you'd never ask."

Racing upstairs, they left a trail of clothing behind before closing the bedroom door on Casey and Charlie and tumbling into bed together, hungry to reacquaint themselves with each other's bodies. For a relationship still in its infancy, the passion they felt grew by leaps and bounds each time they were together, and it was only moments before she lost herself in the feel of Ryan's body covering her own.

"God, you're addicting Andi," Ryan said as they lay snuggled together, heart rates slowly returning to normal.

"Thank goodness I have that going for me," she said as a tired yawn escaped her mouth. "Are you working in the city today?"

"No, and actually I need to start back to the ranch pretty soon or I'll miss a meeting," he said with a quick look at his watch.

"You mean you drove all the way into town and now you're going back?" she asked in surprise. When he had suggested breakfast, she assumed he would work from her house or, at the very least, he would stay at his apartment for the rest of the day. The man had made a two-hour round trip just to bring her breakfast. "Ryan, I'm so sorry," she exclaimed.

"Don't be," he said as he looked down at her. "I'm not. I would drive across the country if it meant we could spend even a minute of time together."

Unable to control the fear that had suddenly erupted in her, she looked back at him with tears in her eyes.

"What? Why are you looking at me that way?" he asked with concern.

"I just don't want our relationship to end up like all the others," she said sadly.

"We won't. Why would you think that?"

"It's just that while I appreciate the gesture of you coming over this morning, I know you don't have two hours to throw away driving back and forth just to spend an hour with me. I know you think it was no big deal, but at some point it's going to get old and then you'll start finding excuses not to be with me and then, well, that will be the end of us."

After her heartfelt speech, it shocked her when he laughed at her.

"My coming here this morning wasn't a 'gesture.' I came because I wanted to be with you... because I missed you... because I wanted to be part of your day."

"But..." his finger on her lips stopped her from finishing.

"No, let me finish. Sure, it's a two-hour trip from the ranch, but I won't always be coming from the ranch and you won't always be working nights. I'm in love with you woman and the most important thing to me is being with you even if it's a little inconvenient or even if it's only for five minutes. Don't you get that? If you haven't figured it out by now, I am a man who knows what he wants and I will move heaven and earth to get it. What I want is you, so stop worrying about me, okay?"

Her heart threatened to burst out of her chest at the intensity of his declaration. All she could do was nod her head before he leaned in for a kiss.

"Now, I think it's time I got going and let you get some sleep. Close your eyes and I'm going to take a quick shower before I leave. I'll call you later, okay?"

"Ryan?"

"Yeah?"

"I love you."

. . .

Waking to a quiet house as Casey and Charlie slept intertwined in a tangled mass of orange and gray fur, the strong light of the late-day sun streamed in through the bedroom windows and the happy sound of children playing in the neighborhood filtered through the glass. Ryan was long gone but pulling his pillow to her face, she could still smell the faint fragrance of his aftershave and she breathed in deeply, hoping the memory of their lovemaking would sustain her through the long shift that loomed ahead that night.

Working nights was nothing new, but after long stretches of days, it was hard to get back into the swing of being up all night. Experience had proven the second night was always the hardest, and she didn't look forward to the next few hours. The new routine was just as strange for Casey and Charlie, but Andi made time to play with them before leaving for work.

It wasn't until she was finally on her way to work that she realized she had seriously misjudged the traffic situation. A mile from the hospital, she found herself in a backlog of rush hour traffic. Fiddling with the radio trying to find a talk radio station to take her mind off the fact that she would probably be late, a glance in the rearview mirror caused her to stop breathing.

Richard Kelly was two cars behind and one lane over in a small, gray sedan. Gasping in fear and gripping the steering wheel so tightly her knuckles turned white, she panicked. How did he get out of jail so fast?

Traffic moved in his lane and she crouched down in her seat as the sedan pulled even with her car. Risking a quick peek, she braced for the worst.

It wasn't Richard. The man driving the car was about twenty years older and looked nothing like him. Catching her eye, he smiled sweetly before traffic once again moved in his lane and he moved past her.

The harsh ring of her cell phone started before she even caught her breath.

"Andi, what's wrong?" Ryan yelled into the phone.

"Nothing. I'm fine," she assured him.

"Your metrics from the sensor nearly went through the roof. Are you sure you're okay?"

Feeling more than foolish, she explained what had happened. "I'm sorry for worrying you. I don't know what I was thinking. The man looked nothing like Richard, and I know he's in jail. I panicked for no reason."

"As long as you're okay, that's the important thing," Ryan said more calmly, the relief in his voice clear as she reached up to wrap her hand around the pendant. As silly as her reaction had been, having the sensor on and knowing that Ryan was ever vigilant meant the world to her. "Why don't you call me when you get to the hospital just so I know you're safe?" he suggested.

"Have I told you today that I love you?"

"I can never hear it enough. Now put the phone down and drive safely. I'll talk to you later. I love you."

It had been a jarring way to start her day, but that extra bit of adrenaline was the push she needed to get through the night shift. Mr. Michaels was doing well and although she still wasn't ready to vocalize her hope to his family, she was starting to think he might just make it.

The ER was busy all night long, requiring the entire staff to juggle several patients at once, each one more critical than the one before. Dr. Connor, who had been so worried she had made a mistake with Mr. Michaels, soon proved to be more than competent and Andi was enjoying her company.

"It looks like we might have a breather," Andi told her after seeing another surgical patient safely to the ICU with no further pages to the ER. "Want to grab a cup of coffee?"

"Sure," the intern said with a confused smile. During Andi's internship, not one surgeon had volunteered to spend time with the interns, and the offer probably surprised Dr. Connor. Things weren't much different at Presbyterian, but Andi hoped to change that if she could.

"So, tell me a bit about yourself," she asked as they settled down in a quiet corner of the cafeteria. Coffee was about all that was available in the early morning hours, but it was black, strong, and hot, and that's all that mattered to her.

"I'm from Seattle, went to the University of Washington medical school..."

"I already know all that. Tell me about yourself."

"Oh, well, like I said, I'm from Seattle and I have five brothers and sisters..."

"Wow!" As an only child, Andi couldn't imagine what it was like to grow up with that many people in the house.

"Yeah, my mom always said that Dad wanted an entire football team of his own, but he had to settle for just six of us."

"You must have had a massive house."

"Not really. The boys doubled up in a couple of rooms, and my sister and I shared. Do you have brothers and sisters?" she asked.

"I don't, but there was never a shortage of kids in the house either. My mom was the only one in the neighborhood who didn't work when I was growing up, and most of the neighborhood kids congregated at our house after school. Are you the oldest?"

"Middle child I'm afraid, but I'm the first one to graduate from college. My older brothers went into the military and the younger kids are still in college."

"Your parents must be proud of you."

"They are, but if my mom had her way, I wouldn't be a doctor."

"That's funny. I would think she would be proud of what you've become," Andi said in surprise.

"She is, but she worries being a doctor means I won't ever get married and that means no grandchildren. I probably shouldn't ask this, but, well, how do you make it work?"

"Make what work?"

"Relationships. How do you make it work with a guy when you spend all your time at the hospital? You're the most successful female surgeon I know and you make it work. I mean, we all know about you and Mr. Jacobs."

A brief flare of annoyance erupted, and it tempted Andi to lecture the woman on the pitfalls of gossiping until remembering how much she would have loved to have had a female mentor when she was just starting out.

"No matter what the gossips are saying about me, the truth is I have no answer for you. A wise friend told me recently that when the right man comes your way, it will just work out. Now, why don't you go check on our patients in the ICU while I stop at my office and catch up on some work? Page me if you need me."

She had failed to answer the intern's question about relationships, but short of going into private details of her relationship with Ryan, it was all she was would say on the matter.

It seemed Lillian had finally gotten the hang of electronic messages and it took Andi longer than expected to wade through the large number of emails she had forwarded earlier in the day. Tackling the important ones first, her mind wandered as she opened and just as quickly deleted spam messages until her eye caught the name Richard and a flashback to the earlier incident on the highway caused her to stop. They locked Kelly up and she was safe, thanks to Ryan. She had been silly to get so flustered by it all. A strong longing to be near Ryan washed over her, and she wished she could hear his voice. Knowing he had an early flight to a business meeting out of state, she wisely decided against calling and instead grabbed her things from the corner of her desk, intending to start her rounds, when the phone rang.

Forgetting her decision to let unidentified calls go to voicemail, she picked up. "Dr. Taylor," she said brusquely.

No sound came through the receiver.

"Hello? This is Dr. Taylor."

Still nothing. Looking at the phone display, it simply said "Unavailable" and a chill went through her before she slammed the phone down.

It couldn't be him! He was in jail. It was just a coincidence. There had been no heavy breathing on the other end, like all the other calls. It was simply a wrong number. A wrong number in the middle of the night.

"Stop being such a baby, Andi," she said aloud in the empty office. Allowing herself to get worked up would most likely trigger the sensor and wake Ryan in the middle of the night. Taking several deep breaths to calm her heart rate, convinced she was just being paranoid and she and Ryan would share a laugh about it when he got back, she headed out to rounds.

CHAPTER TWELVE

Ryan had been on his business trip for several days, but to Andi's great joy, he made his way straight to the hospital upon his return. The late-night hang-up phone call days earlier was long forgotten as they celebrated their reunion with a late supper in the nearly empty hospital cafeteria.

"The Tigers sent over the schedule for the honor ceremony at tomorrow's game," he told her as they held hands across the table like a couple of teenagers.

"I still say it's kind of silly to make all this fuss. It was no big deal," she told him. Public recognition had never been her thing, and she regretted agreeing to the entire event.

"Maybe it wasn't a big deal to you, but it was to Mark and his family. I know you don't enjoy being in the spotlight, but the hospital will get great PR out of it."

"Yes, I understand all that, but after working nights all week and you being gone so long, I was kind of hoping we could spend the evening together, just the two of us," she said rather selfishly.

"We both want that, but it will be a good game—the division championship is on the line—but after it's over, it's just you and me, baby."

The desire in his eyes sparked her own, and she leaned over to kiss him.

"I better head to the ranch," he finally said. "Tom and I will pick you up for the game tomorrow at six, okay?"

"I'll be ready. But before you leave..." Even in the sparsely populated cafeteria there were eyes and ears on them so she leaned in and whispered in Ryan's ear just what she planned to do to him when they were finally alone, causing him to gasp in excitement.

"Pleasant dreams, my love," she teased before giving him a quick kiss on the cheek and walking away. She knew full well he was watching every sway of her hips as she did so.

· · ·

"Okay guys, what should I wear for the game tonight?" she asked Casey and Charlie as she pulled outfit after outfit out of her closet on Saturday afternoon. Even though they had hardly seen her all week, the two pairs of golden-hued eyes watched intently, their heads swiveling as she threw each outfit on the bed until they pounced on an unsuspecting belt and they forgot her as they played.

Normally happy to throw on any old thing, tonight was different. Not only would it be the first night she and Ryan were together in several days, but she would be on the ice in front of ten thousand fans and television cameras, and she had to look her best. Having already spent an extended amount of time on her hair and makeup, she just needed to decide.

A quick look at the bedside clock prompted her to hurry, finally deciding on black jeans with a knee-high pair of black boots, an emerald green blouse and a black waist-length leather jacket. The color combination matched the team logo, which she thought was kind of cool. One last look in the mirror was all she had before the doorbell rang and she heard Ryan come in.

"Andi, you ready, sweetheart?" he shouted up the stairs before she joined him. "Wow, you look fantastic!" he said as she walked carefully down the stairs. "And you have the team colors on too!"

"Thank you for noticing," she said before giving him a kiss. "I wasn't sure anyone would catch that.

Ryan's jeans and pullover warm-up jacket emblazoned with the team logo matched her casual style. As part-owner of the team, she half-expected to see him in a suit, but whatever he wore, he still took her breath away.

"Sorry I'm late. We made a breakthrough with the sensor programming and I think we're ready to do a large-scale beta test, so tonight we're celebrating!" he announced.

"That's terrific," she told him warmly. More so than the anti-spam app, this project meant the world to him and the continual delays had been frustrating for him. "Champagne is on me after the game. Are Carol and David already in the car?"

"They are, and Carol is very excited about your award tonight. She hasn't stopped talking the entire drive over here."

"Sweetheart, if you haven't figured it out yet, she doesn't need me as an excuse to talk a lot. It's just who she is!" she said with a laugh. "And it doesn't hurt that she thinks they have finally won."

Ryan looked confused. "What do you mean? Won what?"

"Remember when I told you it was her goal in life to get me married with a houseful of kids?"

"Yes," he said cautiously.

"Well, she and David have had a little competition about that and even though David knew you first, she thinks she got us together. Since it seems we are now officially a couple, she thinks she won," she told him, not sure how he would react to that thought.

"And what do you think? Is she right?"

"I could be persuaded," she teased with a quick kiss before walking out the door to the car and Ryan, massive smile on his face, hurried to catch up.

The looks Ryan kept directing her way in the car, a mixture of excitement, desire, and love all rolled into one, made the drive even more thrilling. Andi knew he was also looking forward to being alone at the end of the night, but first they had to get through the award ceremony. Pulling up to the arena, the limo came to a stop in front of the main entrance, where officials from the team waited to welcome the group and guide them inside.

"Dr. Taylor, you'll come with me for the pre-game ceremony and Mr. Jacobs, you and your guests can go right up to your suite. There's already a large group waiting for you there. After the on-ice ceremony, I'll escort Dr. Taylor back to you."

"Thanks Roger," Ryan told the man. "Are you okay with that, Andi?"

"Sure," she said nervously. The doubts she had been having about whether this was a good idea had returned at the thought of all those people staring at her. "I'll see you guys in a bit, I guess."

Ryan, accompanied by Carol, David, and of course Tom, turned to walk away when the ringing of Ryan's phone stopped him.

"That's weird," he exclaimed as he stared at the phone. "It's the Sheriff's Department."

"What do they want?"

"I'm not sure. Jacobs," he said into the phone. "What do you mean, it wasn't him? I thought you had him in custody."

Suddenly, her whole being focused on the look of fury on Ryan's face. Something was terribly wrong.

"What is it?" she asked, reaching out to touch Ryan's arm. He held up a finger to silence her.

"And you just found this out? She's been in danger this whole time and nobody could warn us?" he shouted into the phone as people around them stopped to look.

He listened for several more minutes before finally hanging up.

"Ryan, what's wrong?" she asked, her heart beginning to race.

"Come on, we're not doing this tonight. I'm taking you home," he said as he grabbed her elbow and tried to direct her back to the exit before she jerked it away.

"No, I'm not going anywhere until you tell me what's going on," she said stubbornly as he dialed a number on his phone, ignoring her question.

"Get back here with the car. We're not staying," he said brusquely before putting the phone away and once more trying to get her to leave.

"Damn it, Ryan! Tell me what's going on," she said fearfully, as Carol and David watched in confusion. She had never seen Ryan behave so disrespectfully before. "Is Richard Kelly out of jail?"

"We will not have this discussion here," Ryan insisted. "Roger, we're going to need your office."

"This way, sir," the man said as he directed the group through the crowds to the administrative offices for the team.

When the four of them were finally in the man's office with the door closed firmly behind them and Tom standing sentry outside, Ryan looked at her.

"Andi, I'm sorry, but they never had him." There was no need to ask who he was talking about. It was Richard Kelly.

"What do you mean?" she said, her anxiety growing by the minute. "They told us he was in jail."

"It wasn't him. The man they arrested looked just like him, but the fingerprints didn't match. They're so backed up it took this long to clear the prints. I'm sorry, my love, but it wasn't Kelly. He's still out there somewhere and we don't have a clue where he is. That's why we can't do this tonight. It's too dangerous."

"Okay, wait a minute," she said with more confidence than she actually felt. "Let's just calm down and think logically. The Tigers have gone to a lot of trouble to pull this all together, and as much as I didn't want to do it in the first place, I can't back out now. You have building security, right? Let's just go ahead with our plans. Then tomorrow, we'll go back to my having a bodyguard and we'll start trying to find him again."

"No, I don't think we should take the risk. The team will understand and..."

"Ryan, please. I don't want to explain why I am backing out, even though I'm already here. This thing, this man, has controlled my life for too long now. Let me just do this and get it over with. Please?!"

A standoff took hold as they each stared defiantly at the other; she determined to stay and finish what they were there for and Ryan convinced the only safe and reasonable thing to do was to retreat.

"I think Andi's right," David offered.

"David, I don't think we should get in the middle of this," Carol said. The quiver of fear in her voice was palpable. It was the first time she had spoken since Ryan got the call.

"No, honey, Andi's our friend and she's the one who's in the middle of this. If she feels strongly that she can do this ceremony, then I think we should support her."

"Dave, I appreciate your concern, but I don't think either of you realizes what Kelly is capable of," Ryan insisted. "Andi, I know you feel you have to do this, but everyone will understand. Please, let's go home."

Reaching up to take the pendant once again in her hand, she struggled with what to do while everyone else watched in uncomfortable silence.

"Okay, this is my decision," she said. Her voice was quiet but determined. "I'll take part in the ceremony and then Tom can take me home. The rest of you stay and enjoy the game and we can meet back at my house afterwards."

"Andi, I don't think..." Ryan began before Andi interrupted.

"No, that's my decision. If you don't agree with it, that's fine, but I'm going through with the ceremony."

For a moment, it looked like he would continue to argue his point. Instead, he gathered her into his arms as Carol and David quietly slipped out of the office.

"If anything happens to you..."

"I'll be fine," she assured him with as much conviction as she could muster. Terror flooded her soul, but nothing had happened since they thought Richard was in custody and she had to hope that would continue.

A quiet knock on the door interrupted them. "Mr. Jacobs, we need to get Dr. Taylor down to the ice right away."

"We'll be right out," Ryan told them. "Tom will go with you and bring you back to me when it's over. Then we can leave and if you're okay with it, let's spend the weekend at the ranch."

"That sounds wonderful," she told him with the brightest smile she could muster. Everything really would be all right with Ryan watching out for her. She just knew it.

Walking out of the office arm in arm, they both put on brave faces. A quick consultation with Roger about Tom's presence took place before Ryan said goodbye and directed Carol and David to the suite while Andi and Tom accompanied Roger down to the ice. The look of concern on

Ryan's face as she took one last backwards glance while they walked away broke her heart and she blew him a kiss, praying it wouldn't be the last time she saw his handsome face.

"Now, once we get down to the ice, you'll immediately be introduced and escorted across the carpet to center ice, Dr. Taylor," Roger said as they hurried through the maze of concourses to the tunnel leading onto the ice. Even as he spoke, she could hear the arena announcer replaying the story of what had happened that morning with Mark's injury. As the crowd quieted, she imagined the internet video was also being shown. With only moments to spare, she had little time to catch her breath before her name was being announced to thunderous applause and she was escorted to center ice.

With the houselights dimmed for the ceremony, the glare of the spotlight that followed her onto the ice was blinding and she fought the urge to cover her eyes while the announcer's voice continued to reverberate throughout the arena. Players from both teams stood at attention on the blue line, banging their sticks on the ice in what Andi recognized as an honored hockey salute tradition. Receiving the storied accolade brought tears to her eyes as she listened to the complimentary words being spoken by the Tigers' President of Operations. Concluding his speech, he offered both his hand and the award before a loud sound rang out in the arena, stopping her hand in mid-air.

As if in slow motion, she raised her head, thinking it couldn't possibly be a gunshot, just before another one sounded. This time there was no doubt about what had happened, and she felt the bullet whiz past the corner of her ear a millisecond before Tom tackled her to the ground. Bullets rained down as the arena erupted in terrified screams and fans raced for cover. The stairways of each section became packed with people trying to escape, with some crawling over rows of seats trying to get out of the arena.

It was bedlam on the ice as the players from both teams raced to safety, giving Tom the opportunity he needed to jerk Andi to her feet and rush her back to the closest bench and the relative safety of the tunnel to the locker rooms. Andi's eyes naturally went towards the suite where Ryan and their friends were supposed to be watching the ceremony, only to see a jumble of overturned chairs.

Safe in the confines of the players' tunnel, Tom looked her over, trying to find a wound.

"I'm fine," she assured him, brushing his hand away.

"We need to get you out of here," Tom said brusquely, grabbing her arm as he did so before she shrugged him off. His wince of pain made her realize he was the one that had been wounded.

"You're hurt. Let me look."

"It's fine," he insisted. "Just a flesh wound. We need to get you out of here."

Blood had already soaked his shirt and created a pool on the concrete.

"Damn it Tom. That's no flesh wound! If I don't do something right now, you're going to bleed out in front of me." Looking frantically for someone to help, she forced Tom to a sitting position and yelled at a nearby security guard, who looked as if he was about to pass out from shock. "You there. Find the team trainer. Tell them to come with medical supplies."

Hoping that he would do as she asked, she applied pressure to the ugly wound in Tom's neck before a young man arrived with a bag of medical supplies and knelt at her side.

"We have little for bullet wounds, but how can I help?" he asked.

Digging through the bag, she found what she was looking for.

"Place this on the wound and apply pressure on it. Don't release the pressure until I tell you. I'm going to wrap this gauze around his neck and then he needs to get straight to the hospital." Thankfully, the bullet had missed the major arteries, but that didn't mean it wasn't serious.

Even as she barked out orders, the faint whine of an ambulance pierced her subconscious and she prayed there was an entire army of them coming because there were sure to be multiple victims.

"Tom, hang in there. You're going to be fine, but you've already lost a lot of blood and it's going to make you feel faint."

"Dr. Taylor, we have to get you to safety," he said weakly as he tried to get up from the floor.

"I'm safe enough," she told him. "Don't worry about me." Turning her attention to the trainer, she instructed him to stay with Tom until they put him in an ambulance.

A nearby player slumped to the ground as a steady stream of blood dripped from a bullet wound in his shoulder and she hurried to his side. Using a pair of scissors from the trainer's bag to cut away the man's hockey sweater and the straps on his shoulder pad, she got a better look at what appeared to be a through and through shot with a visible entrance and exit point. To her trained eye, the bleeding was minimal, meaning no major arteries had been affected, and after a quick bandage and telling the man to hold his wrist up to his chin to minimize the pain from any movement, she left him to the others who had arrived to help.

The sound of gunshots, which hadn't stopped completely, was becoming more sporadic, but the screams and cries of the victims were still prominent in the arena, and she had no choice but to go back in. Grabbing the medical bag, she started for the tunnel when Tom yelled at her to come back.

"Dr. Taylor, stop. You can't go back out there," he shouted at her.

"I don't have a choice," she told him, realizing how pale his face had become from blood loss. He certainly was in no condition to stop her. "There are people who could die out there. I'll be careful."

"Please, don't do this. Mr. Jacobs trusted me to keep you safe."

"It's okay," she assured him. "I'll tell Ryan you tried to stop me, but I ignored you."

"If you won't listen to me, at least take this," he said as he handed the gun in his hand to her.

Guns weren't all that foreign to Andi, although she had never owned one herself. Her father had been a hunter and being raised in Minnesota where most children took gun safety classes, she wasn't unfamiliar with their operation, but that was years ago. Still, it would make Tom worry less if she had a weapon, so she reached for the gun before bending down and giving him a kiss on the cheek as paramedics arrived to help.

"I'll meet you at the hospital as soon as I can. Don't you die on me," she told him with a squeeze of his good shoulder before identifying herself to the paramedics and updating them on Tom and the other man's condition. As the first responders helped them to the waiting ambulance, she turned to go back into the arena.

"Can you use some help?" the young trainer asked. Intent on controlling her own fear about going back out there, she had forgotten he was standing at her side.

"Are you sure?"

"I was a medic in the Army," he said with a wry smile. "Never thought I'd have to use what I learned there in real life."

"Well then, let's go."

Together, they made their way down the tunnel, staying as low as possible until they had a good view of the arena. The steel catwalk above the ice was crawling with police and security people, guns at the ready as they frantically looked for the shooters. Squeezing past the barricade that separated the crowds from the player's bench area, they kept their heads low, carefully making their way to the areas that seemed to have the most injured. At first all they encountered were those with crush injuries from the groundswell of people trying to get out of the arena, a few sprains, a couple of broken bones here and there. The only thing the victims had in common was the fear etched on their faces. Leaving her young friend to deal with those, she continued on to the sections that appeared to have been in the shooter's direct line of fire. Blood spatter covered every surface and rivers of blood ran in a slow, steady stream down the nearby stairs.

Stopping at the first victim, a young fan in a Tigers jersey soaked with blood, she carefully turned him over, before letting him down again. He was obviously dead. Two more fatalities stood between Andi and the first live victim; a woman with a simple flesh wound which Andi covered in a clean dressing before leaving her with others who had appeared nearby trying to help. Soon enough, Andi had triaged all the victims in that section and moved on to find others who needed her level of expertise. No further gunshots sounded and in the back of her mind, she took it as a sign that whoever had perpetrated the shooting was now in custody. It gave her confidence to move freely between victims before being roughly grabbed from behind.

For a moment, her heart stopped until she turned to see Ryan, angrier than she had ever seen him, pulling her into his arms.

"Thank God you're okay, I thought you were dead!" he told her as he crushed her to him.

"I'm fine. Tom saved me, but he got shot. They've already taken him to the hospital. What about you and all the others? Are you okay? Was anyone else hurt?"

"We're all fine. As soon as the shooting started, everyone got out of the suite and out of the building. What were you thinking coming out here all by yourself?" he spat at her. "Damn it, Andi, they could have killed you! I should never have let you talk me into staying."

His anger was fueling her own, and she snapped back at him.

"It's okay, I'm fine. I couldn't stand by and watch these people die in front of me. You know I couldn't and you would have done the same thing, so let it go, please. You can either help me or get out of my way because these people need me."

A lingering flash of anger appeared in his eyes before he placed a gentle kiss on her forehead, his lips remaining there as if he couldn't bear to let her go.

"I love you, Ryan, but I have to keep working," she told him gently, her hand caressing the side of his face. "As soon as I tend to these last few victims, I'll catch a ride to the hospital and we can meet up there later, but it's going to be a very late night. I'm sure as a team owner, you are going to need to deal with the police and the media. Go do what you have to do and I'll take care of the injured."

More emergency personnel had arrived to help and with one last kiss and an exchange of "I love you's," they went their respective ways.

Within an hour of the first shot ringing out, all the victims were triaged and most transported to hospitals across the city; the worst of those ending up at Presbyterian, where it was all hands-on deck to deal with the influx of patients. Even Dr. Thompson, who had retired from active surgery, was called into action. By the time she arrived in the ambulance with the last victim, the operating rooms were full.

The entire hospital knew the shooting had taken place at the game where Andi was receiving the award and everywhere she went, whispered snippets reached her ears. It wasn't until she was about to begin her first surgery that it finally dawned on Andi that she might very well have caused the whole thing.

Ryan had told her once that Richard trained in weapons in the Army, but could it really have been him? None of the constant news coverage had included information on the identity of the shooter and she couldn't help but think that with the first shots directed at those on the ice, she was the reason so many people died. Tears formed in her eyes, draining beneath her mask as her scalpel halted in mid-air, leaving her desperately trying to control the guilt that threatened to overwhelm her.

"Dr.?" Ashley asked. Her words barely registered. "Dr. Taylor, are you okay?" she asked again.

"What?" she said finally. "Sorry, I'm fine."

Her team exchanged concerned looks. She couldn't blame them. The whole shooting event had been jarring and had left them off their game.

"Ladies and gentlemen, let's save a life today."

. . .

The sheer number of victims meant back-to-back surgeries for the next thirty-six hours. From the excruciatingly tedious work of repairing blood vessels to the simplest of repairs, the patients blurred in front of her. Still everyone she helped made it through surgery, and that was something at least. It was late afternoon on Monday before any of them could take a breath.

"Great work Dr. Taylor," Dr. Thompson said as Andi poured herself a cup of strong coffee in the doctor's lounge. She was too tired to make it all the way back to her office and collapsed onto the couch.

"Thank you, sir," she told him, unable to conceal a yawn as she did so. "Have you heard anything more about the shooters? Are they in custody?"

"It looks like it," he said as he joined her on the other end of the sofa. "There's a lot of confusion, but one of the Texas Rangers was just giving a press conference and he said there is one person in custody."

"Any word on fatalities?"

She had already seen several bodies in the arena, but hoped the rest of the wounded would make it.

"Five so far, but many more wounded, unfortunately. Still, it's a good thing you were there, or we might have had even more deaths."

Should she admit her being there might be the cause of it all she wondered? Not wanting to play the martyr until knowing more about who the shooter was and his motive, she was mentally preparing for the worst.

"I don't think any of us imagined going through something like this when we brought you on board, but I, for one, am very glad you were here. We saved a lot of lives today and much of that is thanks to you."

The guilt magnified within her.

"The credit belongs to the entire staff, sir. They did a magnificent job. Now, unless you have any objections, I need to go home and get some sleep. It's been a long couple of days, and I need to be back for my regular shift in a few hours."

"Heavens no, and don't worry about reporting tonight. We've got plenty of old men like me that will stay through the night. You get a full night's sleep, and we'll see you Tuesday night."

"Thank you, sir," she said with as much gratitude as she could muster, too tired to do much more.

Heading for the front of the hospital hoping to catch a cab home, she reached for her cell phone before remembering it was still somewhere in the bowels of the arena with one of the team staff who had held her purse when she went on to the ice. More than anything, she wanted to talk to Ryan, but without a phone, it would have to wait until she got home. Hailing a cab, she sank into the back seat and tried to stay awake for the ride home.

As had been the case so many times before, the neighborhood was quiet and dark by the time the cab pulled into the driveway and her heart hung heavy with sadness as she plodded to the front door. She didn't even have

Casey and Charlie to welcome her home, as Carol and David had cared for the cats at their house until the emergency was over.

Setting her things down on the hall table, she wondered where Ryan was. Media reports said the team had brought in a series of counselors to talk to the players and staff, but that should have finished hours ago. Maybe he had gone back to the ranch. Calling his cell from her house phone and receiving no answer, she left a message asking him to join her as soon as he could. Even if he couldn't change what had happened, having him with her would make her feel better.

The frenetic pace at the hospital had left little time to process what had happened since she stepped onto the ice on Saturday, and she slowly walked up the stairs as flashes of memory from the shooting peppered her mind. The first shot had been surreal, but thinking back, she wasn't the only one who had stood on the ice in a stupor. Tom was really the only one who hadn't frozen in place when the shots came and the fact that he reached her and tackled her to the ice just as the second shot zipped by her head showed just how good he was at his job.

The commotion that ensued from that point on was just as every shooting victim ever described - an initial moment of disbelief followed by gripping terror and complete shock. Stuff like what they had been through only happens somewhere else. So why had she braved going out to tend to the wounded? Her training had allowed her to push her fear aside. Ryan had been right. She could have died, but it didn't seem to matter. Helping prevent the deaths of others was all she could think about.

Sitting on the edge of the bed, the tears fell, and she cried until there were no tears left. If the shooter was Richard Kelly, it would become public knowledge and she would have to live with the fact that at least five people died because she had been too stubborn to listen to Ryan. All the lives she had saved over her career would mean nothing if it turned out she caused those innocent victims' deaths.

For now, she just wanted a long soak in a hot bath before she crawled into bed. Taking off her jacket, an unexpected heaviness caught her attention. Putting her hand in the pocket, she found Tom's gun. She understood Tom's intentions in giving it to her, but she would never use it.

Something in her would not allow her to pull that trigger and she placed it carefully in the top drawer of her dresser, intending to return it to him at the earliest possible moment.

Leaving her clothing in a pile on the bathroom floor, a sudden and very insistent growl of hunger erupted. She had had almost nothing to eat for nearly two days. As unappealing as the thought of food was, the doctor inside her said to eat and she slipped on one of the dress shirts Ryan had left behind earlier in the week. Enveloped in the voluminous material, breathing the faint aroma of his aftershave, she could hardly stand being without him. Where was he?

In the kitchen, the tile cold on her bare feet, the sudden glare of the overhead lights was jarring, and she grabbed an apple before stopping to look at her reflection in the darkness of the kitchen window. Worry and sadness lined the face looking back at her; a look that would take a very long time to disappear if it ever did. How could she not be changed by what had happened? A deep sigh escaped her lips before she closed her eyes for a moment in silent prayer for the victims and those who loved them. Opening her eyes again, she reached for a small knife for her apple when another face joined her in the window's reflection and her heart stopped.

"Hello Dr. Taylor," Richard said, his voice even deeper than she remembered. "Did you miss me?"

Dressed all in black, his smile showing the rotten teeth of a heavy drug user, the man looked nothing like she remembered from Minnesota, yet there was no mistaking the lecherous way he looked at her, for she had seen it too many times before.

Grasping the paring knife so hard her fingernails drew blood in her palm, she looked around frantically for a better weapon.

"Aren't you going to turn around and say hello?" he asked.

Slowly she turned to face him as if that could forestall what would eventually happen to her.

"Richard, what are you doing here? How did you get in my house?" she asked, her voice trembling as she tried desperately to think of some way to escape the kitchen.

"You didn't think something so trivial as an alarm was going to stop me now, did you?" he taunted.

"It was you Saturday, wasn't it?" she said. "You killed all those innocent people."

"I wish I could take the credit for that," he said coolly as he played with the large hunting knife in his hands. "I would have been quite upset if that guy had killed you before I got the chance to taste your sweetness. After all, I've been waiting a very long time for my chance. Still, it was fun watching you scramble for safety and seeing that bodyguard get shot."

"You were there?"

"Of course! Don't you know by now that I am everywhere you are? Bet you didn't know it's not the first time we've been in this house together," he told her. "Remember your party? You nearly caught me that time when that stupid woman from next door pointed at me. So where is your rich friend tonight? I have to admit that having him and the bodyguard around has made this harder than I expected, but I've always liked challenges and you have been one of the best."

"Richard... why are you doing this? Didn't I save your life back in Minnesota? Why would you repay my kindness by tormenting me this way? Why don't you just leave, and this can all be over?"

Slamming his fist down on the countertop, he screamed at her, his face crimson with rage.

"It's not over until I get what I want. You don't seem to understand, Doctor, I've waited almost two years to have you. And if you're a good little girl, I just might let you live after I've had my fill of you."

Images of what he had done to his other victims flashed through her mind, and she knew he wouldn't keep that promise. He would never let her go. Seeing him look down at the knife in his hands, she bolted for the front door. As quick as she was, he was on her in a heartbeat and she barely reached the door before he had grabbed her from behind, lifted her off her feet, and threw her back onto the floor. The blow as her head bounced off the tile left her dazed as he came towards her, the knife shining menacingly in his hand.

"For someone who is such an athlete, I thought you'd put up more of a fight," he sneered as he crept closer.

Well over six feet in height, his reach far exceeded hers and he watched as she staggered to her feet. She presented little physical challenge to him but gathering her courage and lowering her head she rushed at him like a fullback with the scream of a crazy woman, plowing into his midsection and driving him back until the small of his back connected with the knob on the front door leaving him gasping for breath. As he clutched at his back, she sliced the inside of his wrist with her own little knife. Screaming in pain, his now useless hand dropped the knife. It skidded away from him.

Her moment of victory was short-lived as her feeble attempts at disabling him had done little more than enrage the man. Gaining back his equilibrium, he came at her with all two hundred-plus pounds of him, his one good hand curled into a fist that he launched at her head before she ducked at the last moment and his fist crashed into the drywall behind her. Struggling to put some distance between them, she lunged for the hall closet, hoping to barricade herself inside. She had barely opened the door before he was on her again, throwing her face first onto the floor of the foyer as the contents of the overly full closet crashed to the floor around her head and she struggled to get her breath back.

"As much as I've enjoyed our little wrestling match," he taunted before violently turning her over as he knelt to straddle her, "I'm going to enjoy this so much more."

Wrapping his good hand around her throat, his injured hand attempting to work the zipper on his jeans, he used his knee to spread her legs while she fought back with all her might. Scratching desperately at his hand on her neck as his fingers tightened with a viselike grip, things began to fade to black before unexpectedly there was air in her windpipe again. Gasping for breath and rolling her head from side to side, she spotted the one weapon she could use as he continued to work to lower his zipper.

Fallen from the closet with the rest of its contents, her hockey stick lay at the tip of her fingers. Wrapping her hand around it, she swung with every ounce of strength she had. The stick connected with the side of his head, breaking in two as Kelly collapsed on top of her.

Summoning a strength she didn't know she possessed, she pushed him off of her only to discover his body now blocked the front door. Grabbing the remnants of her hockey stick, she raced upstairs to the bedroom, locking the door behind her and shoving the heavy dresser in front of the door. If Richard was still alive, the barricade wouldn't hold long.

Frantic with fear, she realized too late her poorly chosen escape route now had her trapped in the house and she reached for the bedside phone to call 911. Like every nightmare she had ever had, the call wouldn't go through, and she tried again and again until realizing there was no dial tone. Sometime between her calling Ryan and now Richard must have cut the phone lines.

Now she truly was on her own and, as much as she hated to pick it up, she hurried to the dresser to get Tom's gun. Trying to remember what the gun safety instructor had told them about handguns, she took the safety off and listened carefully at the door, hearing nothing but the sound of her own heavy breathing. Had she actually killed Kelly? The blow she had struck on his head was substantial, but she didn't for a moment think that it was enough to kill him.

Suddenly, she heard the voice she loved more than anything.

"Andi, where the hell are you?! Please answer me!"

It was Ryan, and nothing had ever sounded sweeter. Using what little strength she had left to push the dresser away from the door, she raced to the top of the stairs, gun still in hand, to peer carefully down to the foyer. The front door stood wide open, the foyer littered with blood and broken household goods she had thrown in Kelly's path on her race to the front door. The only thing she didn't see was Kelly's body.

"Ryan, I'm here," she yelled from the top of the stairs. "Richard's here and he's got a knife." Both men came into view and what she saw was more frightening than anything that had happened before.

Waving the large hunting knife like a madman, Kelly was within arm's reach of Ryan as the two men circled each other like wrestlers looking for a takedown. Her heart in her throat at what she was witnessing, Andi crept down the stairs and raised the gun in front of her; her hands shaking as she tried to take aim at Kelly.

As she stood there, hands shaking so hard she could hardly hold the gun, Kelly lunged at Ryan with the knife. Andi heard and felt the odd sucking sound as the large blade slid into Ryan's belly before he went down to his knees with a grunt. Clutching his hands in front of him, blood poured through his fingers as he looked up at her in disbelief before falling face first to the floor.

Andi's scream of horror shook the windows before she dropped the gun to the foyer below and launched herself at Kelly, landing on his back, arms tight around his throat in a chokehold. Legs strengthened from years on the ice locked around his midsection. Fueled by pure rage and fury, she choked him with every ounce of strength she had as Ryan lay dying beneath their feet. Minutes passed before she could feel Kelly stagger and he crumbled to his knees. Yet even as he was falling, her hold around his neck tightened with a fury she didn't know she possessed. Finally, the knife fell to the floor, and he went slack. Releasing her grip, she checked his pulse, hoping she had actually killed him and was disappointed to find he was still alive.

Kicking the knife away and grabbing the gun from where she had dropped it, she raced to Ryan's side as the sound of emergency sirens came closer and the red, white, and blue lights cut through the darkness of the night to reflect inside the house through the open door.

"Please don't be dead," she whispered repeatedly as she placed the gun within reach on the floor and pulled Ryan into her arms. Her fingers on his throat, a weak pulse offered a glimmer of hope. Moving to lower him back to the floor, she elevated his feet under her hockey bag to provide as much blood flow to his heart as possible before applying direct pressure to the gaping belly wound.

"Please, my love, please wake up," she begged as tears flowed from her eyes and mingled with the blood from the many cuts on her face. Ryan's shirt, which had provided such comfort and security just minutes before Kelly appeared, now hung in tatters on her body and was heavy with blood.

"Don't move," an officer shouted from right outside the door, his gun pointed directly at her.

"Please, I need to get him to the hospital. He's dying!" she cried as she looked back at the officer.

Without lowering his gun, the officer used his foot to kick Tom's gun away from her before moving towards Kelly and checking for a pulse.

"Please... I have to get Ryan to the hospital," she begged.

"The ambulance just arrived, ma'am. Can you tell me what happened here?" the officer asked as he motioned for his partner to put handcuffs on Kelly.

Ignoring the officer's question as the paramedics walked in the door, she provided as much information about Ryan's condition as she could before they moved her hands from his wound and took over. It seemed to take forever before they lifted him onto a stretcher and wheeled him out to the ambulance.

As soon as Andi attempted to follow, the officer grabbed her blood-stained arm. "Wait a minute ma'am. You're not going anywhere. We need to know what happened here."

"Get your hand off my arm," she said furiously. "That man is Ryan Jacobs and I'm Dr. Andrea Taylor. If you don't let me go, he's going to die before he even gets to the hospital. That piece of filth," she said, nodding in Kelly's general direction, "has been stalking me for two years and tonight he broke into my house and tried to rape and kill me. If you need more than that, you can follow me to the hospital, but nothing and no one is going to stop me from getting in that ambulance."

Glaring at him in defiance, he must have realized the futility of detaining her before he removed his hold on her arm. Her mind failed to register the dozens of neighbors watching from their driveways in their nightclothes, some standing with hands over their mouth in shock as she ran to the ambulance covered in blood.

The paramedics hung an IV to replace some fluids Ryan had lost and were continuing their attempts to stem the bleeding as the ambulance pulled away and the siren broke the still of the night. Relegated to the role of helpless spectator, she sat on the bench holding Ryan's hand while whispering words of love to him until they pulled into the emergency bay, and he was rushed inside. Trailing behind, she prayed for the best, but prepared for the worst.

"Dr. Taylor, you need to wait out here," a nurse told her as they closed the treatment room door in her face.

"I want to be with him," she insisted, her eyes never leaving his pale face even as a dozen people worked to save him. Watching the routine she had been a part of for so many years should have been a comfort, but she knew too much about what they were doing and was terrified for him.

"I know you do, but you know it's better if you wait here," the nurse said before Dr. Miller rushed into the room.

Minutes later, the door opened again and Ryan was being wheeled upstairs for immediate surgery.

"Andi, I promise I'll do my very best," Dr. Miller said as he took her hand. "But you know how serious this is." Even though she was fully aware, hearing him say it caused tears to start once more.

Watching the elevator doors close behind them and wrapping her blood-stained arms tightly around her, she bowed her head in prayer as the activity of the emergency room continued unabated around her.

"Dr. Taylor?"

At first the voice didn't register. It took a gentle touch at her arm to realize someone was standing there. Slowly lifting her head, she realized it was Nurse Ashley.

"Dr. Taylor, are you okay?" she asked with more compassion than Andi deserved after all the pain she had brought to Austin. "Come on, let's get you cleaned up and then you can go upstairs with Mr. Jacobs," she said before taking Andi by the arm and leading her to an empty treatment room.

"Nothing too serious," Ashley said as she peeled Ryan's shirt from Andi's body and looked at her wounds. "But you have a few cuts here that could use stitches and a resident will be here in a minute to take care of those. I know you want to get upstairs and be with Mr. Jacobs, but it will only take a few minutes, okay?"

Andi didn't answer as they worked to tend to her wounds and dress her in clean scrubs. Her mind was in the OR and the man lying on the operating table six floors above them; a man that most likely was going to die. Someone needed to contact his family.

"Ashley?" she asked softly. "I need to let Ryan's sister know what's going on. Can you call my assistant at home and ask her to come in? She'll know how to find Mary. And tell Lillian I need her to call Carol and David Madsen and let them know what's going on. She has their number. Tell her not to alarm them, but ask them if maybe they can come to the hospital right away?"

"Of course, Dr. Taylor. Is there anything else I can do for you?" she asked kindly.

"Can you say a prayer for him?" Andi asked as tears fell again.

"We all will."

Andi's wounds addressed, the nurse gave her hand a squeeze and walked with Andi up to the gallery above the operating room. Even if Andi couldn't be in the room with Ryan, at least she could watch what was happening. Too nervous to sit, her body covered in bruises, butterfly bandages and sutures, she stood with her hands pressed to the glass, rocking from side to side as she watched the delicate surgery below. Time passed slowly as she prayed nonstop for a good outcome.

Occasionally another doctor would stop by to offer words of encouragement, but when she failed to respond, they left her to her own musings. Finally, Dr. Thompson arrived and stood next to her. Giving him a brief glance, she readied herself for yet another platitude.

"How's it going?" he finally asked after minutes of silence.

"How do you think?" she snapped, before realizing what she had said and who she had said it to, but she didn't care.

"Dr. Taylor, I am so very sorry to be asking this, but I need you in surgery."

"No," she said without even looking at him.

"I understand you want to stay here with Ryan, and I wouldn't ask if we had any other options, but... well, I might as well be honest with you. God Andi, I'm so sorry to do this to you, but that man? The one who broke into your house? There was an incident at the Sheriff's department when they were moving him. He got a hold of one of an officer's gun. Without immediate surgery, this man is going to die and we can't let that happen. They just brought him in and you're the only one who can save him. I'm afraid I need you to save this man's life."

She couldn't believe he was asking her to leave Ryan's side.

"You have my word that as soon as Ryan is out of surgery, I'll come and tell you," Dr. Thompson promised. "Please Andi, I know it's a lot to ask after everything you've been through in the last few days, but I wouldn't ask if I didn't think you were strong enough to handle it."

"Okay," she reluctantly agreed.

The look of relief on Dr. Thompson's face was immediate. "He's already on his way to operating room eight," he told her.

With one lingering glance at Ryan lying so helpless on the operating table, she wondered if it would be the last time she saw him alive before hurrying down the hallway to save a life. The hallway, lined with law enforcement personnel, was something she had seen before when an officer was injured.

The operating room, one she had never operated in before, was the mirror opposite of the others. In this room, the patient's head was at the opposite end of the room, his face hidden by the surgical drapes. So consumed with worry about Ryan, she barely noticed. Ashley posted the chest films taken in the ER in the view box so she could see what she was dealing with. The man should be dead, but yet somehow he was clinging to life. Maybe God really did protect those who protected others.

Stepping into the operating theater, her team, many with tears in their eyes, offered words of encouragement for what she had gone through at the house. There were few dry eyes in the room, but with no time to waste, she just wanted to get on with it. The sooner she finished with the deputy, the sooner she could get back to Ryan. She stepped up to the table.

"Ladies and gentlemen, let's save a life today."

The operation was tedious and required her full concentration, which was difficult when the patient she was most concerned about was in a room at the other end of the hospital. Risking more than a few glances at the clock, she tried to calculate how long Ryan's surgery would take. She should have heard something by now. As each full sweep of the hour hand went by, a feeling of dread that something had gone horribly wrong took hold. Her hands shook in fear and she had to stop for a moment as the surgical team cast worried glances her way.

"Doctor, are you all right?" Ashley asked softly.

"Patient is still holding steady, Dr. Taylor," the anesthesiologist said from his position at the head of the table. "You're doing great."

Taking a deep breath, she worked to control the shaking in her hand before continuing. Regardless of what happened to Ryan, she had to save this man so that something good would come out of the whole sordid affair.

"I'm fine, Ashley," she told her, even though she was anything but. "Let's keep going."

An hour later, it was finally over. The deputy had made it through surgery. As Ashley helped her out of her gown and gloves, Andi asked if she had heard anything about Ryan.

"No, but Dr. Thompson is outside waiting to talk to you," she said. "I'm so sorry you had to go through all this, Dr. Taylor," she said with tears in her eyes. "If there's anything any of us can do for you..."

Looking from one sad face to another, Andi knew without them even having to say it that Ryan didn't make it. That's why Dr. Thompson hadn't come in to tell her the good news himself and was instead waiting for her to finish operating on the deputy. Her knees went weak, and she slumped against the door as Ashley tried to steady her before being brushed off and Andi's grief overwhelmed her. The tears that came so easily earlier in the day were now replaced by unbridled anger at the unjustness of the love of her life being taken away from her.

Did Mary know? Had she even gotten to the hospital yet? How would Andi ever tell his mother? So many thoughts were flying through her mind she didn't realize she was still standing there as everyone in the room looked on, unsure what to do or say to ease her pain. But nothing would help and outside the door she would hear the words that would make it all too real. Ripping the scrub cap off her head, she turned to face the news.

Dr. Thompson stood all alone at the nurse's station and Andi walked slowly to him, every step leading her to the horrible news until she stopped in front of him and waited for him to say it.

"Dr. Taylor, I am so very, very sorry..." he started before she buried her face in her hands and sobbed.

He pulled her into his arms and held her until the anger came once again and she pushed him away, not caring that he was her boss.

"How could you make me do the surgery?" she railed at him as she stood with fists clenched at her side. More than anything, she wanted to hit someone or throw something. "I should have been with Ryan."

"I know," he said sadly. "And I'll never forgive myself for that, but you were the only one who could have saved that man, and I thought you'd want to see him spend the rest of his life in prison."

"What did you say?" she said in confusion as his words sunk in. "What in the hell are you talking about?"

"Kelly," he said, equally confused by her reaction. "I'm sorry I had to ask you to operate on the man who attacked you."

"No! You're lying! I operated on the sheriff's deputy he shot," she insisted. "It was a cop."

"Andi, I'm so sorry. I thought you knew. The man you just operated on was Richard Kelly."

Everything became dark, and she passed out cold on the floor.

CHAPTER THIRTEEN

Waking in a hospital bed with an IV attached to her arm as Carol slept soundly in a nearby chair, Andi's head throbbed, but she was otherwise unhurt. Turning onto her side, remembering Ryan was dead, and they had conned her into saving the life of the man who killed him, she pulled a pillow close to her mouth to muffle the cries that immediately started.

Suddenly overcome with a steely rage that knew no boundaries, she wiped away her tears and sat up in bed. Disconnecting the IV, she got quietly out of bed and entered her credentials into the nearby computer, looking for Kelly's room number before slipping out of the room.

The nearly empty hallways made it easy for her to evade detection as she made her way to Kelly's room, not surprised to see an officer stationed at the doorway. Still in her scrubs, he barely glanced her way before she walked into the room and pulled the curtain around Kelly's bed.

Thanks to her, his color had returned to normal, and the monitors all showed strong vital signs. Watching him lying there, both hands shackled to the bed frame and completely unaware of her presence, a deep-seated need for vengeance took hold in her. Why should he live when Ryan was dead? What plausible reason could God have for saving his life and taking that of a good and kind man like Ryan? Where was the justice in this world when such filth lived?

Barely realizing what she was doing, she grabbed a spare pillow and clasped it in both hands in front of her. The oath to "do no harm" kept running through her head at what she was preparing to do but she forced herself to remember the feel of Ryan's lips on her own and the sound of his laughter, to remember the tenderness with which his hands cupped her face and the love in his eyes each time he looked at her, all taken away by the human garbage laying on the bed in front of her.

She took a step closer to the bed. If Ryan was gone, Kelly didn't deserve to take even one more breath. She was going to end his life, just as he had done to Ryan. Another step closer and her hands held the pillow even tighter.

Kelly's head turned slightly towards her in his sleep and in that moment, sanity returned. Dropping the pillow at her feet, she backed slowly away from his bed, shocked by what she had been about to do. True justice would be knowing that the man would spend the rest of his life in prison and may even face the death penalty. She would have her day in court and when that time came, she would face the man who had killed the love of her life, knowing that she had resisted the urge to play God by ending his. It was slight consolation, but at least she could live with herself.

Turning to leave, she saw Kelly's eyes were now open and staring at her with such lust it made her stomach turn.

"You couldn't stay away from me, could you?" he taunted with a sickening smile. "I knew you wanted me as much as I wanted you."

Temptation to finish what she had come there for flared within her, but only for a moment. She spoke quietly but with great strength.

"Never in my wildest dreams did I think that saving your life would cause the torment you've put me through. The only reason I don't end your life right here and right now is because I took an oath to do no harm and even though you're a piece of filth that doesn't deserve to live, I won't stoop to your level. You should know this though... you might spend the rest of your despicable life thinking of me and how much you wanted to control me, but I will never waste one second thinking of you again."

A string of obscenities shouted at her from the bed as he strained to get to her with only the handcuffs keeping him in place accompanied her exit from the room. The commotion startled the officer standing guard outside the door and he looked at her with his hand on his gun as she walked out of the room.

"He's all yours," she told him with a self-satisfied grin.

Finally, after all this time, Kelly's torment of her was at an end. She had gotten the upper hand and she would now do what she said and never think of him again, but that didn't change the fact that Ryan was gone and tears once more wet her cheeks. As much as she tried to prevent it, she had caused him the ultimate pain and would have to live the rest of her life knowing that loving her had cost him his life. Not knowing what to do, too restless to go back to her room and sleep, and too lonely to go home, she wandered the hallways before finding herself in the ICU.

"Good morning, Dr. Taylor," one nurse said to her. "I wondered when we'd see you. They said you were in surgery, but that was hours ago."

Wondering who 'they' were, she kept on walking.

"Dr. Taylor, you're heading the wrong way," the nurse said as Andi walked past her.

"What?"

"His room is this way."

"Who?" Andi asked tiredly.

"Why Mr. Jacobs, of course," she said with a confused look. "That is why you're here, right?"

Was she hearing the woman correctly? Was this woman telling her that Ryan was alive?

"Ryan? Ryan's here?" she asked in disbelief.

"Cubicle seven, and he's doing really well."

Ignoring the curious look on her face, Andi turned back; her steps hesitant as she walked to the room. The woman must have made a mistake.

Sliding the glass door open and pulling the curtain aside, her knees buckled before she reached for the wall to steady herself. Bathed in the artificial light of the ICU was the face of the man she loved more than life itself. His body was still pale against the stark white of the bed linens and attached to more equipment than most patients, but every beep, chirp, and pulse of the monitors showed he was very much alive.

Gently taking his hand in her own, she kissed his forehead, desperate to feel the warmth of his skin beneath her lips. Smoothing his hair back from his face, tears of love for the man fell unabated.

"Oh, my poor love, I'm here now. Please, Ryan... please be strong."

The nurse guided Andi into a chair close to his bedside. For hours she sat holding Ryan's hand, offering words of love and encouragement, until finally she fell asleep at his side.

. . .

"Andi?"

As if in a dream, Andi raised her head and opened her swollen eyes to see Mary at her side, one hand touching her brother.

"Andi, are you okay? The whole hospital has been looking for you."

"Oh Mary, I'm so glad you're here," Andi told her before releasing Ryan's hand just long enough to offer her a hug.

"Dr. Miller said Ryan's going to be okay, so let's go outside and talk. Everyone's been looking for you, including the police."

"But I can't leave him," she said as she sat back down beside Ryan.

"I'll stay with him, Dr. Taylor," the ICU nurse offered with a kind smile. "I promise I won't leave his side."

Against her better judgement, Andi let the two of them talk her into it and she walked with Mary to the family waiting room surprised to see Jackie, Tom in a wheelchair, and Carol and David, along with some faces she recognized from the ranch and a few new ones.

Carol sprang to her feet and pulled Andi into her arms.

"Where have you been, Andi? The whole hospital was looking for you. When I woke up and your bed was empty, I was frantic."

"I'm sorry I worried you," she said tiredly.

"Hey there, Andi," David said as he offered his own hug. "We were pretty worried about you, but I'm glad you're okay."

Would she ever be okay again? Maybe not, but at least Ryan was alive.

Jackie and Tom offered their own hugs, and it surprised her to see Tom had tears in his eyes as he held her hand when she kneeled beside him. "I'm so sorry I wasn't there when you needed me," he said sadly.

"Hey, none of that," she told him with a slow smile. "If it wasn't for you getting me off the ice, I might not be here at all. You saved my life. I'm just glad to see you're on the mend, because I've grown quite fond of you."

"Andi, I'd like to introduce you to my family," Mary said as Andi stood up. "This is my mom Nancy and my brothers Steve and Joe."

"Dr. Taylor," Ryan's mom said as she beamed at Andi. "I'm so pleased to finally meet you. Ryan has told us all about you."

"Call me Andi, please. I've wanted to meet all of you for a very long time, although I never imagined it would be under these circumstances. You must hate me for all this."

"It's not your fault," they all assured her. What they didn't realize was that because of her, everyone in the room had suffered. It was totally her fault.

"Dr. Taylor," the nurse said from the doorway. "He's awake."

The warmth of the smile that erupted on her face rivaled the sun.

"Mrs. Jacobs, I think you should go in," Andi told her. ICU restrictions limited one visitor at a time, and she knew that if it were her child, she would have been eager to see him.

"I'm sure he's going to want to see you first," she countered, although Andi could see the excitement in her eyes.

"Tell him I need to talk to the police first and then I'll be right in," she asked. "And tell him I love him, will you?"

"I'm positive that's the one thing he'd rather hear from you, dear," she told Andi with a pat on the arm before following the nurse to the ICU.

"Dr. Taylor, if we could have a few minutes, please?" The Travis County sheriff and two deputies had been patiently waiting nearby for a chance to get her statement.

Leading the way to a small room used for private conferences with patient families, she closed the door as the three men took a seat at the table and placed a digital recorder in front of her.

"We think we have a pretty good understanding of what has been going on with you from our interviews with other witnesses, but why don't you tell us what happened at your house last night?" the Sheriff asked.

For the next half hour, she detailed everything that had happened after arriving home and discovering Richard Kelly in the house. Years of dictating surgical notes came in handy, and she could tell the story from start to finish in surprising detail until they seemed satisfied with her statement.

"We'll get that typed up and in a couple of days, you can stop down and sign it," Sheriff Williams said. "When Mr. Jacobs is well enough, we'll get his statement also, but from what you've told us here today, I don't think we'll have any problems pressing our case against Kelly. And if I might say so, I think it took a hell of a lot of guts to operate on your attacker. If it were me, I don't know that I could have been so willing to save his life."

If only he knew just how close she came to ending it.

"Thank you Sheriff. Just give my office a call when you're ready for me to sign."

With the police taken care of, she went back to the ICU, where Mary was just coming out of Ryan's cubicle.

"He's waiting rather impatiently for you," she said, before giving Andi's hand a squeeze.

Taking a deep breath, she pulled back the curtain to see Ryan, the breathing tube already removed, holding out his hand as she hurried to his side. As gently as possible, she peppered his face with kisses.

"I love you so very much," she whispered as she pulled back to look into his eyes.

"And I love you," he said before scooting over in his bed and patting the space next to him. "Come here."

Carefully moving the IV lines off to the side, she climbed up on to the bed as he wrapped his unencumbered arm around her. Placing her head gently on his chest, she savored in the sound of his steady heartbeat.

"I thought you died," she admitted.

"What do you mean?" he asked as he stroked her hair.

With as little fanfare as possible, she explained about being tricked into operating on Kelly and believing that Ryan had died.

"Oh my God, Andi, I'm so sorry they put you through that. How could Everett put you in that position?"

"Looking back now, I guess I understand. If we had just let Kelly die without trying to save him, it would have looked terrible for the hospital."

"Damn the hospital. It's you I care about," he said as forcefully as his weakened condition would allow.

"And I care about you. But I need to tell you something else, and I don't want you to think badly of me when I do."

"What do you mean?"

As ashamed as she was about her actions in Kelly's room, she knew Ryan was the one person who wouldn't judge her for it and she told him everything she had done, or rather, everything she hadn't done.

"I was so filled with the need to avenge you, all I could think about was watching Kelly die. Then, when I found I couldn't go through with it, it was almost a relief. It doesn't make much sense, does it?"

"It does to me," he said. "You stopped yourself before doing something that ultimately you wouldn't have been able to live with. If you had taken his life, you would have destroyed your own. I'm proud of you Andi and I love you more than ever."

"I love you too, but you need some sleep. The faster you recover, the faster you can get out of here and we can start our lives over again."

"That sounds great, but I don't want to start over. Everything that has happened is now part of us and it's going to strengthen us."

Before she could even kiss him, he had drifted off to sleep once more.

CHAPTER FOURTEEN

They moved Ryan to a private room the next day and Andi spent all day with him thanks to Dr. Thompson's kind offer to allow a leave of absence from her job. The leave, which she suspected was residual guilt over conning her into operating on Kelly, not only allowed her to spend time with Ryan while he recovered, but also gave her a chance to decompress from everything that had happened.

Even with the real Richard Kelly locked up, Ryan's security team remained vigilant, albeit without Tom at Ryan's side. Well on his way to recovery, it would still be several weeks before Tom could hold a gun in his hand, leaving him restricted to his Head of Security administrative duties for the time being. A new bodyguard stood sentinel in Ryan's doorway.

"How's our patient today?" Andi's mom asked as she breezed into Ryan's room, interrupting their reading of the dozens of get-well cards that had arrived earlier that day.

Ryan had generously provided for a private plane to fly her parents to Austin and, together with Carol and David, they had been taking care of things on the home front; arranging for a professional cleaning crew to remove the blood that stained most of the first floor of her house, repairing the phone lines and damaged security system, and for Andi, bringing Casey and Charlie home. That they could accomplish all that within the first three days and still have time to visit with Ryan in the hospital was a miracle.

While her mom went to Ryan's side and leaned down to kiss his cheek, her dad held fast to Andi.

"How are you holding up, honey?" he whispered in her ear.

"I'm good, Dad… really good," she beamed up at him. "Ryan is mending well, although he has gotten little sleep with all the visitors he's had the last few days."

Overhearing their conversation, Ryan chimed in.

"Sleep is overrated," he said with a smile as he greeted her dad warmly. It touched her heart to see how much they already cared for each other. "Andi and I can't thank you enough for dropping everything and flying down. I know she really appreciates not having to come home to an empty house."

Until her parents arrived, she had stayed in Ryan's apartment in the city rather than face the house and the demons that still lurked there.

"We're happy to help and I have some good news for you both," her dad said. "The house is back in order, although there are a few bare spots where things broke during the struggle, but your Mom moved some things around so those aren't so noticeable."

"Thanks Mom," Andi said, giving her hand a squeeze. The fewer reminders she had of what had happened in the house, the better.

"And they completed the last of the repairs to the phone and security systems this morning. All the lines are now encased in steel conduit. If, heaven forbid, someone else tries to break in, at least they won't be able to cut the lines. Here's one more piece of news. Jack from next door told me he and some of the other men have organized a neighborhood watch. After what you went through, they don't want to take any more chances."

"That's nice of them," Andi said.

It didn't take long for the publicity Dr. Thompson had once coveted to become a reality as the entire story came out in the press and her neighbors learned what was behind the scene they witnessed the night of the attack. Public figure that he was, well wishes from all over the country, including a personal visit from the Texas Governor and video conferences with more than a few of the gods of the tech world occupied a majority of Ryan's recovery. Andi's part in the whole mess being relegated to the sidelines allowed her to devote her full attention to Ryan and their burgeoning relationship.

They visited together for the next half-hour before a nurse popped her head in to mention that visiting hours were ending.

"Andi, do you want a ride home?" her father offered as they stood to leave, and she stifled a yawn.

"Thanks, but I've got my car. I'll be home in a little while."

"Do you think that will be us one day?" Andi asked with a smile as she gingerly climbed into bed next to Ryan. Arms wrapped around each other, they watched her parents leave.

"I sure hope so," he said tiredly. He was progressing nicely in his recovery, but the constant stream of visitors was making it hard for him to get enough sleep and had left little time for the two of them to talk about what they had been through.

"Ryan, do you want to talk about everything?"

"I was wondering when you would ask that," he said, as he stroked her hair absentmindedly. "Where do you want to start?"

"I want to know everything you were feeling, but for now, where did you go right after the shooting... after you came up to me in the arena when I was triaging patients?"

"Remember, you said I should deal with the media? Eventually that's what happened, but at the beginning, it was more important to make sure the team and rest of the staff were okay. We had a few injuries, but thank God, no one was seriously injured. Mentally though, it was another story; we had a lot of broken people... some who just wanted to go home and some who wanted to be around everyone else and talk about what had happened. We brought in counselors to give them a chance to talk about what they had been through."

"How are they all doing? Do you know?" she asked. Post-traumatic stress could be a serious issue if not dealt with, and she was proud of Ryan for realizing it.

"Roger dropped by yesterday when you were getting something to eat and he said that a few people are too shaken up to go back to work and have submitted their resignations, but everyone else seems to be okay. We're going to have the counselors on-site every day for the rest of the season, just in case."

"That's wonderful, but how about you? Did you go to the ranch to sleep each night, or did you stay in the city?"

"Honestly, there wasn't much sleeping those two nights. I called your cell phone constantly... hey wait a minute. Why didn't you ever call me back?"

"I'm sorry, I didn't know. I haven't been able to find my phone or my purse since the night at the arena. An usher was holding it for me when I went on the ice and I never got it back."

"That explains a lot. Anyway, when they showed the picture of the shooter on TV, and I realized it wasn't Kelly, I was desperate to find you. I had just hung up with the hospital, who said you had already left for home, when your sensor went crazy. Andi, I am so sorry I wasn't there for you." His arms tightened around her.

"But you were—through this," she assured him as she wrapped her fingers around the sensor which still hung from her neck. "If I had felt the least bit afraid, I never would have left on my own. By the time I got home, I was so tired I just wanted to crawl into bed, but I missed you desperately and I even slipped into one of your shirts just so I could feel you near me."

"Were there any signs that Kelly was there?" he asked.

"Nothing," she admitted. "I've gone over it a million times in my head wondering if I missed something, but it wasn't until I saw his face in the kitchen window that I realized he was in the house."

"You must have been terrified."

"It's weird, but I really wasn't. Don't get me wrong. I froze at first, hoping maybe I could appeal to him by reminding him I had saved his life, but it didn't take long to realize that no matter what I said he was still going to kill me. That's when I ran, but I wasn't fast enough. I don't think I'm ever going to forget the look of pure evil in his eyes as he threw me to the floor with his hand at my throat."

Lost in her memories of that night, she shivered uncontrollably as tears welled up in her eyes, but she had shed enough tears in the previous few weeks and never wanted to cry again. Brushing them away, she sat up on one elbow to look into Ryan's face.

"All I could think about was you and how much I didn't want you to be the one to find my body. I didn't want you to have to live with that."

"Oh my God, Andi, I am so, so sorry," he said as he pulled her back to him, his own eyes glistening with moisture. "I nearly wrapped my car around a tree trying to get to you and when I walked in and saw all that blood and broken furniture and everything else, I was sure you were dead. After following the trail of blood back to the kitchen, I was expecting to find your body. I sure as hell didn't expect to find Kelly standing at the kitchen sink eating an apple like he owned the place."

The memories of what both of them had gone through that night were still fresh in her mind, and she doubted they would ever fade.

"I thought for sure I was a goner when he stabbed me. The last thing I remember before I blacked out was the look on your face when you threw yourself at him."

"For me, everything seemed to happen in slow motion. When he stabbed you, I felt unadulterated, white-hot rage." Her voice wavered with the memory. "The only thing I could do was get him away from you and as hard as he tried to shake me off, I knew if I let go, we'd both end up dead. I'm just sorry I didn't kill him."

"I'm not," Ryan said so quietly she almost didn't hear him. "Just like in his room that night, if you had killed him, it would have changed you and not in a good way. Taking a life is not something you could live with. You know that."

"You're probably right, but still... if I ever come close to experiencing that kind of hatred again..."

"Let's hope we never have to find out," he said sensibly before they both lapsed into silence.

Finally, almost too tired to drive home, she got up before Ryan pulled her back down next to him.

"Stay the night."

"Don't tempt me," she told him as she caressed his cheek. After days in the hospital, his beard had grown in covering the scar on his chin and she brushed her finger over it absentmindedly. "You need your sleep, but I'll be back first thing in the morning to take you home."

For the foreseeable future, and even though she wasn't officially Ryan's doctor, she had banned him from all work, and he would stay at her house until fully recovered. It might not be laying on a beach somewhere like they both had dreamed of, but the relative peace at her house would still be an improvement over the hubbub of the ranch.

"Sleep tight, my love," she told him before their lips locked in a kiss passionate enough to leave them both breathless.

"You also, little one," he whispered.

EPILOGUE

Going through a traumatic event changes a person in ways they might not even realize. Maybe that's true, but Andi and Ryan knew exactly what had changed between them. Any lingering doubts they were meant to be together had long since disappeared and they rejoiced in the fact they were both alive and well and the next chapter of their lives together had finally begun.

That was not the only change they noticed. The neighborhood that had appeared to reject Andi when she first moved in welcomed the couple home with open arms and there was a seemingly never-ending parade of their new friends appearing at the door offering food and flowers as their lives together settled into a welcome routine. They filled days with laughter and more love than she could ever have hoped for when she moved to Texas.

The house, which originally seemed cavernous, was now bursting with family; her parents and Ryan's family all under the same roof - at least temporarily. After everything they had been through, no one wanted to be separated. Being together gave them a chance to get to know each other better before they all left for home.

Casey and Charlie, after their forced vacation with Carol's family, were now glued to Ryan and Andi's sides and they could hardly take a step without one or the other of them tagging along. With a full house, the now full-grown cats received more love than they could have ever hoped for.

Ryan finally gave his statement to the Sheriff and as word of how Ryan knew Andi was in danger spread around the law enforcement community, the sensor and what it could do for those with reason to fear for their lives got a lot of publicity. People from all over the world reached out to PrivaTech to purchase the equipment and with the most dramatic and successful beta test behind it, Ryan's company immediately began mass production of the sensor as sales went through the roof. PrivaTech, already well known for the spam filter, became an even bigger powerhouse in the tech world and Ryan's dream of using his tech prowess to protect people had come full circle.

Eventually, after their families had headed back up north and with Ryan chomping at the bit to get back to the ranch to discover even more opportunities for PrivaTech, it was also time for Andi to go back to work. Back in the comforting routine of the hospital and holding a scalpel once more in her hand, she felt like she was finally normal again.

That one day they would be married became an accepted fact between them, but for the moment, neither she nor Ryan felt the need to put a ring on her finger. Somewhere in all the havoc Kelly had played in their lives, the love between them became even more of a commitment to each other than saying "I do" could ever be, but that didn't stop Ryan from talking about it every once in a while. One such quiet night at home in front of the fire, Ryan's arms around her, he asked once more.

"Don't you think it's about time we talked about getting married?" he asked.

"Maybe someday."

"Why someday?" he said with a chuckle. "Don't you love me?"

Turning to look at him with her own smile, she laughed back. "You know better than to ask that," she admonished gently. "Of course I love you and someday we'll get married, but I don't need a piece of paper to feel married to you. We're already a family. You, me, Casey, and Charlie. I have everything I want right here."

"I agree, but say it."

"Say what?" she teased.

"You know..."

"It's you," she told him, her eyes looking at him with every ounce of love in her body. "You, my love, have always been the right one for me."

ABOUT THE AUTHOR

Minnesota author Barbara A. Luker is a master of weaving love stories that will leave readers reaching for the tissues. Luker is an ardent fan of the Minnesota Wild and Minnesota Vikings and a supporter of numerous animal rescue organizations. She lives that passion everyday through her devotion to her polydactyl rescue cat Annie. Luker has honed her writing skills as a Certified Municipal Clerk working for the City of Saint Peter. Her previous works include *Remembering You* and *I Carry Your Heart*.

I Carry Your Heart

Barbara A. Luker

NOTE FROM BARBARA A. LUKER

Word-of-mouth is crucial for any author to succeed. If you enjoyed *The Right One*, please leave a review online—anywhere you are able. Even if it's just a sentence or two. It would make all the difference and would be very much appreciated.

Thanks!
Barbara A. Luker

We hope you enjoyed reading this title from:

BLACK ROSE
writing™

www.blackrosewriting.com

Subscribe to our mailing list – *The Rosevine* – and receive **FREE** books, daily
deals, and stay current with news about upcoming
releases and our hottest authors.
Scan the QR code below to sign up.

Already a subscriber? Please accept a sincere thank you for being a fan of
Black Rose Writing authors.

View other Black Rose Writing titles at
www.blackrosewriting.com/books and use promo code
PRINT to receive a **20% discount** when purchasing.

www.ingramcontent.com/pod-product-compliance
Lightning Source LLC
Chambersburg PA
CBHW050157120726
47903CB00002B/659